Jeff -
This should be
Alley!

Mymidons

by
Struan
Forbes

Distributed in the United States by The Author's Press.

Cover Art by David Knox
Cover Layout by Punch Design
Layout and Design by The Author's Press
First Printing: August 2006

Library of Congress Catalog Card: Pending

US ISBN: 1-933505-07-9
978-1-933505-07-7

Myrmidons

The Author's Press
Atlanta Los Angeles

Dedication

To my wife Lisa, for all her support, encouragement and love.

Acknowledgements

My thanks to H. Christine Lindblom, editor, mentor, creative genius and intolerable nag. Thanks for perservering when my resolve flagged.

To Sara Gardner for her production work and friendship and for a multitude of suggestions that made this project a better piece of work.

Also, I would like to thank Megan Eleazer for her early efforts at illustration and creative cover design suggestions.

Thank you to John and Samuel, for being my sounding boards, your inspirations and a constant reminder of why I do this. I thank you all for your efforts, for your support and for your hard work in creating this novel.

Finally, I'd like to thank that myriad of researchers, scientists and thinkers on whose work this book is based for their inspiration and for doing the hard part. Though you'll never know how much you've helped, I know and I will remember.

Thank you all.

Prologue

A LIGHT RAIN WAS FALLING, which was unusual these days. Normally, it either was bone dry and brutally hot or chilled, with sporadic torrential downpours coming out of the north occurring at odd moments during the day and night, leaving little or no water in its wake. The weather had been that way for years now. For the man staring through the window of his small bedroom, the light drizzle was just another oddity in a long line of oddities that had inflicted him this year.

Three times he had found himself waking up to a nightmare not of his own making. A bizarre combination of events left him puzzled, horribly frightened and totally unable to remember what had happened. He looked over at his left hand that was missing a ring finger and a pinky. That had been the first frightening incident in this macabre play. He remembered awakening as usual just as the sun was beginning to peek above the tops of the apartment buildings that filled this corner of the Southern Complex's central core; feeling particularly drowsy, as if he had been on an all night binge, yet he clearly recalled slipping into bed about ten in the evening.

As he lay there, he had stretched, grasping the rungs of the headboard to help him curl his lower body so that he could swing out of bed, but this morning, his hands didn't seem to do their job. He slipped back down on the bed, his left hand swinging wildly in an arc and coming to rest at his side. That was when he felt the pain and saw that he was missing fingers, the hand itself wrapped neatly in surgical bandages. Of course he had panicked, checking the other hand for damage and trying to wiggle all his fingers. He could feel them all moving, but clearly two digits of his left hand were not there.

Distantly, he observed the phenomenon and wondered what had happened. He couldn't explain it, nor the peculiar disinterest that he felt after a moment's reflection. Somehow he couldn't bring himself to report the event or even seek medical help. He just noted his predicament, released a silent anguished scream from deep within his soul, and felt himself slip into a coma, blissfully unaware.

The second time, he was stepping into the shower when he became aware that flesh was taken from his right side, just under the arm. A large bandage covered the wound. Eight inches in diameter, it was all neatly wrapped with gauze and tape around his torso, reminiscent of an old war movie. How could he have not noticed it immediately when he awakened? What was happening to him? Again he inexplicably accepted the event with a terror that could not be voiced. His whole being cried out silently, bile rising in his throat as he began to feel the violation his body had experienced. He gulped for air, trying to calm himself and think, but the more he tried to remember what had happened, the more difficult it became to concentrate. In a very short time, he had forgotten the incident and went about 'business as usual.' He vaguely remembered explaining to his co-workers, at the newspaper, that he had an accident while climbing on a friend's roof. They were repairing a leak and he fell. During that fall, he experienced some deep lacerations from a trellis on the side of the house. They accepted the explanation without comment.

Now a third incident occurred only days before. His right cornea had been surgically removed, leaving him blind in one eye. Again there was the scream, more insistent now but as silent as before. His eye throbbed in wave after wave of agony whenever he moved it or tried to blink under the bandage, but no matter how much anguish he felt, he could not force himself to call anyone or seek medical help.

Now he stood looking out at the drizzling rain, wondering what was becoming of him and realized that he was being taken apart piece by piece; but why? It reminded him of the old story of the guy who had taken a vacation to Mexico. When he wakes up in a tub full of ice, with a missing kidney and instructions to call an ambulance immediately.

"I am living that horror story," he said to himself whenever it came to mind, which was almost constantly. He would break out in a cold sweat and begin to shake uncontrollably. The horror almost never left him now. How could he work with only one eye? How could an art critic function with such a limitation? He couldn't even carry on a conversation with anyone. He felt as if he were increasingly living in a dream state; some fantasy world where evil prevails and preys on the helpless and innocent. Yet for all his raw terror, he could not bring himself to call for help. "Someday," he said to himself. "Someday I've got to call someone. Why haven't I called the police?" He would reach for his com plate and begin to punch in the code for emergency help, but turn it off before he finished dialing.

Moving away from the window in anguish, he sat on the edge of the bed, his head in his hands, and began to cry. At first he did it softly, but soon a flood of tears and wails poured out of him. Releasing all the built up frustration and allowing the fear to bubble over into the physical world.

"Mister Hayes?" Called a voice at the door. Someone was pounding on his apartment door insistently. "Mister Hayes, are you in there?"

"Who is it?" He wailed.

"I've come to help you, Mister Hayes."

"I don't need your help!" He snapped and began to weep more softly.

"Mister Hayes, I believe you do. I know what's been going on, Mister Hayes. I know you are frightened, confused and that you've been badly abused. I'm here to see to it that all that stops."

He looked up at the door and calmed himself. "Who are you?" He said.

There were shuffling sounds from the hall, as if three or four people were rearranging themselves outside.

"A friend," the voice said. "I'm a friend."

"I have no friends!" He snapped and backed into a corner beside the window. Bile began to rise in his gut as he sensed a very palpable danger building around him.

After a moment, the voice said, "You have more friends than you think, Magnus. We want to help you. What's been done to you is inexcusable and we want to put a stop to it."

"What did you say?" He said hesitantly.

"I said, 'You have more friends than you think, Magnus'," the voice said pointedly.

"How the hell do you know what's been done to me?" He screamed. "You can't know!"

"We know, Mister Hayes. We were there."

Magnus Hayes stared at the door, neither moving nor speaking. He slid down the wall into a near fetal position and sat very still, trying to make sense of what he was hearing.

"Are you still with me, Mister Hayes?"

"I'm still here," he said at last. "What do you want with me?"

"We told you. We want to help you, but we can't unless you let us in. We can give you all the medical attention you need. We can also see to it that nothing like this happens again, but we can't do anything for you if you won't let us in."

"Why should I?"

The voice on the other side of the door took on an air of frustration. "Because you have more friends than you think, Magnus!" It said again.

Hayes stood dazed but maintaining control.

"Step back from the door," he said. After a full minute he crossed to the door and looked at the security screen embedded in the wall beside it. Standing about four feet from the door was a tall man in a dark suit and wearing a tie. He looked as if he were on his way to a banquet or another formal gathering. His com plate was in his hand, propped against his right side. He was smiling, almost sympathetically looking back at the spy lens in the door. Hayes sighed and slipped the bolt on the door. He opened it.

"Hello, Mister Hayes," the tall man said. "My name is Anthony. I'm glad you decided to see me. There are two companions with me. They are around the corner and won't come out until you say it's all right. I'm fully aware of how frightening all this must be, and we do not wish to add to your fears. May I come in?"

"Um, you can. Tell the others to wait outside," he said.

A tall man in a dark blue pin stripe suit entered while the other two stood in the hall, hands folded loosely across their front, expressionless. To his surprise, all three of the men were so similar that they were almost mirror images of each other. They didn't look like brothers or even as if they were closely related. They were nothing less than identical. Each wore the same dark suit and each sported a red and gold striped tie that was far wider than the formal style of the day. They were the same height and build, and whereas the one called Anthony had nearly jet black hair, the other two were a sandy blond and a russet red. The red head had a splotchy, pinkish complexion while the other two were so pale that their skin was almost translucent.

The two stepped into the room quickly into the room and stood behind Anthony, closing the door. Hayes took a step back but said nothing. While Anthony did the talking, the other two scanned the apartment, apparently looking for any surveillance devices or evidence that Hayes was not alone.

"What are they doing?" Magnus Hayes asked.

"Being sure that you are secure, you're in grave danger, you know."

"I know," he said, almost helplessly. "I know that very well."

"It's okay," said Anthony. "You have more friends than you think, Magnus."

Magnus Hayes felt dizzy and steadied himself against the wall. For some inexplicable reason, he felt secure with these three strangers, as if they were old friends.

"We want you to come with us to a safe place where we can protect you. I know that you must have endless questions, and we'll answer them all as best we can, but we must leave right away. Don't bother with packing. Just

grab your personals and your com plate and come with us. There's no time to lose."

"Just like that?"

"Just like that, Mister Hayes. Remember the Mona Lisa."

Again like the other phrase, this one was delivered with a special emphasis and Hayes' eyes glazed over when he heard it. He gathered those items that he always carried with him, his pocket knife, card to his apartment and his ID folder. Picking up his com plate, he walked out into the hall without another word.

"What do we do about the rest of this stuff?" Asked the red head, looking back into the room.

"Leave it. A clean up crew is on the way."

The four of them left through a side door and entered an alley where a single large van stood waiting. As he moved, Magnus swayed and stumbled, as if he wasn't seeing what was going on around him. He began to drool from the corner of his mouth, his eyes still staring aimlessly straight ahead. All resistance gone, they hustled Magnus Hayes into the bay of the van and drove away.

"Where to?" Asked the driver, a burly man with curly hair and an odor laced with garlic.

"South," Anthony said. "Take it easy. We've work to do."

Hayes was quickly stripped of his clothing and instructed to lie on a medical table, which he did without comment. Inside, he felt a terrifying memory of having done this before. He tried with all his strength to fight their orders. His body seemed to have a mind of its own, separate from whatever shred of free will he still possessed. Beginning to breathe heavily, he emitted little distant moans, barely audible above the thrum of the engine. He could feel the adrenaline coursing through his body in his panic. His muscles began to cramp and twitch as they fought to take action but would not obey him. The three men took off their coats and ties, stepping into coveralls that enveloped them from head to toe. They donned surgical masks and soft protective helmets with clear visors and pulled their garments' hoods over their heads. With a final glance at each other, they began their work.

Anthony began with the hands. Tying off Magnus Hayes' wrists, he picked up a surgical saw and started to sever the hand. Magnus Hayes finally reacted, jerking his ruined arm across his chest. Anthony grabbed it and pinned it again by Magnus' side.

"Remember the Mona Lisa," he whispered, and Magnus relaxed. Holding the nearly separated hand, he began to saw through the bone. After the bone was separated, he grabbed the dangling hand with both of his and yanked, ripping it from the body, dumping it unceremoniously in a plastic pail at his feet, repeating the process with the other hand. The sandy haired man was simultaneously working on the head. He made neat surgical incisions along the base of the jaw from either side and separated the ligaments holding the mandible in place. Finally it was ripped away like some Neanderthal twisting a joint of beef free from a carcass. Immediately, a spray of blood erupted from the gaping wound.

"Watch the blood," Anthony said. "He can't die on us."

A spray was quickly applied to the open wound, sealing it. The second man proceeded to the ears and eyes while Hayes lay perfectly still, not moving in spite of the lack of sedation. His tongue twirled, grotesquely in circles as if searching for the missing jaw.

The red head monitored vital signs and occasionally injected this drug that to keep the man alive, as piece after piece of human body found its way into the pail. Each slab echoed with a resounding slap as it hit the growing pile of discarded parts. When they had finished, Magnus Hayes, now breathing heavily, lay on the table, each wound temporarily sealed, without hands, eyes, ears, testicles, a penis, one of his feet or his nose.

Anthony bent over and bit what was left of his right cheek, sinking his teeth deeply into the flesh and ripping it away. The wound was a gaping hole that went clear through the flesh, exposing molars.

"Jesus," snapped the red head.

"Orders. You get to take a chunk out of his leg."

The man's reddish complexion was suddenly a pale green but he did as he was told. Wrenching a plug of flesh the size of a golf ball out of the man's left thigh, he spitted it into the bucket.

"Now for the delicate work," Anthony said. "Scalpel, please."

ONE

HE WAS DAYDREAMING, sort of. He knew he was awake, but his eyes stared out of the window at a spot on the horizon, unable to pull away from the featureless bumps of distant foothills. Although he was perfectly aware of where he was, his mind processed dream matter in a rapid staccato rush of scenes and emotions. Children surrounded him, some of whom he recognized from his own childhood and others whom he had never seen. They were playing, but with pathos to their faces that made it all seem so orchestrated. None of them exhibited the least spark of spontaneity. It was like watching a play, but there was no discernible audience on the playground. For himself, he was just observing and his head ached with the attempts to remember; to separate the portion of the image that was fantasy and the portion that was memory. Simultaneously, he reminded himself that this had all happened before, with different scenes and different content. It was the inability to stop, to divert his eyes or shake off the image that most disturbed him. Finally, with a supreme effort of will, he shifted in his chair and forced himself to look away from the point on the horizon. Heaving a great huff of air from his lungs, he shook off the reverie, if it could be called that, and he was back. He looked again out the window.

The sky seemed to have a turquoise quality, and after five straight days of rain that was a welcome respite from the usual winter doldrums that the city experienced. Instead of the perpetual slate grey overcast, white cotton clouds lazily paraded across the sky. From his vantage point twenty floors above the street, Charles Peavey could tell that the weather pattern extended into the foothills of the Smokey Mountains on the horizon. He looked out at the late winter scene and its promise of an early spring, thinking to himself how totally boring it all was.

Charles sighed, looking again at the screen in the center of his desk, shuffling aside three notes that were hiding the corners of the photograph it displayed. He traced his finger over the image. It ran down the mast and along the spar of the sailboat beneath his hand, then up the angle of the pristine white sail. He traced the image down again along the billowing spinnaker. On the side, in flowing script, was the boat's name, the *Nattie Bumpo*, thinking again how much he missed his old boat, and how long it had been since he had been anywhere near it.

In the photograph, he stood at the wheel, his wife Karen beside him. He was grinning and looking very much like the master of his world. His light brown hair was highlighted with those sun bleached streaks that always appeared in the summer months back in his sailing days, and his body was hard and well muscled. Absently, he thought about how he'd let himself slip out of that level of fitness in the last few years. He was still broad shouldered and powerful for his age. At six foot three he was tall but not disproportionate to the general population, and his light blue eyes gave him a softness that often put people at ease.

Karen on the other hand was small, with curves in all the right places and a smile that carried a sharp edge to it. Never seeming completely relaxed, even in those days, she was a good companion for the most part, and a very attentive lover. How they loved that boat and how they loved to sail her off the coast and down to the Keys. All that was gone now. How long had it been? Was it really seven years already? Since then, he could not remember a point in his life where he had felt alive. Every day seemed to bleed into the next. Every moment seemed like the one before. He had hoped to bury himself in his work when he took on this job, but it was like any other vigilance position, full of boredom with brief moments of excitement. Lately there had been very little excitement. This was definitely not what he expected, but then neither was anything else in his life.

Perhaps he'd find an excuse to leave. He could always claim he was fact finding. His specialty, Human Dynamics, allowed him to get away with that. One of the few benefits he had working Homeland Security here was that any time he felt like it, he could just take a walk or prowl the back alleys of Atlanta. He could claim that he was just 'feeling the pulse' of the people, looking for 'abberants' and the like. Actually, he didn't know why he bothered to justify such excursions. No one really cared anyway. Punch in, punch out. It was all the same to his superiors.

On impulse, he stood, sweeping his jacket and cap from the back of the chair as he walked to the elevators at the end of the room. He entered, pushed a button and leaned back against the cold, enamel-clad wall. Again he sighed for no apparent reason and slipped his smog mask casually over his mouth and nose. For a brief moment he considered the goggles as well but dismissed the thought. He hated those things. They always made him look like some sort of angry frog. From the lobby, Charles made his way out of the main entrance and onto the street. As expected, the low, thick pollution that often hung over the streets, no matter what the weather was like on the twentieth floor, was present, though thinner today. He stepped out into the stream of foot traffic and stalled, having no idea where he was going. Automatically, he checked his cap-camera to be sure it was functioning, more from force of habit than anything else. He then turned right for no good reason, moving north along Peachtree Street.

He wandered, paying almost no attention to where he was going or to the others walking along the wide sidewalks. All of the buildings looked the same to him. All the noises of the city, from the whoosh of traffic to the soft lofting of rubber soled shoes on the black porous sidewalk sounded identical in his mind. It was but a hodgepodge of noise and a blur of color. In his mind, he was back on that sailboat, cruising along the coast toward Free Cuba with Karen. His heart ached at the thought of it.

"I just want to do a little shopping," she had told him. "I need some downtime from the boat. Besides, you need to fix that halyard, don't you? I'll only be a little while."

Off she had gone, like so often. Nevertheless, he pretended not to notice how anxious she was to get away or how she had changed and primped for the shopping trip.

It was somewhere around the Fox Historical Museum that he came back to awareness. He found himself standing nearly against a knot of people gathered on a corner waiting for the gate to open that would allow them all to cross the street. He looked around him. The hairs on the back of his neck were standing straight out. His sixth sense told him to be careful. As unobtrusively as possible he looked around at the faces in the crowd, but nothing seemed out of the ordinary, no one seemed significant. Turning a full circle, he pretended to be looking for someone in the distance while his cap-camera recorded everyone and everything around him. He did it casually as he had been trained.

"I'm over here, Mr. Peavey, across the street," a voice said. The soft deep voice speaking to him in his ear, the signal coming clearly through the voice inductor. Charles scanned the four corners of the intersection. His gaze came to rest on a smiling man, looking at him from the old hotel's veranda across the street. He was tall and extremely thin with long white hair pulled back in a pony tail and a full tightly curled black beard. He wore no mask and no goggles. It was a terrible disguise, but it was enough to hide the man's identity.

"That's right, Mr. Peavey," the figure said nodding and smiling. "I'm over here. I want you to listen to me carefully."

"Who are you?" He said aloud and several people in the crowd looked at him quizzically. He separated himself from the group and moved back along the sidewalk a few paces.

"First, who I am really doesn't matter. Secondly, I'm not at liberty to say. I have a message for you, and the only way to insure privacy was to wait for one of your meandering walks where the short range of my device would minimize the probability of someone else picking up the conversation."

"This is ridiculous! You must be agency, if you're scrambling and descrambling signals on this frequency," Charles said flatly.

"Clumsy try, Mr. Peavey. As I said, I'm not at liberty to discuss who I am with you."

"Suppose I just come over there and you can give me the message face to face, then?"

"I . . . don't advise it. I'd be gone before you could cross the street, and I'm afraid close proximity would endanger both of us."

Now his interest was peaked. Whoever this character was, he was doing a good job of relieving Charles' boredom. He casually looked away, examining his watch and then his fingernails. "So what's the message?"

"Things are never what they seem."

"Okay. I can buy that. You needed to hide in the shadows to tell me that?"

"Yes, I did. You're under surveillance, you know."

Charles frowned and looked back at the man. "By whom?"

"I could tell you, but since things are never what they seem, it would just lead to confusion."

"Look," said Charles, "This is the most ridiculous conversation I've had in my entire life. You sound like a Sufi spouting *koans*. If you've got something to say, just say it!"

"Actually, that's all I have to say, but to convince you that I'm serious about all this, I might remind you that this is not the most ridiculous conversation you've ever had. How about the one you were engaged in last week with Cinnamon? Remember? You argued over the origin of pudding. Now that was a truly ridiculous conversation."

"Pudding? What are you . . . ?" Charles remembered the conversation now. It really was silly. How could this man know about that? He looked back to the veranda only to find the man gone.

"'Guy's a lunatic," he said to himself, turning on his heels, and hurrying back toward the office.

The more he thought about it, the weirder the incident seemed to him. If it were a prank, it was an elaborate one, considering the technology necessary to pull off that little conversation back on the corner. If the man were serious, lunatic or not, he had access to some very sophisticated and very secret technology that civilians were not even supposed to be aware of. Then there was the 'message'. *Things are never what they seem?* What was that supposed to mean?

As soon as he was back in the office, he poured himself a cup of Black Rock Tea from the ever brewing pot on the far corner of his desk. Afterward he accessed the data from his cap-camera. Giving it a quick perusal, what he found simply added to his confusion. When his unit was pointed at the veranda of the hotel, it showed no one standing there. Skipping ahead to the conversation, prepared to replay what was said and begin an I.D. inquiry on the image, nothing was there. No man was standing on the porch of the hotel, and there was no audio record of the conversation. It was as if it had never happened. Charles shook his head, a knee jerk reaction to the confusion. At this point, anything that would help clear his head was fine with him. Could he have imagined the whole episode?

Slipping the cap-camera into the diagnostic slot on his console, he ran every check he could think of, trying to find some flaw in the equipment. Repeatedly the readouts came back: No flaws, no malfunctions, no tampers of any kind evident in the device or its operation were to be found. Charles was beginning to suspect that his daydreams were beginning to creep into his mind ever more forcefully. It was all so real. He simply couldn't believe it was all in his head.

Composing an inquiry to the central communications administrator to check his cap-camera for anomalies, he dumped it before it was sent. If he were losing it, no need to give anyone in the agency ammunition. They already thought him strange enough without this. Almost absently, he made a mental note to look into it later.

Leaning back in his chair, he took a long pull on his Black Rock tea and attempted in vain to cross his legs. Unconsciously he caught the edge of the desk with his shin, wincing at the sharp pain. The tea spilled everywhere, its more caustic ingredients beginning to eat at the floor almost immediately. He could tell that this was just not going to be a good day. Whatever had just happened on the street, had really shaken him up and he knew it. Looking around at the other desks in the office, he noticed some were manned but most were empty, and he wondered why these people even existed as a unit anymore. No one seemed to have noticed his distress or the fumes spiraling up from the floor. Were they really that unconscious? Were things so lax that his mind was making up events just to keep from being bored?

Homeland Security was a dead issue and had been for years. There hadn't been a serious terrorist threat for more than two decades, but government was government, and once created, a bureaucracy takes on a life of its own. Like a living organism, it wants to survive and grow. Only rarely did some agency that had outlived its usefulness actually go out of business without a fight. That was too much like committing suicide and even Homeland Security wasn't that psychotic. It leaned more toward the paranoiac.

Sighing for the hundredth time, he looked up as a movement from the direction of the elevators caught his eye. Charles eyed his FEMA counterpart as he approached, noting the worried look on his face. He had a determination in his walk that looked like urgency. Of course, in Sergei Melinov's case, that was usual. He made an art of making the most mundane of events a national emergency. Charles long ago decided that the man was as bored as he, just more creative in dealing with it.

"I'm glad you're in," Sergei said breathlessly from more than twenty feet away. "I've got something here that requires your special expertise."

"Hello, Sergei," Charles said dully. "How's the family?"

"Hmm? Oh, they're fine, Carl. Listen now. This is important."

"That's Charles, Sergei, not Carl. It's not Chad or Charlie or Carlton or Chuck. Did I miss any? It's Charles."

"Hmm? Yes. Of course. I know that. Is that Black Rock tea you're drinking? You know that stuff will kill you some day. Now will you please pay attention?"

Charles sat up and leaned forward in his chair, signaling Sergei to take the seat. Sergei looked at the straight-backed metal chair hesitantly and decided to remain standing.

"I've got an investigation for you."

"Do you now."

"They've found a body and the investigator in charge has asked for us to send someone. It's rather unusual, you see."

Charles just looked up at the man passively and said nothing. He waited for Sergei to launch into his usual semi panic about what would turn out to be nothing more than a simple mugging or a marital argument gone bad. He waited for the punch line, but Sergei didn't speak.

In final desperation, he said, "A body is not that unusual, so I assume that it's the circumstances of the find that the supervisor finds strange?"

"Well, yes. Of course," Sergei said, and again fell silent.

Charles was losing patience. Sergei reminded him of one of those psychoanalysts who never spoke until prompted. In Sergei's case the behavior was more patient than Freudian analyst.

"Wanna fill me in?" He said at last.

"Um, well, I'm not sure what to tell you except that we have a body and it's been mutilated."

"Mutilated how?"

"Missing limbs, eyes gouged out. That sort of thing. The Super said he's never seen anything like it. He wants some expert opinion, and I naturally thought of you."

"Naturally," said Charles, but he was beginning to think that if nothing else. This might have some potential for bringing him back from whatever fantasy world he'd stepped off into this morning. "Perhaps," he thought, "some deviant was out there playing games, but more likely . . ."

"Did the Super say which limbs were missing?"

"No, Carl, I'm sorry. He didn't."

"That's Charles, Sergei. Damn it, I wish you'd remember that! Probably just a jilted lover gouging eyes out and severing a penis, but we'll see."

"Then you'll go?" Sergei said with a quick breath.

"Straight away," Charles said and stood up. Sergei grinned broadly, pleased that he had instigated an investigation. As contact man for FEMA with the Office of Homeland Security, he didn't often find a chance to do anything but plan, plan and plan again. The sole reason for his planning was a preventive measure, just in case some terrorist attack might actually occur. Sergei would give his pension to work a good flood or earthquake. Nobody wanted terrorist attacks again, not after the Boston incident of '18.

Almost as an after thought, Charles said, "You haven't seen my partner, have you?"

"Um, no," Sergei replied, fiddling with his clipboard viewer. "Here. I'm transferring the information on the case to you."

Pushing a few buttons on the keyboard of his communications plate, Sergei watched the instructions appear on the flat screen with satisfaction. Sergei was the only man that Charles Peavy knew who could take pleasure in something as mundane as using the universal communications device. He played it like a toy.

"No matter. She's probably in the lab. I'll find her."

Charles pressed a red tab on his clipboard and the scene changed. He was looking at the lab on the floor below from the vantage point of a surveillance camera in the corner of the ceiling. Nearby was the figure of a woman, busily staring at a microscope screen and scribbling notes. She was quite pretty, with what seemed light red hair. These days, it was not a sure thing what color an operative's hair would be, either in real life or through a surveillance camera. If she were using a deceptive wash, how she looked in person and how she looked through a camera lens could be quite different.

He studied her for a while, admiring her concentration and the way her forehead crinkled when she was deep in thought. For a long moment, he said nothing, just watched her. He paid particular attention to her eyes, as she manipulated the view of whatever was on the screen, to investigate some nuance or detail. How she could discern those minor variations in a sample of flesh or in the anatomy of some bug was quite beyond him. Still, those details were her specialty, and she was supreme at it. After a few moments, she shut her notebook, turned off the viewer, retrieved the slide from the microscope and slid sideways along the bench and out of camera range.

Charles slapped the small button on his lapel and waited for the beep. "Where are you?" He said.

A clear voice spoke into his ear and said, "Just coming out of the lab. What's up?"

"An assignment, I think. Meet me in transport."

"Anything good?" The voice inquired.

"Probably not, but at least we'll get out of here for a while. I'll tell you about it when I see you."

"I beep," the voice said.

Charles smiled at Sergei. "We'll take care of it. I'll get back to you when we have more information." The FEMA rep turned with a nod and left.

Charles grabbed his com plate beta unit and headed for the elevator. Entering, he punched the appropriate key. In less than a minute, he was exiting onto a platform on the edge of the building some twenty floors above his office. A chilled wind was whistling through the waiting area, blowing in through the gaping hole in the building's wall opposite the tramway floor where he stood. Beyond there was only empty space and the smell of a very fragrant world. At least fragrant was what Charles preferred to call the mixture of odors that always permeated the air at this height. It was sweet and musty, chemical and metallic, thanks to the way the recycled air of the building mixed with the fumes beyond. Fragrant was such an acceptable word for what his nostrils were trying desperately to ignore. He involuntarily wrinkled his nose and blew out, hoping to clear the passage.

"You could just wear a mask, you know," said a voice behind him. He turned and smiled halfheartedly at his partner.

"If I did that, I'd look like everybody else. It's worth it just to have an identity. So how's everything, Cinnamon?"

His partner smiled at him. Even through her mask he could tell she was smiling from the way her eyes crinkled up at the edges. As usual, he looked her up and down, still able to appreciate feminine beauty and wishing that it did something for him beyond the aesthetic. She wore the same uniform as everyone else in the department, straight legged grey wool slacks, a black turtleneck and a dark blue blouse over it, and the ever present jacket emblazoned with the Homeland Security shield. Somehow, on her very shapely five foot ten inch frame, it took on a whole different look than when worn by the other women. Even the way she moved was different; lithe, more catlike than athletic. He'd seen her respond to threat with a quickness that was astonishing. He was lucky to have her for a partner, he knew it. Why she'd chosen him he could never fathom. He'd done nothing but give her trouble.

"Things are fine, Charles. And to answer your next questions, Peter is doing well, we're not engaged and I don't know when or if we ever will be. No, I don't want a new partner. Now that's out of the way, what's up?"

Charles said nothing for a moment, then, "Am I really that predictable?"

"Yup. It's time for a new routine."

"I'll work on it," he mumbled.

"So what's the assignment?"

They waited while the tram arrived with a loud hiss to take them to the transport hub and they got in. As usual, they were totally alone in the car.

"What'll it be today, skyway or highway?"

Charles gave her a look of consternation and turned away.

"Skyway it is," she said and stabbed at three buttons on the console.

"Hmm," said Cinnamon. "So what's the location?"

"I'm not sure. It's in the on board Travelstar. We'll be vectored automatically."

"I hope it's somewhere really seedy," Cinnamon said with a grin. Charles looked over. She was almost salivating. Was it possible that she was bored with all this also? Maybe the whole damned world was bored. "Now that would be something, wouldn't it," he thought to himself.

"It's one of Sergei's alerts, I'm afraid. They've found a body, and there's mutilation. The Super on the scene seems to think it's strange enough to get outside input. He called local control, who called FEMA, who threw the job at us. I doubt if it's anything, but if you're as bored as I am, it could be a good excuse to be out. Besides, there's always hope."

At transport they transferred to the Travelstar and in moments were quietly winging their way out over the city. They turned east and accelerated without gaining altitude. Charles looked down as they began paralleling one of the prime arteries that connected the central city to what were known as the 'burghs'. Of course what had once been smaller communities surrounding Atlanta were now just part of the metro area, extending nearly one hundred twenty-five miles in every direction. The road below, once an artery, was now just a thin grayish line cutting through denser living space. Traffic was at a standstill.

"You really travel to work on those roads," he asked Cinnamon.

"Every day and you know it. You should try it some time. It's very relaxing. I just sit back, catch up on my reading, talk to Pete or friends and if I'm late, it's the traffic's fault, not mine."

"Must take hours," he snorted.

"Hour and a half to two, but that's not bad. Think about those people who live further out. If they're not on a rail line, they're really cooked. I remember one day last summer, the day of the killer smog alert. You remember it? Well, I was just starting out and had gotten onto the beltway ready to merge with the main flow when the word came down. People scattered like rabbits. I mean, cars went everywhere. I thought I was going to be stuck for hours. You know with all these people trying to get off the freeway, I just headed for the almost empty center lane and sealed the compartment. Thank goodness for all that extra air exchanging equipment I had installed. Anyway, to make a long story short . . . "

"That would be nice," Charles mumbled, but she ignored it.

"I got to work in record time, and no more than ten minutes after I pulled off, the whole system came to a dead stand still. Four people had suffocated or died of respiratory distress from the pollution levels just north of where I got on. By the time they cleared the vehicles, a dozen more had died."

"I remember," said Charles. "That's one reason you'll never catch me in that mess," he murmured. "Why you don't take a sky car, I'll never know."

Cinnamon cast one of those exasperated looks she did so well. "Because I don't have two hundred K plus to buy one and I'm not going to hire one. Who knows whose been riding in one of those things?"

"Me," he said trying to appear insulted, and failing miserably.

The Travelstar lurched to one side and turned to the south, now picking up speed. Wherever they were going, it was somewhere between the city central and the Florida line.

"I don't know why you want to get to work so early anyway," Cinnamon said. "God knows there's nothing going on, Charles. What you need is a good playmate, someone to take your mind off the routine."

"You mean someone like your Pete?"

"Don't be difficult," she said turning away. He looked over at her again, studying her. Her chestnut hair fell to her shoulders perfectly. Even her ears were works of art. Charles shook himself free of the thought. They'd been partners for a very long time now, and he still fought the urge to reach out and caress her hair. He looked away.

"I just can't afford a toy right now, Cin."

"He's no toy!"

"Okay, a pet then. Maybe you can support Pete while he tries to become the next Copeland or Bernstein, but I can't play that game."

Cinnamon said nothing, which was somewhere between miraculous and astounding. She continued to look out the window at the passing terrain but Charles caught every subtle hint of her anxiety and her control. He'd learned to read her "tells" long ago. Charles had hurt her more than he'd intended and he knew it.

"I'm sorry, Cin. You know I don't mean anything by it. How's it going with Peter anyway?"

She sighed. "I don't know. Sometimes I think he's more trouble than he's worth. My mother always told me never to get involved with a professor or an artist."

"Your mother's a wise person. Both can be self absorbed."

"Oh, if only that were the case."

Charles looked past her out the window.

"I think we're slowing down," Cinnamon said. Charles took a moment to recover from that remark, his mind having gone in an entirely different direction. He tried to ignore the bumps and shudders of the decelerating craft.

"So what's the problem with Pete anyway?"

"He dotes on me. It's as if he has no life outside his relationship with me."

"In every relationship there is a dominant and a submissive, no matter how well camouflaged the dynamic may be," he quoted. "The submissive is always more committed to the relationship than the dominant, creating an imbalance that, if not managed, can lead to serious and sometimes dangerous consequences."

"Thank you Dr. Harlan," she said sarcastically.

Charles started again to say something, but the moment was lost as a wave of nausea accompanied the slight weightlessness of their descent. The sky car spiraled down toward a large complex surrounded by interstates, rail lines and parking lots. It took him a moment to recognize it, but he finally said, "That's Perry. We just blew past Macon. We're pretty far south this time."

The sky car zeroed in on a parking spot beside a service entrance to the mall complex. Below them they could see perhaps a dozen official ground and air vehicles, all state and locals, with flashing blue and green or red lights. To one side and farther out was an ambulance with its rear doors opened widely. More than a dozen uniformed men and women were arranged just beyond the vehicles. On the ground, covered with a tarp of some description, was what Charles could only assume to be the victim.

The sky car came to rest just beyond the ambulance and they stepped out, Cinnamon retrieving her voluminous handbag from the cargo area behind the seats. They walked quickly toward the spot where the police were gathered. Charles took it all in, cataloging every person at the scene, their gestures, their tells, their clothing and the way they stood. The cap-camera insured that there would be a record of everything he saw for later analysis. Cameras were literal but he still depended on his own first impressions to give him direction in how to proceed in any investigation. At the moment, all he could detect was fear and confusion. Beside him, Cinnamon was similarly engaged but required no cap-camera. Her eidetic memory insured that she'd find any details that he missed. That eidetic memory of hers was also how she could predict what he might say next and how she recognized the quotation from Dr. Julian Harlan.

Near the body was a tall older man dressed in a supervisor's light blue uniform. His cap was pulled forward, the bill half covering his eyes as if protecting him from the sun, but Charles recognized him immediately. There was no mistaking that stance or the way he rocked when he was noodling out some problem. Standing in the shade of the building, he looked over at them from beneath the cap as they arrived, then grinned and popped a hand full of small hard candies into his mouth.

"Good God, it's Charlie Peavey. I thought you died."

Charles nodded.

"I did, Ben. I'm back to haunt you," he said pleasantly.

"Brought me an angel I see."

Cinnamon extended her hand to the super and smiled.

"Cinnamon Harper," she said. "I'm Charles' partner."

"Always liked cinnamon," Delano said with a broad grin. "It's a good way to spice up life."

Cinnamon ignored the remark and shook his hand. She released it quickly and looked at Charles questioningly.

"Cinnamon, this is Ben Delano. He and I go way back, I'm afraid. He used to be a Federal."

Ben nodded.

"The pay's better at the local level," he said simply. "I'm glad you two are here."

Charles managed a reasonable smile, but his mind was working overtime. Ben Delano was nobody's fool. He was well trained and he'd had experience with Federal task forces during the last terrorist scare nearly ten years ago. If he were the one that called in Homeland Security, there just might be something to all this.

"What have you got, Ben?" Charles said bluntly.

"Damn, Charlie. Didn't your parents ever teach you to warm up to a conversation?"

"Never knew my parents, Ben. You know that. You called us, now what are we here for?"

Delano nodded toward the tarp. "Well, we've got a body, but this is definitely not the crime of passion here. I wouldn't even call it a hate crime. I've never seen anybody chewed up like this before. It looks ritual to me, but it's got me downright scared. My intuition tells me there's something very weird about this one. I'd like your take on it."

They walked to where the body lay beneath the tarp spread out over the corpse. Blood and other fluids oozed beyond the edges of the eight-foot square covering the corpse. Much of the blood was dried, but there was a peculiar pearly substance still lying wet on the surface of the spatters. Delano reached down and carefully pulled back the sheet for them to see.

"Holy shit!" Said Charles. Cinnamon let out a brief breathy 'whoof' and retreated several steps.

"That's about what I said, Charlie."

"Mother of God!" Charles said in a whisper. "That's the damnedest thing I've ever seen!"

TWO

BEN DELANO POPPED ANOTHER HANDFUL of small candies in his mouth and began to chew and talk at the same time. He was like the Greek orator who used pebbles to overcome a speech impediment. As before, he rocked from side to side as if he were listening to music in his head. Crunching the small candies vigorously, popping a second handful into his mouth, he gulped down what was already macerated.

"This is exactly how we found him," he mumbled, spitting tiny flecks of white sugar in the process. "I'm afraid the lady that reported the body was so traumatized that they took her off in an ambulance. Her medchip must have gone berserk. The medtechs were here before we were. Anyway, his pockets are empty and all his clothing is standard, as near as we can tell. We'll be able to tell more when we get him to the lab."

Charles forced himself to take a closer look at the body, but it wasn't easy. Both hands and one foot had been torn away, as had both ears. It was if they had been ripped away by powerful jaws or a heavy machine of some sort. The nose had been severed cleanly, as if done by a scalpel, and the eyes were missing as were the man's testicles and penis. Even his lower jaw was gone, as were his upper teeth. His chest had been opened with surgical precision though the ribs were pulled away haphazardly, and it appeared the heart was missing. The shriveled lungs lay across his ruined sternum. What disturbed him most of all was that the fact that the body had apparently been gnawed, particularly the cheeks and one leg. None of this made any sense at all.

"Are you sure this guy's medchip didn't go off? Maybe the medics were here because he died."

Delano shook his head. "According to the medtech, it was the woman's chip that got 'em out here. Makes you wonder if he were killed somewhere else and dumped, but all that blood says otherwise."

"There's no identification on him at all," asked Cinnamon, now recovered from the initial shock, exchanging glances with Charles, hers a silent apology and his an assurance that it was all okay.

"None. Like I said, it looks ritual to me, and the way he's laid out, all spread eagle like that. Someone is very, very sick."

"Did you check for a penis?" She said.

"Not there. It's the first thing I checked for. It's gone."

"Well," said Charles, "with both hands gone we can't use prints, and without eyes, there will be no retinal scans to work with. Whoever did this even took the teeth so that we couldn't use dental records. Someone doesn't want this guy identified. We'll have to do it with DNA,"

"That's my thought too. So you want this investigation? I got a dozen other murders to work on between Macon and Chattanooga. I'd love to dump this one."

"Have your lab boys been here yet?" Cinnamon asked, bending down to examine the white pearly substance glistening beside the body.

"All done. We were just waiting for you guys before we packed him up."

Cinnamon looked up at Charles, squinting against the sunlight. "I don't know anything we need to do here, Charles, do you? I don't see anything that suggests a national threat."

Charles nibbled on his lower lip which he did when he was troubled. He wished that this were more than just bizarre, if for no other reason to give them something to do for a few days. "Not much that I can see. Sorry, Ben, but I think we'll let you play with this one. Can you let us know what the lab finds? Oh, and if you need anything from our database, just say so. I'll get you whatever you want."

Ben Delano frowned, disappointed. "Well, that'll help, but I was sure hoping to dump this one. Okay. We'll let you know."

They stood to one side, looking around to watch the crowd gathered around while the medtechs came forward to load the body. They were just sliding the cart into the ambulance when a familiar high-pitched wail filled the air.

"Damn!" Said Charles.

"Another alarm? That's the third one this week."

"The sky was clear as a bell when we left," Charles added, looking up at the grey-green clouds rolling in from the west.

"Okay, folks," yelled Delano. "That's an alert, folks. Everyone inside. It's probably nothing, but inside anyway."

Around them, the crowd began to disburse as the police attempted to seal the death scene with a tarp. The ambulance driver began maneuvering their vehicles under the cover of the inside garage area. The police soon followed suit. They didn't bother to look for a parking space. They merely slipped the body into the ambulance and pulled into the aisles and parked as far away from the open air as they could. Ben looked at the two Federals and shook his head.

"Can't control the weather," Cinnamon called back to the Super with a smile. "Maybe I'll get some shopping in while we're here."

"Or lunch with me?" Ben asked grinning.

"Not likely, Delano. Not after seeing that body. Besides, Charles owes me a lunch. You can join us if you'd like."

Delano shook his head and tried to look pleasant, but his disappointment was obvious. He gave Charles a conspiratorial look. "Too much to do here. Thanks, though."

As Delano turned away, Charles and Cinnamon moved along with the crowd toward the nearest mall entrance. At the door, Cinnamon stopped. "Should we try to move the sky car?"

"Too late," Charles said and nodded in the direction of their vehicle. A heavy rain was beginning in earnest out in the parking lot, and bright flashes of lightning were splitting the air all around them. It was a very hot storm, violent and fast moving. It would be over soon, but it would probably do some damage along the way. They moved quickly through the doors and as soon as they were inside, Cinnamon exchanged her pumps for tennis shoes, carefully placing the low heeled dress shoes in a plastic bag and sealing it. She slipped the bag into her industrial sized handbag, and then stepped onto the escalator, carrying them toward the main floor and the retail concourse.

The wind was picking up as they entered the mall and the sound of rain was replaced with the rattling hiss of hail beginning to fall. A look of recognition passed between them. This could be a very serious storm. Charles was glad for the strength of the building. They did their best to ignore the din as they emerged from the stairs into the vast open shopping area.

"So what's this about owing you a lunch?"

"Hmm? Oh, that. I just didn't want to suffer through the attentions of your friend Mr. Delano. Come to think of it, I bought last time, didn't I?"

Charles did some quick mental calculations and nodded. "Where do you want to eat?"

"How about Georgiana's? I hear they have an incredible pasta dish there."

"Sounds expensive," he said flatly.

"I'm worth it," she teased. He looked down at her, trying to forget another time and how appealing she could be; laughing almost too loudly, they headed for the directory at in the center of the mall.

Cinnamon didn't say much throughout lunch, which was not like her. It was so not like her that Charles actually noticed. He'd been ruminating about what they'd seen in the parking lot when he suddenly realized that any of Cin's usual chatter had not interrupted his thoughts. Looking up, he saw her silently toying with the remains of a much too large pasta salad and frowning.

"What's up?" He asked.

"Hmm? Oh probably the same thing that's up with you. That body just doesn't seem right somehow. It doesn't fit any pattern I'm aware of."

"Yeah, but what does it mean?"

"I think this was the act of a very calculating and sane person."

"The pattern's too random to be random?"

She brightened and nodded. "That's it exactly! It's so perfectly insane that it can't be what it appears to be!"

Charles nodded, giving up on the *coq au vin,* he'd tried desperately to like but didn't. He placed his utensils a bit too neatly on the plate and slid it back precisely two inches on the table.

"I agree. Things are never what they seem to be," he said, remembering the morning walk. "I'm not sure what's going on, but it's not sexually oriented, obviously not an act of rage and obviously not strictly cultish in nature. It's got elements of all three. Nobody's that screwed up!"

Cin shuddered. "What if they are?"

"What do you mean?"

"You saw the way the body was gnawed. I mean, I've seen that before, Charles. We both have, but only with a completely dissociative personality. There'd have to be no shred of humanity left in the psyche for someone to do that, even if they are a calculating personality. If that's what Ben's dealing with, then he's got a very bad situation."

Charles frowned and said nothing. He didn't want to think what he was thinking right now, much less share it with anyone. He had seen it before, but not in a civilized culture. Involuntarily, he shuddered and called for the check.

As they stood, he glanced across the room toward the far wall and froze. He laid the check down on the table and started toward a couple in the corner.

"Hey!" called Cinnamon. "'You gonna leave me with the check again? What about taking Cin to lunch?"

Charles ignored her. He stared fixedly at the couple ignoring everything else. When he had covered nearly half the distance to the opposite wall, the woman looked up and did a masterfully executed double take. There was barely a flicker of the eyes, but it was enough to let him know that she had spotted him. She spoke briefly to her companion and then they rose, laying a fist full of bills on the table and headed for the door.

Charles broke into a run, making contact with one auto waiter which deftly sidestepped the collision with a whine of its servos. He then wove his way through a cluster of tables separating him from the retreating couple. By the time he reached the door, half the patrons of the restaurant were staring at him. He pushed aside the doors and stepped out into the main mall, searching for the fleeing couple. They were nowhere to be seen.

Cinnamon hurried through the doors behind him a moment later and nearly ran into him. He stood silently staring out at the crowd.

"What the hell are you doing, Charles?"

He didn't reply.

"Charles? I said what are you doing?"

"I, uh . . . I thought I saw someone I knew," he said, half in a daze.

"Who? Was it Jack the Ripper?"

He looked down at her only vaguely aware of her presence and said nothing.

"Okay, Charles. What's going on? You might as well tell me. I'll see it all later on the cap-camera readout anyway."

He jerked his head, clearing it and exhaled for the first time in what seemed like minutes. "It was nothing," he said. "Sorry. Let's pay the check and get out of here."

When they reached the table, he picked up the check, but Cinnamon grabbed his hand. When he looked at her, she was looking up at him intently.

"Who did you see, partner?"

"I, um, I thought I saw Karen."

"She's dead, Charles. She's dead, isn't she?"

Charles offered a shudder and nodded. "'Couldn't be her, could it?" He said.

"'Couldn't be her," she agreed.

"I'm sorry, Cin. I really am. It's just that she looked so much like her, and the way the two of them got up and left in such a hurry. I thought it had to be her."

"If I'd seen you coming at me like that I'd have left in a hurry too. You're lucky they didn't call security."

Charles looked down at her again and laughed. "I suppose you're right. I guess it was stupid, wasn't it? Let's get out of here. We need to be back in the office."

Outside, it was worse than they'd feared. The storm had not quite been a tornado, but it was severe enough. The huge expanse of the parking lot was white with hail. Charles knelt and picked up one piece, about the size of a soft ball, and tossed it in the air. He looked for the air car but couldn't find it.

"This thing's still hard as a rock," Charles said, rolling it in his hand. "There's been some real damage done here. The insurance companies are going to have a stroke."

"So's the motor pool," Cinnamon said, nodding toward a low mound of white ten yards away. "I think that's the sky car."

"Damn!" He said. "Now what do we do?"

"Um, well you remember that ground transport you hate so much? Looks like you're going to have a chance to ride. The rail line is on the other side of the mall. It'll take us right into town and drop us off about a block from the office."

Charles growled and heaved the hail stone as far as he could. It was an impressive throw, but short of what he used to be able to do in college. Still, it was enough to impress Cinnamon. She whistled and gave an appreciative nod.

"Just shut up," he said and walked back the way they had come.

THREE

THEY MADE THEIR WAY QUICKLY to the train station on the far side of the mall and bought commuter class tickets. Charles shuddered when they entered the half-filled car, thinking about what lay ahead. This was a commuter line, but a very ambitious one, that ran from south of Perry through the Atlanta complex and northwest to Chattanooga, total distance more than two hundred miles. When it first opened, it was a wonder, a rapid and comfortable way to get from the burghs to the central core of the city. It had been spacious, sweet smelling, clean and safe. With use, it had naturally deteriorated so that now it was still an effective way to travel, but a bit on the shabby side, and as people moved to fill the small towns along its route, the stops became more frequent and the clientele more varied. Now it reminded him of the rather archaic *Circum de Vesuviana* that ran around the Bay of Naples. This line had air conditioning, saving him the smell of blue collar workers ripe with the aroma of their trades that he had experienced on the way to Sorento. Charles was glad that the Perry station was just 'down the road' from Macon, at the beginning of the run. This of course meant that they actually had seats on the train. The closer they came to Atlanta, the larger the influx of passengers. Charles tried to ignore the masses surrounding him, standing over him, pressing against him as the train shifted in the high speed turns that it occasionally made.

He looked out the window at the passing countryside pocked with housing developments and apartment complexes, over crowded neighborhoods and manufacturing facilities. Occasionally he sighed, yearning for the clean landscape of his childhood.

"See, Charles? This isn't so bad, is it?"

"Compared to what?"

She slipped him a piece of paper, folded in half. He opened it and read the words printed there. "Compared to what?' It said in bold block letters.

"Really that bad, huh?" He said, crumpling the paper and tossing it aside.

Cin laughed and squeezed his forearm. "Just keeping you on your toes. You really do need new material."

"Hmph," he said, and looked out of the window again. "That's what I get for having the same partner for three years."

"You couldn't get along without me and you know it," she said, teasing.

He turned to her with a look so penetrating that she blinked. "You're right about that, Cin. I don't know what I'd have done if you weren't around for the last three years to keep me straight."

The ride was mercifully short. In less than forty-five minutes they were walking toward their offices. Charles automatically studied those around him, reading their body language. Nothing unusual here, he decided. He could sense no dynamic of panic or fear, no anger beyond the norm. They entered the Fourteenth Street Federal Building, passing easily through security that didn't even bother to ask for their I.D.s and went up to their own floor. It was deserted as expected.

"Coffee?" Cin asked as she headed for the back room.

Charles hesitated for a moment, thinking how much he wanted a very large mug of Black Rock tea, but reminded himself of the lecture that would accompany the request. At last he said, "Cream and two sugars."

Cinnamon looked at him over her shoulder. He was smiling.

"New material," he said. She nodded and kept going.

There was a stack of notes on his desk blocking his view of his beloved sailboat, which irritated him as it always did. He looked through them to see if there was anything worth pursuing. Most of them were routine inquiries, follow-ups and inane pronouncements from the powers that be. The motor pool was asking about a missing sky car that should be in the garage, since they were now in the office. The director of public affairs wanted to know if Charles would be available for a news conference on some burgeoning initiative the department had developed. Charles could only hope that he would be informed of its origins in due course. A note from Sergei Melinov inquiring about his field investigation also lay on his desk. Most interesting of all, however, was a scan note from Delano, asking him to call when he could. He laid the stack of messages aside and stared down at the *Nattie Bumpo*. Its pristine sails eternally billowing, shining in the sunlight of a perfect day in the gulf.

Cinnamon was suddenly at his side, placing a cup of steaming coffee on the edge of the desk. From the smell, it was the real thing, part of Cin's private stock. He sipped it slowly, thinking, and then swung his chair around toward her.

"I think we need to run a trace on our dead friend's movements for the last two days. It shouldn't be too difficult. We can start with where we found him and work our way back. If his hands were severed on the spot, the medchip should have a recording of where he was."

"Can we do that without the chip scan?"

"No problem. Just scan for anyone at that spot and see which one suddenly disappears. If we're lucky, we might be able to follow the severed hand before the chip died. What do you think?"

Cinnamon frowned. "I don't know, Charles. You're talking about breaking a primary directive. The public doesn't know that medchips do surveillance on them. Think about it. Just the hint of medchips having that capability could send shock waves through the political structure of the whole country. Surveillance was one of the primary reasons for the original opposition to the program. People still want to maintain the fiction of privacy in their lives. If you do this, what can we do with the information? I'm not sure we should tell Delano. After all, he's not one of us."

"It's okay. Remember that he used to be Federal. I think he had this in mind when we were talking about any help the department could give him. Nobody needs to know how he got the information."

Cinnamon busied herself with her own com unit. Unlike Charles, she ran everything through her clipboard screen, which was now propped up against her desk lamp. Her fingers moved swiftly over the keyboard, accessing files in a sequence that would read the location of everyone at the mall during the last twenty four hours. When one trace disappeared, they knew they'd have their victim. From that point on it was a matter of isolating his individual trace and running it backwards.

In two minutes she sat back in her chair and retrieved her cup from the desk.

"Answer in ten minutes."

Ten minutes went by, but there was no response. At twenty minutes, Cin sent an inquiry, but it came back saying that the search was still running. At thirty minutes, she decided to re-input the data and try again.

Charles was about to help when his desk com interrupted. He slapped the button on his lapel as Ben Delano's name appeared on his desk screen.

"Hello, Ben," he said.

"Hey. I was wondering if you might have any helpful information for me."

Charles nodded as if Ben could see him. "Not yet. We're . . . working on some leads right now, but the information is hard to come by for some reason. Our . . . usual contacts are a little slow."

From the hesitation in Ben's voice, Charles knew that he'd gotten the message. "I understand," Delano said. "We seem to be having trouble at this end too."

"Oh?"

"Yeah. The body's late getting to the lab. It should have been here by now."

"Probably traffic," Charles said. "The trouble with a meat wagon is that it uses surface streets and after the storm that could take a while. Have you checked in with the medtechs on board?

"That's just it, Charlie. We can't seem to raise them, and I can't get a read on their vehicle. It's very strange."

Charles sat up and leaned forward, grabbing a piece of plain white paper and a pen. "Do you . . . want me to ask around?"

"If you can," Delano said casually.

"I'll see what I can do. Do you have any coordinates for me?"

Delano read serial numbers to Charles, which he promptly wrote down. They identified the medchips for the two medtechs who were transporting the body. Anyone monitoring the call would simply think they were grid coordinates from the way Ben Delano parsed out the twelve digit numbers.

Charles hung up and turned back to Cinnamon, who was obviously irritated.

"Whasup?" He asked.

"Friggin' program! It won't give me anything. I don't know what I'm doing wrong."

Charles handed her the paper. "Let it go for the moment. See if you can find these two. It seems Ben's lost his meat wagon."

"You've got to be kidding!"

Charles shrugged and chuckled. "That's what he says. I told him we'd see if we could find it for him."

Cinnamon typed the data and they waited. Again there was no response. They looked at each other and then back at the screen.

"Maybe the system's down," Charles offered.

"It's up. I've already run parallel diagnostics and followed several known' movements for the last two days. Which reminds me. Just why were you eating in a Chinese restaurant last night alone? You know I live for Chinese food!"

"You'd have to bring Pete along. So the system's up. Where does that lead us?"

She shrugged. "Damned if I know."

"Well, keep at it," he said needlessly. She was already torturing the keyboard and shooing him away.

Charles sat back down and leaned back in the chair. He locked his hands behind his head and stared out the window at what appeared to be another approaching storm from the northwest. Silently he cursed the shift in global temperatures that brought on all the bad weather. At least it was temporary, or so they kept saying. The more he thought about the anomalies of the morning the more concerned he became. If the medchip trace was failing, this could be a very dangerous thing. Was it the program or just local conditions? Maybe it was the storm. "Still, better safe than sorry," he thought. He punched numbers into his com.

"Sergei, is that you?"

Sergei stared back at Charles from his clipboard screen, smiling. He started to speak, then stopped and frowned. "You don't look happy, my friend."

Charles cocked his head to one side. "I'm not."

"Then there's something to all this?" Sergei asked, brightening a bit.

"Where did you hear about this body, Sergei?"

"I told you. The supervisor called Central who called me and said it looked strange. I agreed and brought it to you."

"Was it the supervisor on the scene?"

"Um, yes. It was Delano."

"Did he say why he called you instead of me?"

Sergei frowned. "Actually, he didn't. I wondered about it at the time but didn't say anything."

Charles was about to ask another question when a beeping in his ear told him there was another caller. "Hold on," he said, and tapped his lapel button.

"Yes?"

"Hey. It's Ben."

"Good. Why did you call FEMA about this mess this morning?"

The question obviously caught Delano off guard. He waited several seconds before answering. "I called it into Central and they told me to call FEMA, so I did. They said they'd notify Homeland Security. Why?"

"Do you remember who actually told you to call?"

"No . . . I really don't. I can find out if it's important."

"Definitely."

"Listen, Charlie, I need to tell you why I called. We found the meat wagon. It was in a ditch on an access road near Peachtree City. No one's in it."

"And no dead body, I suppose."

"Right. How'd you know?"

Charles scraped his lower lip along the edge of his teeth. "Hold on, Ben. Sergei?"

"Yes?"

"This just became an official Homeland investigation. Tell your people. I don't think there's anything to worry about, but something's going on besides just a dead body. I'll call you back."

Sergei looked almost joyful at the news. He brightened again and nodded, then signed off.

"Ben?"

"Yeah. Still here."

"We're taking over the investigation. Have you got that?"

Silence.

"Ben?"

"I'm here. You think it's that serious?"

"I don't' know. It could be. I'll need all of your information from the scene and the lab results of any trace evidence you've gathered. That includes the air analysis. I assume they're working on that now?"

"As we speak. You want to run your own tests?"

Charles thought for a moment. “I don’t think so. There’s nothing we can do here that you can’t do there. Just get me results as soon as you can. Oh, and Ben? We need to talk face to face. I’m not about to take your department out of the loop on this one, my friend. Meet me here in the morning.”

“You got it.”

“Oh, and Ben, can you tell me exactly who found the ambulance?”

“Satellite feed, actually. I’ve a team on the way to the scene. Right now all we have is photos and scans.”

Charles cut the connection without saying good bye and spun around to find Cinnamon looking at him, concerned. “I’ll alert the team,” she said. “Five this afternoon okay?”

Charles looked at his watch. It was a little after three. He nodded.

“By the way,” she said, “the meat wagon’s beacon is functioning again. I still can’t get a reading on either of the medtechs or surveillance on any deaths nearby.”

“I don’t think you’re going to. Tell the team that this is a level three. They need to be armed.”

FOUR

BY 5:00 P.M. ALL EIGHT TEAM members of Charles' investigation team were seated at one end of the office. Nearly everyone else was gone for the day, which gave them a degree of privacy. Charles looked over the seated agents, pleased to have them all in the group. He had assembled the finest investigative team in Homeland Security, and he knew it. A projection of Charles' clipboard was staring out at them from the wall. Charles played his fingers over the virtual keyboard on the clipboard screen, cycling through pages, checking them quickly, and moving on. He finally came to rest on a screen that displayed a series of still pictures from the mall, showing the output from his cap-camera. They were even more gruesome in high definition than they were in person. Only the smell was missing. Charles droned orders as he manipulated them.

"This is the scene at the Perry Mall this morning when the body was found. Note the missing limbs and the mutilation. The locals did a good job on processing the scene and gathering information, but the body was lost in transit; we don't know how. We have made many attempts to scan medchips to determine either the identity of the deceased or the presence of others in the area at the time of the murder. All have failed."

A general murmur passed among the team members. Several let out low, soft whistles.

"That's why we're here. Anyone who can block medchip scans can potentially represent a threat to National Security. If we can't trace 'em, we can't catch 'em. I want to know who and how as well as why. The murder itself is secondary to our main concern regarding the medchip traces. Since they're obviously connected, we're taking on the investigation of the death as well."

"Any telemetry from the victim's medchip prior to death?" asked one of the team.

"Not a sound. It's as if he didn't have one."

"That's not possible, is it? Everyone gets a chip at birth. It's the law."

"That may be, but the facts are that his didn't register either distress or death. That's another reason we need to figure this one out. Craig, I want you and Susanne to get the scan on the lady that found the body. That's what started this whole thing, and even if we can't access her movements, the record should be at the hospital that sent the ambulance. Check it out personally."

A tall swarthy man with penetrating ebony eyes and a woman of middle age with salt and pepper hair and a small scar on her right cheek nodded.

"Bobby J., I want you and Meg to work the surveillance program backwards until you can find a most recent scan of people at the mall. We'll start with anyone near the location where the body was found. Create a file including their profiles and photos. We'll have Cin look at them and see who matches with those around the body when we got there. We'll do the same for my cap-camera recording. Cinnamon and I are going to monitor the locals' investigation of the meat wagon and follow up on the missing medtechs."

At the far end of the table, the two somber looking young operatives nodded as well.

"Questions?"

In the corner sat an attractive young woman with flame red hair and an aristocratic looking man with a complexion the color of coffee and cream. They hesitantly looked at each other and back to Charles. One of them raised their hand.

"You new guys haven't seen us work yet, have you?"

The newest members both shook their heads.

"First of all, if you have a question just ask it. This isn't a classroom. Everyone's input is important. Secondly, since you're both new to the office and new to the job, you get to split the worst and best jobs on the team. Anton, you get to man the com links. You're now the information coordinator. You take in everything, figure out if it's valuable and see that we get what we need. That's the worst job. Keep in mind that everything is going to be valuable in some context. Sarah, you get the best job. You're our floater. They used to call it the 'odd man'. You have no assignment other than to figure out what we've missed, play with the wildest ideas you can come up with and support anyone who needs another brain. Got it?"

The red head beamed, grinning from ear to ear, her green eyes flashing with excitement. Anton simply nodded stoically, apparently resigned to his fate.

"Okay, guys. Pay attention to this one. There's real potential for harm here, and we need to take care of it stat. Let's do it."

Charles ended the meeting by simply walking away. In his mind he was running scenarios, including one that said he had no idea what he was doing, praying to God that no one noticed. He and Cin began analyzing all the information that Ben was sending them about the body transport. Apparently the ambulance had left the interstate just south of Peachtree City and simply disappeared. An accounting clerk accidentally found it on his way home from work. He'd been checked out thoroughly and found innocent of any involvement Photos of the vehicle showed it laying sideways to the road. Its nose buried in a huge oak tree trunk, back wheels suspended in the air above the rock outcropping on which it rested. Something was odd about the way it sat, but Charles couldn't quite see it.

According to local authorities' information at the scene, the cab and cabin of the ambulance were both completely empty. The gurney was still there but the body was gone. In the driver's area, there was no sign of violence and no blood. Everything looked as if the driver and attendant had simply turned off the truck and stepped out with their deceased passenger for a quick lunch.

Charlie sipped his Black Rock tea and frowned, hoping that the tea's jolt would cure his headache, or at least give him one of its famous fully lucid buzzes. He loved the combination of alertness and feeling of well being that came with the tea. So what if it were addictive? What if it were bad for him?

Cin sat across the desk from him and gave him that maternal look of disapproval. "You know that stuff will kill you one day."

"That's what they say."

"Does it really help?"

Charlie looked up at her from the clipboard and shrugged. "It helps fight off the demons and the boredom."

"Now you're bored?" She said like a New York teamster.

"Nope. This time it's demons. I'm just trying to stay sharp."

"Then stop it with that stuff," she said, and took the mug of tea from his hand. She replaced it with strong coffee, which he accepted without protest.

"Thanks."

She came around and looked over his shoulder at the photos. Charlie watched her out of the corner of his eye and could feel her tension. Her tells were so strong to him that they were almost palpable. It didn't take much to read her.

"So what's bothering you?" He said.

"There's something wrong with the photos. Do you see it?"

"I've been seeing it for hours," he said, rotating the picture slightly to get a better look at the back wheels. "I just can't figure out what it is."

"Have you tried holos?"

"Actually, no," he grumbled. "That would be too much like a good idea."

He manipulated the virtual keyboard and laid the board flat on his desk. An image began to coalesce above it, like a genie forming from the neck of a magic lamp. In moments, they were looking at a three dimensional image of the photo. It began to rotate slowly, offering views of the wreck from every angle. The two of them watched in silence but still saw nothing unusual. It simply didn't look right, and that was all. Finally, Charles typed a single word into the search key. They stared for a moment at the word, ANOMALY as it blinked at them while the system thought the problem through, then reported, NONE DETECTED.

"Got any other ideas, Cin?"

She shook her head and sat back in the chair. "I'm fresh out, but I don't care what the system says, something's not right."

There was a sharp buzz in Charles ears and he automatically tapped his lapel button. His screen cleared, the holo disappearing in the process. The image of their immediate superior, Homeland Security Section Commander Darren Rich replaced it.

"Peavy, I hear you're running an investigation."

"How'd you know that so fast?"

"It's my job to know such things, Peavy. Now what's it all about?"

Charles thought for a moment. The last thing he needed was Rich looking over his shoulder. "It may be nothing. We were asked to consult on a murder case. Someone was killed down at the Perry Mall and mutilated. It was unusual enough that the locals asked for a consultation."

The image of Darren Rich glared out of the screen at him. The man was not pleased. "And you were going to tell me about this when?"

"Um, sorry boss. I hadn't gotten around to it. I was a bit busy working the information."

Rich looked like a thundercloud and Charles was about to get rained on. "Cut the crap, Peavy. If you're working a case, I'm supposed to know about it! Protocol, Peavy. You've heard of it?"

"Sorry Darren. I'll send copy on it immediately.

"See that you do," Rich said, suddenly pleased with himself. Charles had always thought the man would have made a great silent movie star, the way he overacted his every gesture.

"Yes sir."

"And don't spend too much money! Are you spending money?"

"No sir. So far it's all been computer time and people who are getting paid anyway. Of course, there was the sky car, but that wasn't our fault. I can't control the weather."

"That was you? The transportation pool has been on my ass all afternoon about that missing flyer. What happened? Never mind. We'll discuss that later!"

The screen went blank.

"And a good day to you too, sir," Charles said quietly.

Cinnamon was suddenly at his side again, another cup of coffee in hand. Charles turned up his lip at it and shook his head. "C'mon, Cin. I'm floating now."

"So pee."

"Um, not a bad idea. I'll be back."

Charles sat in the stall with the door closed, his feet propped up against the door to avoid anyone noticing that he was in there. He found that it was one of the few places where he could have complete privacy when he had to think. He reminded himself to flush before he left, just in case he was showing up on security cameras. Rich didn't like people using the bathrooms as a second office.

His mind drifted, alternating between trying to feel his way through the 'evidence' of the case. He could not cease replaying the utter shock of seeing who he thought was his wife in the restaurant earlier.

"I'll be back soon, darling. I just need a little down time. I'll be back soon."

He could hear her words, the tone in her voice; as if nothing was different about that day and that it was just a short trip to pick up a few things before they set sail. In his mind's eye, he saw himself repairing spar bracing and resetting halyards. He stood, tuning the guys on the main mast and looking at his watch, wondering where his wife could have gone.

I'm sorry, Charlie," Marge had said. "I haven't seen her since lunch. She was on the terrace with that man from the marina; you know the one that brokers the yachts? You two aren't thinking of trading in the Nattie Bumpo, *are you?"*

Nearly half an hour later, he was walking back to the office from the men's room. He shook off the memories of his and concentrated on the task at hand. How could there be so many glitches in a trace program that had been keeping track of the population for more than ten years without a hitch? The more he thought about it the more it sounded like some virus, either intentional or random, but that was impossible. The firewalls on the software were inviolate. Not to mention the proprietary language the programs were written in couldn't be hacked for the simple reason that no one could figure out the commands. There was simply no way to get in except with authorization.

"Except with authorization," he thought again. "Someone in the agency?" He thought back to the incident that morning with the man on the hotel veranda. There was at least one person that had been able to side step all their normal firewalls. There had to be a connection.

Back in the office he called technical support and ordered a complete diagnostic on the system for the last forty eight hours. If anyone had purposely changed the programming, it would be found. This was a major surveillance package, used by every investigatory branch of the government. If it had been tampered with, there would be hell to pay. More and more it looked like a serious breech of security, dead body or no dead body.

He checked in with his team, hoping for some sort of break in the case but nothing was forthcoming. They had luck backtracking the events at the mall; there was no news from Ben on the missing ambulance personnel and no news on the body. He felt stymied, but he knew it was part of the process. The one thing he knew for sure was that he was not bored. "Careful what you ask for," he thought to himself. "You may get it."

Cinnamon had been constructing a timeline on the case as they understood it, developing a graphic, showing each moment since the body was found based on their own data and what they'd received from Ben Delano. Unfortunately, Delano's input was precious little. Outside of some photographs and a few preliminary statements from potential witnesses, he didn't know much more than they did. Technical support had called and demanded a work order for the diagnostic, not an unusual event, but they refused to proceed without it. That was unusual. Charles fired one off to them and went back to studying the timeline chart with Cin and Sarah, their floater. While they were trying to piece together any anomalies or links, his lapel com buzzed again. He looked up to see that it was Rich on the screen.

"Now that's a record," Charles said. "He usually waits at least two hours before getting in our face again." He tapped his com board and said, "Yes?

"I need to see you," Rich said flatly.

"Yes sir. We'll be right up."

Rich shook his head and said, "No, just you. Ms.. Harper stays where she is."

"Pardon?"

"I only need to see you."

"Sir, Cinnamon is my partner. We need to maintain continuity if we're going to be maximally effective."

Rich stared out at him from the screen with obvious frustration. Charles could see him grinding his teeth, a habit the man had when he was trying to control his rage at some real or imagined affront.

"I need to see you alone, Agent Peavy. If I had wanted the two of you, I would have requested the two of you. This is to be a very private conversation. Do we understand each other?"

Charles mumbled assent and hung up. He turned to Cinnamon who was still sitting at her terminal, but she was looking over at Charles. There was no way she could have avoided hearing the conversation."

"He should have asked you to use your ear unit, Charles. The man's being sloppy. Don't worry. I'll be fine right here. I've got a lot of work to do. It's hard to keep things confidential with a human recorder in the room."

On the way up, Charlie decided that he should have anticipated this trip. They were using resources now; spending money. In a bureau where the director gets paid a bonus for how much money he saves, any increase in expenditure was bound to send up red flags, and Rich was very good at the game. He was aptly named.

When Charles went in, he passed a large man on the way out who diverted his face and pretended to be wiping his nose. It was a bit obvious, but Charles was used to that. Every movement the man made said he was trying to hide something. The assistant asked for his clipboard and cap-camera, which he carefully placed on the edge of her desk. Waving him through the security scanners, Charles entered Rich's inner office. Rich was seated behind his huge mahogany desk, looking grim.

"Sit down, Peavey," he said.

"What's up, Darren?" Charles said as lightly as he could. Rich looked suitably irritated, which was what Charles had intended.

"I want to know what the hell you're doing."

"My job, I think. You are referring to the investigation, aren't you?"

"You know damn well I am!" Rich bellowed. "Why are we involved in a local murder case?"

Charles nodded toward the hard copy of his preliminary report on Rich's desk. "You've read that?"

"I have."

"Well, that's what it's about."

"It's a murder case, Peavey. We don't do murder cases. We do terrorism!"

"And that's why I'm carrying out this investigation. Did you read the part about the failure of the surveillance net? If that's not potentially a threat to national security, I don't know what is."

"It's a glitch, that's all. It's happened before."

"Look, Darren," Charles said sincerely, "This really is a potential threat. We've had glitches before, but support has always found the problem in a matter of minutes and corrected it. No one seems to know what's going on with this one. People have disappeared without a trace. A man is dead and no one knew it until the body was discovered. We don't even know what hundreds of people were up to at the Perry Mall for about an hour, and we don't know why. This is a serious security issue and needs to be handled."

Rich listened, seeming to hear what Charles was saying, but then said, "It's costing us a fortune."

Charles chuckled in spite of himself. "Is that what this is about? Its how much money we're spending? Jesus, man! Some things are more important than your damn bonus! You ought to be glad we're doing this. Your parsimony is costing us funding as it is. Spend it or lose it. Isn't that the rule?"

"Now hold on, Peavey . . . "

"Sorry. That's probably unfair," he said, though didn't believe it. "But we've got a very dangerous situation here, and it's all wrapped up in this murder at the mall."

Rich looked down at the report, fidgeting with a pencil, his eyes darting back and forth rapidly. He was conflicted and Charlie could see it. The man was showing beads of perspiration across his forehead, his breathing was quickening. If this was a stranger, Charles would have said he was on the edge of fight or flight, and that was not at all like Rich. What was going on here that Rich wasn't telling?

"I want you to drop the case," he said. There was no conviction in his voice.

"You what?"

"Drop it. Wrap it up and clear your desk. Find some excuse. Just take my word for it, Peavey. It's best for all of us if you do. Now get out of here."

He started to protest but thought better of it. The man had finished. It was obvious that he wasn't going to discuss the matter any further. Charles stood and left without another word.

As he entered the elevator he said, "You get that?"

"Every word," Cinnamon said in his ear.

"We need to saddle up. I'll be there in a minute and we need to be ready to go."

"Um, excuse me, but didn't Rich just say to drop the case?"

"Actually, what he said to do was wrap it up, and that's what we're going to do, but we need to get out of here before he can stop us."

"Clever."

FIVE

CHARLES RETRIEVED HIS ASSAULT PISTOL from the drawer and clipped the heavy weapon onto his side. He slipped on his uniform windbreaker to hide it and the whole team, clipboards in hand, headed for the elevators. They were out of the building and moving further toward the downtown area in minutes, then into another government building and up to the fifth floor where a separate situation room had been established for task force use. No one had used it in years.

Charles was pleased with these new offices. At one end, a huge screen dominated the twelve foot wall, flanked by two smaller screens that were for isolating particular data from the main display. No need to clutter up the main screen with parceled sectioning. There were carrels around the outside edge of the room, a large conference table with three built in holos, and a full kitchen opposite the door. They entered and sealed the door behind them.

"Make yourselves comfortable, guys," Charlie said. "This is your home for the next few days."

Coffee and finger food were on the table in minutes, the former gratefully accepted, the latter mostly ignored. Everyone was either in a carrel or hovering over a read out, looking for any evidence of the victim's last moments on earth. Charles and Cin sat opposite each other across the conference table, studying a hologram of the ambulance, hoping that they might catch what was bothering them if they simultaneously studied it from opposite sides. The image itself rotated slowly, shifting to a new angle after each two full rotations. They were beginning to think that they were just stumped, or quite crazy for thinking that there was anything odd about the scene at all.

As they sat studying the image, Sarah came and leaned over the image next to Charlie. She provocatively leaned forward as her long red hair cascaded off of her shoulder. Charles didn't notice. Cinnamon definitely did.

"What's the problem?" She asked.

"We think something's not right about this picture, but we can't put a finger on it."

"Well I can see one thing right now."

"What!" They said together.

"It's the rock the ambulance is sitting on. That's a slab of marble. In fact, I'd say its either serpentine or travertine from the color, but I can't be sure. Holos just don't hold true color, you know. It's definitely not dolomite."

They both stared at the woman. She smiled back. "I was born in Tate, Georgia. That's the home of the largest marble quarries in the world."

"Okay," Cinnamon said evenly. "So why is this anomalous?"

"Well, you said that they found the ambulance near Peachtree City. That's south of Atlanta proper. There are no marble outcrops anywhere near there, and if it's serpentine, it wouldn't be hanging out on the surface anyway. That stuff's generally mined from underground."

"You're sure about this."

She nodded. "That picture was taken somewhere in the southern Appalachians, probably up around Marble City or Jasper, not south of Atlanta."

Cin closed her eyes and nodded. "I'm so damned stupid!"

"No one expects you to be an expert on marble, Cin," said Charles.

"No, it's not that. I just realized what's so odd about the picture. Look at the background. There's no red clay. You don't find it much that far north. And look at the lay of the land. There are mountains in the background. I should have seen it immediately, and so should you."

"Thanks, Sarah," said Charlie. "You've earned your cookie today."

"So that's a new wrinkle," Cinnamon said.

Charlie nodded. "Either that's not the ambulance we're looking for or it is and it covered over a hundred miles of the worse traffic in the south in less than an hour and a half. Who's doing this?"

Cin just shook her head. Sarah stood there for a few more minutes, and then walked away to see what others were doing, satisfied that she had nothing else to add.

By midnight the team had done all it could from here. Without actually interviewing people face to face, they had run down as much information as they could. Cinnamon spent hours looking at head shots until they started to all blend together, which was saying a lot for her. Charles had caught three duplicates using different names, but they decided the way the software was acting up, there was no telling what that meant. There were also two cases of individuals who appeared to be in two places at once according to the face recognition programming in the visual scans of the mall. That was also an obvious glitch in the software. They were all beginning to be a bit concerned about their surveillance capabilities, but occasional anomalies were not unusual and under the present circumstances to be expected. After a final briefing they opted for bed.

The situation center had two dormitories attached, one for women and one for men, each with its own shower facilities. As usual, the team ignored the segregation and simply tumbled into bed where they wished. Except for the two rookies, they had all known each other for several years and were used to intimate circumstances. It was also not uncommon for affairs, romances and simple trysts to develop among operatives working so close together, but everyone pretended it wasn't happening. In the end, two of the team occupied the smaller of the two dorms and the other five opted for bunking in the larger. As for Charles and Cinnamon, as lead investigators they each had quarters of their own. Charles took a very quick shower and was just slipping into bed when Cinnamon came in. He instinctively pulled the covers up around himself and immediately thought how silly that was.

"What are you doing?" He asked.

"It's Anton. He snores. The damn man sounds like a fog horn and he's taken the bunk on the other side of the wall from mine. There's no way I'm going to get any sleep in there, so you've got a bed buddy for the night. It's a big bed. I promise not to disturb your dreams."

Before he could object, she had unzipped her slacks and stepped out of them. She unbuttoned the blouse, dropped it to the floor and pulled the turtleneck up over her head.

Charles inhaled a quick, jerky breath as he watched. She was wearing a black chemise and panties, the one thing that always set him off when he had been married. Karen was infamous for using it to get what she wanted. Cin's top was abbreviated to say the least, her ample charms thrust proudly over the margin of the material. The panties were thongs, something you didn't see too often these days, but on her it looked almost regal. He exhaled and stepped out of bed.

"Where are you going?" She said. "I'm not going to run you out of your room. You can't sleep with Anton on the other side of the wall anymore than I can."

"I'm going for Black Rock tea. It'll calm me down."

Cin lowered her gaze to his midsection and the obvious bulge in his boxers. She raised an eyebrow.

"I'd say you need some calming down. Thanks for the compliment."

"'Not funny, Cin."

"No, I'd say it's not funny at all," she said, continuing to look at his crotch.

As tired as he was, Charles was not the least embarrassed.

"Ignore him," he said. "There are no brains in his head, just animal instinct. I'm just glad to know the equipment can still function."

"How long has it been?" She asked seriously.

He said nothing for a moment, and then blurted out, "Since Karen died."

He slipped on his pants again and padded to the door. Three steaming cups of Black Rock tea later he returned in a thick fog, barely able to walk. He found Cin curled up on one side of the bed sleeping soundly.

Karen used to do that. He'd come to bed late and find her all bundled up against the edge of the far side of the bed. In her case, of course, it was to avoid any contact with him. It was only later that she railed at him that she was usually awake at those times, pretending to be asleep so that he'd leave her alone. It was one of many hurtful things she would say during those final months of their marriage.

When Cin did it, it seemed considerate, like a gentle pet not wanting to disturb its master. She laid there, her back to him, her breathing deep and rhythmic. Cin was definitely not awake. Carefully Charles crawled into bed next to her and hovered on the opposite edge of the bed, not wishing to disturb her sleep. His body ached with the sudden flush of desire that swept over him. How long had it been? How long since that night years ago?

"Go to sleep!" Karen had snapped when he rolled toward her and caressed her shoulder. He had persisted, and she swung out of bed, grabbing a blanket and pillow and stomped out the door to the living room. He could still hear the door slamming in his mind.

He wept silently and then fell into a stuporous sleep.

In the morning he awoke to find himself curled up against her. One arm was wrapped around Cinnamon's waist, the other casually tucked under his side. It was the cramp forming in that arm that had awakened him, and as he opened his eyes he felt her stir. He realized he was in full erection. She turned her head to look at his disheveled face and said, "Does this mean you've got to do the right thing by me now?"

Charles was immediately wide awake and retreating to the opposite side of the bed.

"Jeez, Cin. I'm sorry. I swear I didn't plan that. I'm really sorry," he said.

She looked at him briefly, stepped out of bed and headed for the bathroom. She slipped the chemise casually over her head and onto the floor behind her as she went in and said, "Don't give it another thought. You're over reacting. I know a gentleman when I see one." He almost wished it wasn't true.

Charles dressed and stepped into the situation room. Only Anton and Sarah were up. Anton was already scanning through the morning reports as Sarah looked over his shoulder, occasionally making comment. They ignored him as he sought coffee and some rather sad looking pastries left from last night. The way he was feeling right now it might as well have been hemlock. What had he done last night? That third cup of Black Rock blissed him out completely. He couldn't even remember anything beyond lying in bed as far from Cinnamon as he could manage.

Cinnamon was the last to join the team. She emerged from Charles' room, combing her still damp hair and acting as if nothing out of the ordinary had happened. For a brief moment, the whole team stared in mute silence.

"Anton," Cinnamon said, "You snore. In fact, you sound like the Queen Mary in a fog bank. Sleep in some other bed next time."

They resumed their work and nothing more was said.

"Let's see what we've got so far," Charles said after gathering the team around the conference table. "We've got a corpse that someone went to a great deal of trouble to mutilate, probably to prevent us from finding out who he was if they could. The body has been chewed; limbs and organs removed, and the probable cause of death either the removal of the heart or, judging from the scene, exsanguination. We'll know more when we get lab results from the locals.

"We have a missing corpse as well as two missing medtechs whose ambulance supposedly ends up abandoned in Peachtree City though the evidence says it's in North Georgia in the foothills of the Smokies. We have surveillance processes that don't work and medchip failures that we can't explain, and we still haven't been able to find any suspects or motive. All in all, I'd say we're in very deep shit except for Ben Delano and his lab work. He's meeting me this morning. I've already alerted his office to send him here rather than our usual haunts. When he gets here, we'll see what we really have. Now then, are there any suggestions?

"You forgot to add the directive from Rich to drop the investigation," said Cinnamon.

"He didn't say that. He said wrap it up, and that's what we're doing. If he meant anything else, I must have misinterpreted him by taking him literally."

"That's not what I mean," she said. "I think he was told to drop the case from higher up. This is all beginning to look like someone at the top doesn't want this investigation to take place."

Charles remembered the man who was leaving Rich's office as he went in yesterday. Why hadn't he thought of this before?

"Let's rerun my cap-camera from my visit to Rich's office. There should be a man leaving his office as I entered."

"Already done," said Cinnamon. "There's no man leaving Rich's office on the tape."

"What? There was a man. He was leaving Rich's office when I arrived and I did get it on my cap-camera!"

"I know. I was watching, remember? It's just not on the record. It's been expunged."

Charles fell silent.

"Somebody sanitized the record, Charles. There's got to be somebody inside."

"Um, there's something else too," said Sarah. They all turned to her.

"Death could have been caused by asphyxiation. It's a trick the Serbs used in Bosnia-Herzegovina during the breakup. Removing the jaw causes the victim to suffocate painfully over time. It's a form of extreme torture."

"Okay. So now we have another possible connection, this time with Eastern Europe, possibly terrorists. Anything else?"

No one spoke.

"So keep at it," he said and left to take a shower.

SIX

IN THE AFTERNOON, Cinnamon, Sarah and Bobby J. left, ostensibly to clear their heads, though Charles suspected that they had personal business that had been interrupted by the sudden 'gathering of the clan' that led them all to the situation room. Cinnamon was certainly with Pete, if for no other reason, because of his inability to function for long periods of time without her. He suspected that Bobby J. had a girlfriend outside the agency whom he mysteriously met periodically. Considering the amount of headway that they were not making with the case, he let it go.

The rest of them continued to pour over the shreds of information that came into the situation room, looking for the slightest clue or connection to the murder and breech of security posed by the faulty surveillance program. For his own part, Charles decided early on to check the input from his cap-camera of their time in the mall, hoping to shed some light on the mistaken identification of the woman at the far end of the restaurant. Karen was dead and he knew it. He was the one who identified the body, and there was no question of who she was. It was Karen right down to the mole on her right shoulder, and the slight cleft in her chin. Yet this other woman was a dead ringer for her. Why had they left in such a hurry? Had he really been so threatening?

He was still ferreting through the visuals, now appearing in three dimensional holos above his com plate on the table, when Sarah and

Bobby J. returned. The red head breezed into the room shaking water off of her raincoat and headed for her terminal with determination. Bobby J. followed shortly thereafter, but he was quite dry and much more sedate in his manner.

"It's raining out there?" Meg asked.

"Just started," answered Sarah. "I was lucky to only be two blocks from here. I thought I was going to drown as it is."

"So how come you're so dry, Bobby J.?" asked Craig, looking up from his screen.

"Took a taxi. I got out right in front."

Craig gave Meg a knowing look and they both smiled. "Who paid for the cab," he asked, "you or her?"

"Mind your own business," Bobby J. said and grabbed a rather limp pastry as he passed the conference table. He put it in a napkin, set them both on the table at his com plate and poured a mug of coffee.

Cinnamon came in five minutes later. She looked irritated and tired. Charles could guess the reason why. She sat at the desk next to his and began reviewing the hourly reports from the team.

"How's Pete?" Charles asked and immediately regretted it. If looks could kill, he'd be not only dead but eviscerated by now.

"I wasn't being sarcastic, Cin. That was a real question."

She offered a forced smile and a shrug. "Pete's as expected, ornery, demanding, self absorbed and very much the brat."

"I'm sorry. I guess that wasn't much R and R for you, was it?"

"It's okay," she said, conveying more fatigue than she intended. "I didn't expect it to be. What are you working on?"

"Take a look."

She looked over at the holo display. It was a split cube of light, each of the two halves displaying images of the restaurant where they had lunch, showing people scurrying about, eating and talking. The one on Charles' left was from above and to one side, encompassing the entire floor area, a long shot that took in the whole room. On the right, was a representation from eye level and it jumped around, obviously displaying the output from Charles' cap-camera. A few moments of looking confirmed that they were synchronized.

"Well, the image on the left is from your cap-camera, but where'd you get the one on the right?"

"It's the surveillance camera output from the mall," Charles said. "I was able to download it by just asking. It took me half an hour to synchronize them."

Cinnamon studied him for a moment. "Is this connected to the case or are you just looking for Karen in the crowd?"

"Yes," he said.

"Charles, you've got to stop this. You're beginning to obsess. It wasn't Karen that you saw and that's all there is to it. I don't see how you can connect this to what we're working on, anyway."

"Uh huh," he said, watching the display. Now watch this closely. You see what's happening with my cap-camera? See them there sitting at the table?"

Cinnamon followed his finger and noted the two people sitting at the far side of the restaurant by the door.

"I'm moving toward them now, still looking at them and making my way through the tables. See her look up? Now she speaks to him and he looks too. Now they're getting up and leaving. They're through the doors now, and I'm following. In a moment, you can see me go through the door and that they're nowhere to be seen in the concourse."

Cinnamon followed the action as he described it. She'd never seen a picture of his dead wife, but from his description of her she could see how he would believe it might be her.

"And your point is?" She said sardonically. "She could be anyone from what I can see."

"Now watch the rerun, but watch the surveillance camera feed this time."

Again the images danced and Cinnamon concentrated on those on the left side, looking for the couple by the door. They weren't there. She could see Charles making his way through the crowd, but no one was seated at the table where the couple should have been. She blinked to clear her vision and looked again.

"Now here's the interesting part," he said. As she watched, the doors to the concourse opened and closed again of their own accord as Charles approached them and shortly he went through and disappeared from view.

"Run that again," she said. He did, and again there was no couple at the table, and again the doors opened and closed by themselves.

"Holy shit," she said softly.

"Yeah. That's what I said too."

"Someone's sanitized the surveillance tape. They've removed the images of the man and woman by the door."

"Exactly!" He said, smiling.

"But it's still on your cap-camera record. How can that be?"

"It's still on the cap-camera record," he said triumphantly, "because I made a mistake. I didn't tie my cap-camera into the departmental feed when we got back to the office. It was never transmitted to the database but stayed isolated in the cam itself! No one could sanitize it because the only place it existed was in my cap, and I've had it with me the whole time, the transmit function turned off."

"So no one had a chance to change it."

"That's right," he said. "Now we know that someone's manipulating the system, and from my standpoint, what's more important, I know I'm not crazy!"

"It has to be someone inside the department, Charles," Cinnamon said.

"I hope to God it is. If it's from outside, then our whole security net is compromised and somebody can get at everything we know and discover."

Cinnamon looked around the room at the others. She looked back at Charles, an expression of panic growing on her face.

"Don't worry. We're isolated here. The situation room is not connected to the main database. We can draw data from it, but we can't input anything into it. That's on purpose, and I'm glad some paranoid techno-dweeb had the good sense to set it up that way when the room was installed."

Cinnamon sat back in her chair and heaved a sigh of relief. "So what do we do now?"

Charles looked back at the holo for a moment and then shut it down. "We keep looking for answers," he said. "Right now, I'm going to get some dinner, if there's anything fit to eat around here. It's almost seven."

By eight, it was obvious that they were not going to get much more done that night. They were all exhausted. Charles sent everyone home to sleep and get a change of clothes with strict orders to be back first thing in the morning. When Cinnamon volunteered to stay, he barked something unkind about Peter and sent her on her way. He would hold the fort alone.

Once he had locked the facilities down and secured the floor, he stripped and tossed his clothes into the cleaning unit in the utility closet and stepped into the shower. He was sour, every pore emitting the pungent aroma of two days of stress and adrenaline, his hair caked with sweat and oil, his nostrils clogged with too much recycled air. Even his joints hurt him now, convincing him that he was right to send everyone home for a rest. If he felt this way he was sure everyone else must be equally worn out.

After the shower, he pulled his now warm, dry underclothes from the cleaning unit and put them on. They smelled wonderful, fresh and fragrant, like they'd been hanging on a clothes line. Absently he wondered how many people even knew what that was like these days. If it hadn't been for the orphanage, where sheets and cottons were routinely hung out to dry, he wouldn't know it himself. It was a lost pleasure now. Anyone who was psycho enough to try drying clothes out of doors today would end up rewashing the soot and grime out of them, unless they lived deep in the country, away from any centers of population.

He slipped into his T-shirt and boxers, lay back across the bed and closed his eyes. Strange that he would think of the orphanage now. He had so few memories of the place. His years there seemed more a dream than a memory. He sighed deeply and stretched, feeling his muscles groan as they sought to loosen from the intensity of the day, then closed his eyes and slept.

He was back in Free Cuba again, walking through the heat of the day, the ocean breeze coming from his right the only saving grace of being afoot. He knew instinctively where he was going and what he would find, but he was compelled to keep going. It was just down the block, by the long pier that jutted out into the bay, where the fishing and scuba diving boats lined up for tourists and sportsmen. He knew he was going to go into the hotel, but what he would do next he couldn't say.

Once inside, he entered the elevator and directed it to the fifth floor. How did he know to do that? How did he know? Inside his head, he screamed to be set free, to turn and leave, but somehow he couldn't bring himself to do it. He was going to room 5004 as inexorably as one facing their Maker. He knocked once and waited.

A tall, dark haired Latin answered the door and instantly tried to close it, but Charles pushed his way in, sending the man tumbling, across the floor. On the bed Karen lay, naked and red and shaking, like a small baby after a warm bath. She stared at him, first in horror and then in defiance. At first, Charles said nothing. He just stood there, staring.

His own cries awakened him. Charles sat upright on the bed, dripping with sweat and breathing heavily. He shook his head, trying to clear the memory, but it persisted, unwilling to let go of him. He screamed and shook himself again, relieved to sense the image in his mind drifting back into the void in response to his immense self control. He looked at the clock, which read 11:47 P.M. "Damn!" He said. "Now I'll be up half the night!"

Charles pulled himself out of bed and forced his body to step into the situation room, now dim in the glow of the situation board which was the only illumination in the room. He crossed to the kitchenette and made himself a huge mug of Black Rock tea, gulped it down in spite of the steaming temperature and then made himself another. By the time he had finished the third, he was woozy, wondering what all the fuss had been about and stumbled off to bed where he slept the sleep of the dead.

At six, he was up and dressed, by seven, he'd brought all the systems online, scanned the news for any related headlines and reviewed all of the preliminary reports that the team had created before leaving the night before. By seven thirty the team began to drift in, the irritating sound of the warning horn announcing the arrival of someone in the building. Every time it went off he jumped, as did anyone else in the room at the time, and he swore he'd find the cut off switch for that monster before the day was out.

Cinnamon was the second to arrive, right after Sarah. She came in full of energy, obviously rejuvenated by her down time, but the smile on her face faded when she saw Charles at the conference table.

"Hello, Cin," he said, forcing a smile. "Feel better?"

"Better than you," she said, cutting to the chase as usual. "What'd you do last night, get drunk or have an orgy?"

The remark stung, but he tried to ignore it. "Neither. I just didn't sleep well. Ready to get at this again?"

She set her voluminous purse and raincoat aside and poured them both a cup of coffee. Sarah had watched this all play out and chose to make herself scarce, disappearing into the women's dormitory with her overnight case.

"Here," she said handing it to him. "This'll fix you up. Caffeine's the best thing for a Black Rock PDD."

"You think you know so much," he said sarcastically.

"After almost three years, Charles Peavy, I think I know you pretty well. Now drink this or you're going to be worthless for half the day. Have you eaten?"

"You're not my mother."

Cinnamon laughed. "If I was your mother, I'd probably kick your ass and send you to your room! Now get that coffee down."

"Leave me alone, Karen. I don't want to play."

Cinnamon froze and the smile vanished from her face. She looked at him with sadness in her eyes. "My name's Cinnamon, Charles. Karen's dead, remember?"

After a very long moment, he said, "Sorry. I guess we're both kinda 'walkin' wounded' here, aren't we?" and began drinking the coffee.

"It's okay, Charles. We're all entitled to our pain. We all earned it."

Twenty minutes more and the whole team had shown up and all looked better except for Bobby J. who looked positively ecstatic. Everyone else chose to ignore his state, hoping they wouldn't have to endure the details of his latest conquest later. Charles really didn't care, as long as it brought him back sharp and ready to go. At nine he called everyone to the conference table to map out the day's work.

They had just settled in, convinced that there was nothing that they could do until they had forensics to work with when the Claxon sounded and they all looked at the main screen. It showed the hallway outside the situation room door and a lone figure standing there, waiting with impatience. It was Ben Delano. When they opened the door he stepped, and looked around at the room.

"Situation room," he said simply. "Nice. Wish I had one of these to work with."

"Come on in, Ben. Join the party," said Cinnamon.

"Ah, my delightful little spice. Has Charlie been treating you well?"

"Stop calling me Charlie."

"Okay, Chuck, but I've got bad news for you."

Charles groaned. "What now?"

"We have no evidence."

Charles stared at him blankly. Finally, Cinnamon said, "Say again?"

Ben shook his head. He looked almost apologetic.

"It's gone. All the physical evidence has disappeared from the lab and all of the records have been dumped from our database. Hell, Charlie, I can't even find out who brought in the ambulance. When it wasn't brought in, we sent out another team to pick it up, but all they found was the ambulance's transponder. There's no evidence there either. I don't know what's going on, buddy, but watch your back. When I told them upstairs about all this, they said to forget about it and they'd take care of it. This sounds like some agency's playing with us. You know how nasty that can get."

"As nasty as I can," Charles mumbled. "You don't have anything at all?"

"Nope, and I'm getting damn sick and tired of losing that friggin' ambulance!"

"It's in North Georgia, up around Jasper. Have your people look there."

Delano cocked head reflexively. "How do you know that?"

Charles looked over at Sarah and smiled. "Classified. I don't think you'll find anything of interest when you locate it. What I can't figure out is how all the physical evidence at the lab can go missing."

Delano shook his head. "It's all disappeared. Last night it was all labeled, catalogued and crated, ready to come to you this morning. I also sent what data and conclusions I had over to you, but there's no record of the transfer of information. Your net's been isolated."

"What about the autopsy team?"

"Oh, I've got them all right. Cause of death was removal of the heart. Beyond that, we have nothing. Everything else was run through the diagnostic programs, but they don't show having done it even though we know they did. I have three hard copies of fragmentary data that I retrieved from waste disposal, but no DNA trace, no blood typing and no ID of the victim. All we've got left to prove there was a crime at all is your data, your photos and an hysterical eye witness who has proved to be totally useless."

"Did you find out who put the call through to FEMA to get us out there?"

"Nope. Central says they received my call and bucked the decision up stairs, but the bosses say they never saw it. I believe them, Charlie. That's another strange thing. I got a call from FEMA asking if we wanted their help. I chalked it up to weird communication and just reaffirmed I'd asked for it."

"Hmm," Charles said, "and that doesn't fit anyway. Why would they send us out there if they wanted to cover all this up?"

"Charles, what if there's two people or groups or whatever trying to influence the investigation? What if one's trying to block it and one's trying to help us or lead us away from the truth?"

"Whatever the case, this thing's getting stranger and stranger. Thanks anyway, Ben let me know if you get anything else and I'll do the same. And you watch yourself too."

"You bet." He smiled, nodded to the others and left.

When Ben was gone, Cinnamon asked casually, "So tell me, Charlie, what would you give to know who the victim was?"

"Don't play with me, Cin."

"Oh I'm not playing. I just don't' think we're dead in the water yet."

She stood up and stepped into Charles' quarters. She came out holding her hand bag. With a flourish, she reached in and pulled out a sealed plastic bag containing a pair of high heel shoes. The souls were encrusted with dried blood, mud and a pearly white coating on the sole.

"Cinnamon, I love you!" Charles blurted.

"Don't let Pete hear you say that, but thanks anyway. I'll get back over to the office and run this through the lab. We ought to have an answer by noon."

SEVEN

"VANDERHOORST. PETER HANS VANDERHOORST," announced Cinnamon.

"That's our victim?"

She nodded.

"Well known industrialist and confirmed bachelor. His companies make everything from clipboard viewers to solar cell packs. He was approximately sixty five years old and a native of the Netherlands. I double checked surveillance scans and he doesn't show up as alive and kicking anywhere on the continent. He lives right here in the Atlanta area. I didn't bother with the rest of the world."

"No need, if we have a match. He's a local, too. That makes things easier. You have an address?"

"It's a penthouse downtown at Atlantic Station."

Charles whistled. "The most expensive real estate in the US. I'd say that's about as exclusive as it gets. When's the last time we know where he was?"

Cin referred to her clipboard, punching in data sheets one at a time.

"Four days ago he attended a fund raiser at the governor's mansion. That's his last known public appearance. We don't have any visual surveillance scans on him, I'm afraid. He's exempt."

"He's exempt? That means he has friends in very high places."

Charles stood up from where he sat at the conference table and looked around the room. Craig and Susanne had completed their history of the witness's movements for the past five days and were busily researching other knowns from the mall. Bobby J. and Meg were still mired in the surveillance, trying to reconstruct the sequence of events. They'd actually been able to recover about an hour of movement that was lost, reducing their efforts to only a single forty-five minute period before the murder. Anton sat idly by the phone and Sarah was pouring coffee. At least everyone looked busy.

"Okay, boys and girls," he called. "New plan. We need to find out everything we can about Peter Vanderhoorst and his associates, particularly movements in the last week. Craig, you and Susanne, you're on research. Find out who he knew, who he met with recently and where. He may be exempt from surveillance scans but his friends may not be. Whenever they were together, he'll show up as ancillary data. Bobby J., you keep at the reconstruction of what happened at the mall but I'll need Meg to man the phones."

Anton looked up from his stupor, a glimmer of hope in his eyes.

"Anton, you and Sarah need field experience. I want you two at the governor's mansion to check on the fund raiser he attended four days ago. Talk to anyone who may have spoken to him or just seen him. That includes staff, guests, security...anybody. Then go over to Vanderhoorst's office. Find out what you can from the staff there about what he's been doing lately and who he's been cutting deals with. I don't think this is a simple murder for personal gain, but we need to know for sure. Remember this may be a terrorist threat. You're armed. Be careful. Cinnamon and I are going to visit his home. Questions?"

"I need to speak to you alone," said Cin.

"No problem. Everyone get to it"

When they were alone in his quarters, door conspicuously open, Cin asked, "How soon do we need to be at Vanderhoorst's apartment?"

"Why? What's up?"

Cinnamon sat on the edge of the bed and took a deep breath.

"Well the truth is, Charles," she said hesitantly, "that we've been at this for two and a half days straight. I haven't even had a chance to call Pete, and we're supposed to have lunch together in about twenty minutes. You know how sensitive musicians can be. He's expecting me. Can this wait an hour or do I have to brave the slings and arrows of outraged boyfriends when I get home, if I ever do?"

Charles' first thought was to scream at her, but, as usual, she had that puppy dog look on her face that always melted him. He thought for a moment.

"Where are you supposed to meet him?"

"The Rotunda Grill at the capitol. It's only fifteen minutes from Vanderhoorst's place if traffic's not too bad."

Charles pretended to think it over, enjoying the pained expression on her face as she waited. At last he said, "An hour for lunch and no more. I'll talk to people at the Capitol myself and send Anton and Sarah directly to his office. It'll take you a few minutes to get there, and knowing Pete he'll be late. I'll meet you at Vanderhoorst's in about an hour and a half."

Cin breathed a sigh of relief. "Thanks, boss. I really mean that."

"Don't be late!"

"Oh, I'll beep. I'll be there on time."

She turned and headed for the main doors, grabbing her handbag as she did. Charles watched her as she crossed the room and left. As usual, he was unsuccessful at ignoring the way her body moved inside her clothes. He shook off the feeling, remembering Karen and the flowing movements of her body, like a dancer. Grabbing his viewer, he had just enough time to write some suitably ambiguous progress reports for Rich before he braved the snarl of humanity outside.

The Capitol was even more of a bust than Charles had anticipated. State Capitols are an odd combination of museum, symbol, gathering place for those involved in the day to day process of running a state and community meeting place, and, of course politicians on the make. Knowing that, Charles had sought only those denizens of the halls who might have attended a charity event in the rotunda some four weeks earlier. He failed definitively. No one seemed to know what he was talking about. The governor's social secretary, contacted by com, could find no record of it and was very sorry that the gentleman was so misinformed. Security was most willing to help, but they showed no such event having taken place, and no additional security requested or provided by their office. Even maintenance, which would set up and take down any temporary venue for such a happening, was perplexed by his assertions that there had indeed been a charity event held one evening four weeks ago. On the other hand, perhaps the lack of information was the information he needed. He would discuss it with the team.

True to her word, Cinnamon met him outside the Twelve in exactly one hour. She was in a sour mood.

"Anything at the Capitol?" She asked.

"I was stone walled. No one seems to know anything about a fund raiser. It's probably more problems with the trace programs."

She nodded and said nothing more about it.

"How was lunch?" Charles asked cautiously.

"A disaster."

"I'm sorry" he said.

Cinnamon shook her head. "Don't be. It was a long time coming, but Pete and I had a little talk about his needs and my needs and his work and my work..."

"Cin, you don't need to tell me this if you don't want to."

"'Gotta tell somebody," she said in disgust. "Who better than you?"

Charles would think about that when he had time.

"We basically broke up. I'm just too busy to babysit a spoiled child anymore. A nice body and good sex just aren't worth it."

"Um, okay. So what happens now?"

She brightened somewhat and looked up at him. "Now he moves out. I told him to start today. As it turns out, he's already found another place and he's going to pick up his things this evening. By the time I see my apartment again, he'll be long gone, and that suits me just fine."

"It's too bad it didn't work out, Cin. It really is. People need someone in their life."

"Good advice," she said looking him in the eye intently.

As expected, Peter Vanderhoorst's apartment was a true penthouse on the very top of the Twelve, not one of those penthouses in name only. This one was on one of the top floors just below the roof that sold for twice what the others did simply because of their designation. Entering the lobby, Cin asked the security guard at the desk to direct them. One look at their uniforms and he became instantly cooperative. They took one of the three elevators from the lobby straight to the top. It was one of the newer Bell Corp units, designed to move both vertically and horizontally. Not many of them had found their way into the Atlanta area as they required three times the normal core width in a building, in order to accommodate their horizontal tracks. Bell had recently developed one that would even turn corners, but only two buildings had been designed to accommodate this technology and they were both in Chicago.

"Ever been in one of these?" He asked Cinnamon.

"Once or twice. I've a sister in Boston. Her building has one."

"Bell Corp's made a lot of changes since they merged with Ottis. I never would have thought of an airfoil company and an elevator company being a good match."

"Vanderhoorst has a piece of that action, you know," Cinnamon said.

"Really? No wonder there's a Bell unit in his building."

After nearly two minutes, the elevator reached the top and shifted to the right, traveling along the horizontal track for only a few seconds before coming to a stop. The doors slid back silently and they stepped out into a wide foyer. Some thirty feet to the right of the elevator there were large bronze clad double doors in a style from the 1930s, with raised geometric panels and a stylized sun half on each door.

"Smart design," said Charles. "Anyone coming up here would have to move down the hall to reach the main doors to the penthouse rather than being able to charge directly at the doors."

"Personally," said Cinnamon, "I just like the Art Deco façade."

As they approached the doors the one on their left swung effortlessly outward and a tall, heavy set man stepped toward them. He had the movements of a body builder but the grace of a ballet dancer, a difficult combination to achieve. He was impeccably dressed in a solid black suit with velvet collar, very much up to date and very formal. Protruding from the space between neck and coat was an ascot of burgundy and cobalt blue with a gold crest, like a medieval device from some knight's shield.

He smiled formally and bowed.

"Good afternoon," he said with equal formality. "My name is Hodges. I have been asked by Mr. Vanderhoorst to inquire as to the reason for your visit."

Charles and Cinnamon looked at each other.

"And when did he make this request?"

"Approximately one hour ago, directly after your call."

"That's impossible," Cinnamon said without thinking.

Hodges looked at her blankly and then said, "Pardon?"

"What my colleague is trying to say is that he couldn't have made such a request an hour ago as his body was found at the Perry Mall earlier this week. He was murdered the day before yesterday."

Again Hodges merely stared at them blankly. Charles detected the indecision in his face.

"Won't you come in?" He asked, as if nothing had happened.

He led them through another entrance hall, very Renaissance in design, with heavily carved dark oak furnishings and what appeared to be original tapestries. They followed him into a large living room, perhaps twenty feet square, and he asked them to be seated, leaving without another word.

Charles plopped down in the overstuffed chair near the door, while Cinnamon wandered; sliding her hand along the edge of the grand piano, then along the top of the camel back couch of embroidered silk. Finally she settled into a rather formal Queen Anne wing chair close to the window. Charles made note of the strategic move. In case of trouble, she would be silhouetted against the huge expanse of glass wall, but anyone facing her would be blinded by the sun, now lower on the horizon behind her.

"Nice room," he said absently.

"Late forties or early fifties motif, I think," she said. "Oh don't give me that look, Charles. I've been into interior design for a long time. You can tell a great deal about someone by looking at their taste in décor."

"And what does this tell you about Peter Vanderhoorst?"

Cinnamon thought for a long moment, and then said, "Well, he's eclectic. I've only seen two rooms, but there is absolutely no sense of cohesion between the entrance hall, the foyer and this living room. He decorated the place himself with very little artistic help from a professional. No one in the industry in their right mind would do juxtaposed rooms without some sort of transition. This is jarring. I wouldn't be surprised to turn a corner and find a circular entrance into an oriental motif of Chinese red and black lacquer! This is a designer's nightmare."

"Interesting," was all Charles said.

"And another thing is that grand piano. It's not been played in a very long time. There is no evidence of oil stains on the keys and several of the strings have dust bunnies along the edge where the tuning pegs are. Whoever cleans the room doesn't know to look for that kind of thing. I'd say it's just for show."

"I'm impressed," Charles said honestly. "You have a hell of an eye for detail."

She cocked her head to one side in mock arrogance. "Eidetic memory isn't enough, you know. I need the ability to reach logical conclusions as well."

At this point Hodges entered the room and gave them a short bow. He cleared his throat and said, "I have just spoken with Mister Vanderhoorst and he assures me that he is very much alive."

Charles studied the man's tells carefully. He was speaking the literal truth.

"In that case, would you please ask him to step in here so that we can verify that?"

Hodges seemed not the least perturbed by the challenge to his honesty. "Quite impossible," he said.

Charles nodded, and stood.

"You realize that we are with Homeland Security? That means that we have the power to circumvent normal civil rights and due process. We can do just about anything we want to as long as it doesn't involve murder or mayhem. The point is, my friend, we have the power to turn this place upside down if necessary, and you cannot legally stop us. Now please ask Mr. Vanderhoorst to come here."

Again, Hodges was not in the least disturbed. "It is quite impossible, sir, as he is not here. He is currently in Switzerland, recovering from a rather serious operation. I have spoken to him by phone only. If you wish, I will be glad to replay the conversation."

"You normally save all conversations that come into this house?"

"Mr. Vanderhoorst does, yes sir. Would you like to see it?"

"Definitely."

On the screen a very tired looking Peter Vanderhoorst spoke for some three minutes with Hodges concerning the guests from Homeland Security and their insistence that he was dead. He was patient and very much in control, as if this was a common occurrence, and he explained carefully to his assistant that it must be an error of some kind as he was actually feeling better than he had in years. While this was taking place, Cinnamon was comparing the man on the phone screen with her file data on the clipboard. When she finished she turned to Charles and said, "It's him. We've made a mistake."

"Well," said Charles, "it appears we owe Mister Vanderhoorst and you both an apology."

"Think nothing of it," Hodges said and moved toward the door. They followed and allowed themselves to be escorted out.

"There's one last thing, Hodges. Can you tell me what kind of operation Mr. Vanderhoorst had and when he will return?"

"Heart bypass surgery, sir. It was quite routine. He is expected to return the day after tomorrow."

"I'm glad there were no complications."

"As are we all, sir. Thank you."

"I don't see how that could be," Cinnamon said as they descended to the lobby. "We had a positive ID on the DNA. Unless our data is wrong, the man's dead."

"A conundrum for the ages," Charles mumbled.

"I don't think it's that bad, Charles."

He waved the thought aside. "Just a quote from an old book, Cin. Let's get back to the situation room and see what we can figure out. Somebody's screwing with us. I want to know who."

They opted for ground transportation on the way back to the situation room. It was too far to walk and too short a distance to warrant a sky car. As usual, traffic was heavy, and since it was after three in the afternoon by the time they had left Vanderhoorst's home, the 'crush hour' had begun. They found themselves midstream in what was inaccurately referred to as the fast lane.

"What's today?" asked Charles.

"Thursday, why?"

"That explains it. Atlanta's the only city in the world where the Friday afternoon crush hour starts at noon on Thursday."

Cinnamon chuckled. "You may be right, but that's okay. We're just going to have to start all over when we get back. I think we could both use some time to regroup before we see the rest of the team."

"You are the eternal optimist," Charles said dryly.

"And you the eternal cynic. It's why we work so well together. You know. It's that Hegelian thing."

"Hmm," was Charles' only response. His clip board began signaling insistently and he pulled it from his belt. It was Rich.

"Peavy!" Rich screamed. "What the hell are you doing?"

"Hello, Darn. How's it hangin?"

"Watch it, Peavy. I mean it. What the hell are you up to?"

"Me?" He said innocently. "I'm just following orders. You told me to wrap up the investigation and that's what I'm doing."

"I told you to drop it, damn it, and that's what I meant!"

"Okay, Darn. Now what's the problem?"

"I just got a call from my opposite number at the Pentagon. He tells me you've been harassing one of their prime contractors; some guy named Vanderhoorst. Is that right?"

Charles did his best to sound calm. “His name came up in the course of the investigation and we went to interview him, that’s all. He’s out of town. How did they find out about it?”

Rich was red as a beet. The viewer was almost glowing.

“How the hell should I know? I’m told that you were snooping around at the state capitol too, and that you sent agents to harass his staff at his corporate offices. He’s involved in more top secret military projects than I can count! They’re mad as hell over at the Pentagon. Now shut this thing down, do you understand?”

Charles hesitated for only a second and said, “Okay, chief. We’re about through anyway.”

“And another thing. Why are you using the situation room? Do you know what it costs to use the situation room? You’re costing this department a fortune!”

“Not really. All we’ve used is some electricity, which would be keeping the situation room ready anyway, six dozen pastries and eight pots of coffee. If it really concerns you, take it out of my salary.”

Rich let out a guttural sound in his throat and slammed his fist on his desk. “You smart off to me one more time and you won’t have a salary! Is that clear?”

“Yes sir,” Charles said. I’ll shut it down.”

Rich signed off abruptly.

“Well now,” Cinnamon said, smirking. “I’d say the chief’s a bit upset.”

“More upset than I’ve ever seen him,” Charles thought aloud. “We must be onto something or he wouldn’t be taking that much incoming from elsewhere.”

“I don’t like the look in your eye, Charles. He said shut it down.”

“And we will. By tonight we’ll be out of the situation room and the whole operation will be officially over.”

She eyed him. “I know you better than that, Charles Peavy. What are you up to?”

Charles sat back and looked at her innocently. “Me? Nothing at all, Cin. When we get back we need to call off the crew and they can all go back to the office. It’s a done deal, okay?”

“Charlie…?”

“Damn it, Cin. Don’t call me Charlie!”

When they arrived at the situation room, everyone was there. The team all looked up at the two as they came through the door. There was a thick tension in the room.

"What's happened?" Cinnamon asked.

"What hasn't?" said Craig.

"Specifics please?" said Charles.

Anton spoke first.

"Sarah and I went to Vanderhoorst's corporate headquarters and were asking for general information about their boss. We'd been there for no more than five minutes when two Federal types showed up and told us to leave. We pointed out that we were Homeland Security, which superseded any authority they might have and they pulled weapons. They actually pulled weapons on us, Boss! They pushed us out the door and said that if we showed up again that they'd kill us."

Charles didn't miss a beat. "What kind of weapons?" He asked.

"AKs". They were nines or tens from the look of them. Who caries AK hand guns these days?"

Charles ignored the question. "What else is going on?"

Bobby J. spoke up. "I've got something scary for you, Boss."

"Like?"

"You remember when we were scanning faces at the mall? We found that the program was so screwed up that it had one guy in two places at once. Well, I was wrong. We found he was actually in four places at once, and the analysis confirms it! It wasn't a glitch or a virus of any kind. That guy really was in four places at once. And that's not all. He doesn't show up anywhere on medchip traces. According to the trace, he doesn't even exist!"

"You're sure about this."

Bobby J. nodded. "I've got confirmation from security footage not even connected to the general trace program. I just can't explain it."

"What if someone purposely superimposed one person for another in the record so that the real person could not be visually identified?"

"There's still no medchip trace for anyone in those locations at that time."

Charlie thought for a moment. "Actually, that might explain a great deal. Okay. Anything else?"

Susanne said, "Um..."

"What?" Charles snapped.

"Some guy named Pete has been calling for Cin all afternoon."

"Jesus!" groaned Cinnamon.

"It's okay," said Charles. "Here's what we're going to do. I want everybody to put all your information and analysis on memory pins and bring them back to my office. Don't transmit anything. The operation's been shut down. Thanks for your hard work, guys, but I'll take it from here. Once the data is on my desk, go home and get some sleep, or see your families or whatever else you do when you're not protecting the rest of us. I'll see you in the morning."

Cinnamon eyed him with that penetrating look that always meant she was way ahead of him.

"What?" He said.

"You know the minute you put all this data into the system it will kill it, don't you?"

Charles nodded with a slight smile. "Only after I put it in. Before I do that, it all gets transferred to my own memory pin and sanitized. Now why don't you go home and see about your composer friend. Take what time you need. In the morning we'll figure out what to do next."

"Why do I get the feeling you've already decided what to do next?" She said. "And is this your version of how to shut down an investigation?"

"Go see about Pete," he said again, and went to his quarters to gather his things.

EIGHT

IT WAS SIX O'CLOCK BY THE time Charles finally settled in at his desk, turned on the screen for the news broadcast and began looking over the information they'd gathered. On the way in, he'd done a public search on Vanderhoorst, who he still felt sure was somehow connected to all this and found a great deal about the gentleman. With the exception of some 'most secret' information that the team had uncovered concerning military hardware and foreign transportation contracts, the public sites had most of what was available on the man.

Vanderhoorst had started out in his native Netherlands as a relatively small electronics manufacturer, building specialty devices for the domestic market. One particular device which he developed in his early twenties, an in-house monitor implant that turned out to be the forerunner of the medchip, was so successful that he expanded from the medical field into general manufacturing and began operations in the United States. Here he produced various mass transportation vehicles and control devices for public and military use. Where his backing had come from was suspect, but no more so than many large entrepreneurs in the modern era. His looked to be a typical success story, though he had generally avoided the public eye as much as possible. There were only four photos of the man available from both public and government sources, taken at approximately age twenty, thirty five, fifty and a recent one at age sixty two. They looked surprisingly similar. Charles thought that the man must have a portrait aging in an attic somewhere or incredibly good genes.

As for the other material they'd gathered, the most intriguing seemed to be the strange case of the multiple ghosts wandering the halls of the Perry Mall. There was no apparent explanation for that one. The software checked out as did the scanners. Yet there it was, one single man, about thirty years of age, athletic and intense: walking near the food court, opposite a luggage boutique, near the main entrance and in the transportation concourse all at the same time, and all without any sign of a medchip trace. This was definitely one for the engineers. Something anomalous was happening with the surveillance programs, and that in and of itself was enough to warrant the investigation. Still, he'd been told to shut it down and he would...as far as Rich was concerned.

Simultaneously his clip board, land line and com screamed at him. After a few seconds of indecision, he killed them all. On the screen, the news report caught his attention:

> *"This was the scene late this afternoon in downtown Atlanta, as a massive explosion rocked the city's core. At approximately six thirty this evening, the apartment building at 1447 Baltimore Street suddenly and inexplicably exploded, spreading fire and debris over a six block area. Windows were blown out for another three blocks in every direction. Preliminary reports indicate that it was probably caused by a gas leak in one of the units on the bottom floor, which would explain the nearly surgical precision that leveled only the single building, leaving its neighbors in tact. Police and fire officials promise a more complete report after the fires are out and they've had a chance to investigate. Of the ten residents of the building, all were apparently killed. No survivors have been found and there is no indication of distress calls from anyone remaining in the building. We have with us a neighbor who was just entering the street as the explosion occurred, and..."*

The screen showed a raging fire and rubble strewn about a short narrow street where a gaping hole had been gouged out between two buildings in a long line of brownstones. Charles recognized the neighborhood immediately. It was Baltimore Block, an old Atlanta street whose row houses, more indicative of London than of Atlanta, had stood for nearly one hundred years.

The historic buildings had passed through eras of posh opulence to middle class apartment dwellers, then to slums surrounded by warehouses and commercial buildings. Anyone who called themselves native Atlantans had watched the metamorphosis of the area. Once, in the early and mid- twentieth century, this had been all in-town residential territory, neighborhoods surrounded by retail and commercial interests that had fed the city's core population. The area had marked the boundaries of what was known as 'downtown', but over time, the elite had moved outward from the central city, leaving these streets to less affluent renters and eventually to the bohemian fringe. Over the past forty years, the neighborhood had made its way back to middle class studio housing as part of the flight back to the city and re-gentrification.

Charles visited the area often when he was married. He and Karen either meeting other couples for drinks or dinner at one of the new upscale nostalgic bistros meant to capture the left-bank atmosphere of the old days. It was one of the reasons that he didn't go there often now. He knew only one local resident currently.

That one resident was why he was so intent on the current scene. The brownstone near the middle of the block had simply disappeared. It was nothing but smoke, flame and rubble. He remembered it as one of the best preserved buildings on the street. It was the building where Cinnamon lived, his heart leaping into his throat, as he listened to the announcer's words.

Charles switched off the unit, slumping back in his chair. Cinnamon gone? He felt his heart sink to the pit of his stomach. It was a feeling of loss he hadn't experienced since Karen had left him. Was it possible that she was gone?

Again his clip board and com unit began screaming. One call was from Darren Rich and the other from a café. He opted for the café.

"Charles, come get me. Do it now!"

His heart shifted again, this time into his throat.

"Cinnamon? Is that you?"

"Yes. Come get me, please."

"I thought you were dead. On the news..."

"I know. I almost was, and if you don't come get me I may be. I'm at Griller's Café about two blocks from my apartment. Can you find it?"

"I've got it," Charles said, looking at a map on his clip board. "I can be there in ten minutes."

"Please. And be careful, Charles. They're probably looking for you too. Where are you?"

"I'm at the office."

"For God's sake get out of there. It's the first place they'll look...and warn the others!"

She signed off. Again the clip board signaled. He killed the line and thought for a moment.

"Central," he said, speaking to the automatic messaging center, "This is a message for all members of Team One-one-niner, Atlanta Local Region, Homeland Security. Quote. All members are now on alpha six alert and are instructed to proceed accordingly. This order is to take effect immediately. Head for the hills."

He thought a moment more and continued.

"Central, this message is for Mr. Darren Rich, Area Director, Homeland Security, Greater Atlanta Region. Quote. Darren, I've just heard about Cinnamon. I need time to get my bearings. I will be taking a personal leave for at least the next month, commencing now. All in progress work is covered. I'll be in touch. End. Delay delivery one hour."

Finally, he added a third message.

"Central, this message is for my personal domicile. Quote. Heather, when you get this message, please go ahead and do a thorough cleaning as usual, then do not return for four weeks. I will be out of town. Thanks. I'll be in touch if I decide to return early. Delay delivery one hour."

He signed off, reached in his desk drawer, withdrew his side arm, and headed away from the elevators toward a door marked EMERGENCY EXIT at the opposite end of the office. Entering, he pushed a small red stub on the wall beside the door jamb and immediately descended to ground level.

He stepped outside into a narrow alley. It was chilly and just turning from day into night, the reflection of street lights forming long shadows on the high brick walls of the narrow passage. All around him was the smell of garbage and mold, and small shiny eyes stared up at him from among the flotsam littering the ground. Charles' heart was racing and he breathed rapidly, more as if he were startled than frightened. He shivered in the canyon winds of the alley regretting his decision to not bring a heavy coat with him today. After all, he was supposed to be back home by now, all cozy and snug with plenty of Black Rock tea to keep him company. How he wished he had some now.

He turned left and made his way to a side street. It was nearly devoid of traffic and he seemed to be the only pedestrian around. Opposite the edge of the alley where he still stood in the shadows was a large parking facility, filled with ground vehicles and a host of sky cars on the top deck, all neatly arranged in rows, awaiting their owners. He stepped out onto the sidewalk and turned north, toward Baltimore Block.

"I thought you'd come this way," said a voice behind him. Instinctively he spun around. A hand caught his wrist as he reached for his side arm. He was staring into the face of Ben Delano. Charles relaxed and released the weapon.

"Damn, Ben," he said. "You scared the hell out of me!"

Delano smiled, pumping an atomizer up his nose and inhaling. "Not too surprising. You're getting a little clumsy in your old age, aren't you, Chuck? If I'd have been here for a different reason, you'd be dead by now."

"How'd you know where to wait for me?"

Delano shrugged and sniffled then hesitated for a moment while he blew his nose. "Damned nasty cold," he said irritably. "I used to work in this building, remember? All emergency chutes come out on this side of the building. Now it's pretty obvious you don't want to be walking down Spring Street after what happened at Cinnamon's tonight, so this was the only other way to come. The trouble is, if I can figure it out that easily, so can they."

His eyes darted around as he spoke. Pulling Charles by the arm, Delano pointed him south, away from the Griller Café and Cinnamon. Charles decided to go along. He was not about to mention his appointment with Cinnamon.

"You know about the explosion then."

"Hell yes, I know. It's all over the news. Besides, I'm local police, remember? As soon as I found out who lived in the building I came here to find you. "I'm sorry about your partner, my friend. She was an angel, that little bit of spice.."

"Thanks," Charles said in a noncommittal tone . "So who's this 'they' you were talking about?"

Delano shrugged again.

"Who knows? All I know is that the explosion was surgical. All I had to do was look at the video from the scene to know that. No accidental gas leak is gonna cause that kind of an effect. The police know it, the fire chief knows it, and you and I know it. It was a very professional job. Whoever they are, buddy, they want you and your team out of the way. I thought you could use some help."

Charles looked at his old friend, who was doing his best to muster a smile. "Thanks, Ben, but I think I've got it under control. The rest of the team's been ordered to go to ground and as far as my boss knows, I'm on leave."

"Yeah. That's gonna help," Delano said sarcastically.

"It'll give me a little time, and that's all I need. I've got a safe house that I can use until I figure this out."

Delano pursed his lips and frowned. "I hope you're not talking about the rental on Lindberg Place. The Company occupied it this afternoon. They notified us ahead of time, of course, but I never made a connection between that and you until the explosion."

"Well just damn!" said Charles. "They're really that good, aren't they?"

"Nobody better but you guys. So, what now?"

"I'll think of something," Charles said, anxious to get to Cinnamon before it was too late. He was already formulating an alternative plan.

"Well don't take this the wrong way, Charlie, but whatever you decide, don't tell me."

Delano had a look of pleading on his face. He was stuck in the middle of a very deadly situation and he knew it. Charles knew it too.

"Don't worry, Ben. I can keep you out of it. From now on you don't know me."

Delano thrust a wad of cash into Charles' hand.

"There's about nine thousand there. It's all I could get without withdrawals being reported. You know how that goes. Whatever you do, don't try to leave town on public transportation. That much cash will get you a look-see at any terminal in the free world."

"Yeah. I know."

"And don't use your cash card either."

"I know, Ben!" Charles snapped.

"Okay, okay. Speaking of leaving town, do you need transportation?"

"I... yeah, I hadn't thought about it. I could use some."

Ben slipped a key card into Charles' jacket pocket and stepped back. He took another blast from the atomizer and immediately sneezed.

"It's from the impound lot. As far as anyone is concerned, it doesn't exist except in police inventory. You should be good for at least seven days. I picked one that won't even be processed for that long. The anti theft device and tracers have been removed as well. You'll find it just around the block here. It's the maroon Arrow Marine with the wheel covers."

Charles took Ben's hand. "Thanks, buddy. You seem to have thought of everything."

"Aw, it was easy. All I have to do now is rebuild my own emergency bugout plans. You just got all mine. I only wish I could do something about your medchip, but short of cutting off your left hand, I don't know how to handle that one."

"Thanks anyway, Ben, but if it's all the same to you, I'll keep the hand. Besides, the way the program's acting up, they may not find me for weeks that way. So long."

"Luck, Buddy. So long. You owe me a big one."

Charles turned left at the corner, making his way back toward Spring Street. True to Ben's word, there was a maroon Arrow Marine parked half way up the block, facing away from the main thoroughfare. It was deceptively sedate for such a fast machine, and that was to his advantage. Ben had done him well. He'd have preferred a sky car, but that made this even a better choice. If people were after him, they must know how much he hate surface transport. He used the key card, stepped in and gave the navigation unit instructions for Griller's Café. Finally, he was in motion.

nine

CHARLES WAS STANDING BENEATH the shelter of an overhang about half a block away from Griller's, trying to decide how best to proceed. If Cinnamon was right and the unknown 'they' were after him, he had to assume that they would cover most of the public area around Baltimore Block just in case he showed up. All they needed was an accurate trace on his chip to know his exact location anyway, but if they were out to kill him or capture him, they'd want to do it quietly. Once that dawned on him, he decided that public was better than private and decided to just walk into the restaurant.

Charles had parked the car in a public lot around the corner and made his way to the café, his uniform not the least out of place, considering the number of investigators, both local and Federal, that were swarming over the wreckage of what had once been Cinnamon's studio loft two blocks away.

When he entered the café, Cinnamon looked up, then immediately back to her coffee. Cinnamon was sitting at the far end of the room near the fireplace. She was at a small round table wearing a raincoat that covered her almost completely and hid her weapon well. In the light of the flames from the gas fireplace her hair looked almost alive; the red highlights in the chestnut glowing like a halo around her sad face. He felt an unfamiliar shudder when he saw her, something he hadn't felt for a long time. He was relieved to find her alive.

He made a point to walk boldly, as if on official business and too busy to notice the people around him and took a seat four tables away on the opposite side of the fireplace. He was lucky to find it. The café was nearly full. As the waitress was taking his order, a flash of lightning and roll of thunder announced the arrival of yet another storm. The waitress didn't seem to notice.

"Just coffee," he said.

"Real or fabricated, decaffeinated or regular, spun or brewed," she asked mindlessly.

"Real, regular, brewed," he said.

"That costs extra, you know," she said.

He looked up at her for the first time. She smiled back, an uninterested, plastic, but well practiced 'waitress' smile as she pushed her long blond hair back over her shoulder. He looked her up and down briefly, studying her as much out of habit as anything.

"It's okay," he said, and she disappeared into the kitchen behind the counter. Charles watched her go, thought briefly and stood. He headed for the door. As he passed Cinnamon's table, he said, "Get out of here now."

She stood and followed him.

Outside it was already starting to rain and he motioned her to follow him. He walked briskly both to put distance between him and the café and to avoid as much of the downpour as he could. Around the corner he entered the parking lot and walked straight to the car. Cinnamon was right behind him. The Arrow Marine's doors unlocked with a chirp and she was inside.

"What's the rush?" She asked.

"'Tell ya in a minute," he said, and manually pulled out onto the street and sped away. Neither of them spoke for several blocks. He finally turned control over to the navigator and released the wheel.

"That waitress was no waitress."

"You're sure?"

"I'm surprised you didn't catch it. Wrong shoes, wrong hair and she went into the kitchen to get a coffee that could be poured at the counter. I don't think they recognized you, but they sure spotted me."

"Great," she said. "This is no time for me to get careless."

"Tell me what happened," he asked. Cinnamon gave a great sigh and cleared her head.

"I came home to talk to Pete, but traffic delayed me, and I saw him arrive just as I turned into the street. I was parking the car down the street when the building blew. Charles, he must have triggered the device when he opened the door, or when he put the key in the lock. Oh, Charles. I've never seen anything like that. The whole front of the building blew out into the street and then it collapsed in on itself, like some demolition job. It didn't take long to realize it was not an accident. The car was parked at the dead end and there was all this rubble in the street by then so I couldn't use it. I just went into a building across the street, out the back way and into the café. My God, Charles, Pete's gone! He just disappeared with the rest of the people in my building. Those were friends of mine, Charles. What the hell's happening?"

"I'd say somebody wants us permanently off the investigation. I'm sorry about Pete."

She nodded and looked pained. "He was such an innocent. It's not fair. I'll miss him."

Charles was cruising north toward a residential area, paralleling the main drag, which would be grid locked even now. They drove on for a while in light traffic, but he occasionally took control of the car and made sure that he blended with a cluster of cars all proceeding toward Piedmont Park and the Mid-Town Art Festival he knew was in full gear. As they approached, he could hear the sound of several bands, apparently battling it out for the attention of the crowds amidst bright colored lights. In the distance, a Ferris wheel lazily rotated in rhythm with the music.

"That's what we need," he said and pulled into the far left lane. He turned into one of the larger parking areas and found a place near the center. Cinnamon said nothing, but she gave him a puzzled look.

"We need clothes. They'll have booths and boutiques here, and we also need to see a friend of mine."

Cinnamon raised an eyebrow. "You know some strange people, Charles Peavey. Normally I wouldn't be caught dead in this area at night even armed, at least not far from the lights and security."

"You still have your handgun on you, right?"

"Yes."

"Then don't worry. No one knows where we are, and I'm still in uniform. No one will bother us."

They quickly found a boutique that contained relatively normal clothes and outfitted themselves. Charles felt out of place without his uniform, but the loose-fitting trousers hid his weapon well, and the black shirt and pullover sweater were warm. Cinnamon wore a retro knee length full skirt with a colorful print and a white sweater. They also bought light jackets in a salmon color. These days anything else would have seemed out of place and they needed desperately to blend in. She pulled her hair back and tied it with a ribbon to form a small knot at the back of her head. She kept the raincoat on and carried the jacket, though the sky had cleared. When Charles pulled out the wad of bills and paid cash for the clothing, Cinnamon's eyes were wide with surprise. The proprietor checked each of the four one-hundred dollar bills under his scanner to be sure they were real, shrugged, and gave change.

"Where the hell did you get all the cash?" She asked as they made their way through the crowd.

"Hard to believe, but it was Ben Delano. He got me the car too. He figured out what was going on almost as fast as you did, Cin."

"Oh, my God, Charlie! What about the others? They're as vulnerable as we are, aren't they?"

"I've already contacted them. They've gone to ground. And here we are."

He took her by the elbow and guided her across a soccer field to a run down residential area that bordered the park on the south. Cinnamon looked around nervously and slipped her hand into her coat pocket, grasping the small hand gun.

"Relax," he said, "We're not going far."

Three houses down from where they had crossed were lit up inside and out, with signs suggesting cheap parking on the lawn. The next three houses were dark and across a side street lined with early twentieth century craftsman style bungalows. Charles nodded to the dark house in the middle of the cluster and walked casually toward it. They turned up the walk to a typical bungalow that had seen better days. The yard was overgrown with weeds growing up from the cracks in the circular driveway; the bushes spread off at odd angles, as if they hadn't been pruned in years. In the center of the driveway was an island containing a lone pine tree, gnarled and stunted from the polluted world which it was forced to inhabit. To the left of the tree was a small pond, greenish algae choked water laboriously flowing from a little waterfall cut into the rock bank on one side. It trickled sporadically, producing a sound less like a brook and more like that of a street bum with a kidney problem attempting urination. The house itself looked darker than its companions if that was possible. Charles hustled her along, ignoring her reluctance and stepped up onto the porch which creaked ominously. He stopped and stood at the front door.

"What now?" She said, looking around.

"Now we wait," he said.

They stood for nearly five minutes before the door opened marginally with a sharp metallic click. Charles pushed it open and stepped in, Cinnamon in tow. It closed automatically behind them. Cinnamon found herself in a dimly lit living room, dusty and smelling of old frying oil and oranges with a touch of urine. It was a disgusting combination. There was no furniture in the room except for a single chair situated in front of a central shallow Mumford fireplace.

Cinnamon shivered.

"This looks like the haunted house at Disney North."

"What do you want?" A disembodied voice said from nowhere.

"I want to see the wizard."

"Who are you?" the voice asked.

"Oh, come on. You know who I am. Let us in."

There was a moment's hesitation followed by a now irritated unseen questioner who said, "If you're not going to participate in the niceties, you can just leave now!"

"He's a bit quirky," Charles said softly to Cinnamon.

"I am not! Now who are you?"

"Dorothy and the Tin Man," Charles said, almost embarrassed. Cinnamon chuckled in spite of herself.

"Ah. Back again. Will the man behind the curtain do?"

"I need a heart," he said.

"Where are the scarecrow and that lion fella?"

"The scarecrow went out to the outhouse and the hogs ate him."

"Must have been damned hungry hogs!"

Now Cinnamon was chuckling uncontrollably. This was all so ridiculous that she couldn't contain herself.

"And the lion?"

"Oh, he got bored and took the last train for the coast."

"He always did like the taste of a good Vestal Virgin!"

"This is ridiculous," Cin said. "Did you have to memorize all that just to get in here?"

"Nah, we make it up as we go along," said the voice. "Come on back."

A door opened to the right of the fireplace with the same metallic click. Light beamed out into the living room through the crack and Cinnamon could see movement behind it. Charles went to it without hesitation and swung it open. She followed.

In the back room, they found a comfortable and very modern sitting room, well furnished and neat as a pin. The disgusting odor of the front room was now gone, and a faint hint of lilacs filled the air. Standing at a large mahogany desk, opposite them, was an older man, long gray hair neatly combed and braided, wearing vintage blue jeans and a cardigan sweater. His eyes were sharp and very blue, his features chiseled and his body more athletic than Cinnamon would have imagined from his wrinkled face. He was smiling at them gently.

"It's been a long time, Chuck. I'm glad to see you. And who's this?"

"Stephen, this is my partner, Cinnamon Harper. Cinnamon, this old fossil is Stephen Hillel, one of the most brilliant men I've ever known."

Hillel bowed slightly and said, "Flattery will get you nowhere, Chuck, but Cinnamon is welcome to use it liberally."

She nodded and stepped forward to shake his hand.

"No contact," Charles said quickly and she backed off.

Hillel looked embarrassed, but recovered quickly and motioned for them both to sit down opposite him at the desk.

"So what are your needs, Charles?"

"We need new identities."

Hillel was suddenly all business. He looked each of them directly in the eye and held the gaze for an uncomfortably long minute.

"How permanent, and how extensive?"

"Total new personas, Stephen. As for how long, I don't know."

"That gets expensive, you know."

Charles withdrew the roll of bills from his pocket and placed it on the desk.

"There are eighty-five one-hundred dollar bills there. It's all I have, Stephen."

"Oh, put your money away," Hillel said, trying to sound irritated. "I don't need that. We'll settle up with the agency. Who knows? I might need a favor in the future. In my business, it helps to have people in high places beholden to you. Now I remember when I first started out. There was this federal judge. Come to think of it, he's a senator now. Anyway..."

"Stephen," Charles said.

"Oh...very well. I suppose you want reconstructive surgery, new medchips, credit cards, birth certificates and all that?"

Cinnamon gave Charles a startled look that fluctuated between amazed and frightened. He shook his head and smiled at her.

"No surgery. We don't have time, and just remove the medchips. We need freedom of movement. The rest would be plenty."

"You realize that will leave you without any protection? If you're injured or develop some serious condition, no one will come."

"It is necessary."

"Very well. I'll pull them and deactivate them. Do you want your medchips saved for later reinsertion? Yes? All that I can do here. Now then, I'll need more information."

Hillel was already busying himself at his desk screen, staring down into it as he manipulated his keyboard at lightening speed. Cinnamon noticed that his keyboard only had seven keys and that he used them in combination, often striking more than one at a time. It was a fluid movement born of much practice and she wondered where he had found such a device.

The reflection of the changing display gave him an eerie, almost mad scientist demeanor which was only enhanced by his physical appearance. Cinnamon had visions of him suddenly looking up and announcing "It's alive! It's alive!"

"I resent that," he said, still staring at the screen.

"Sorry?" said Charles.

"Not you, Charles, her. She just compared me to Dr. Frankenstein."

Cinnamon jumped but Charles caught her arm.

"I'm sorry," he said. "I forgot to tell you that he's an adept."

Hillel looked at her, grinning. "A natural one, actually. No implants or enhancements. I find it comes in very handy in my line of work. It saves a lot of time asking questions."

"Damn, you know some weird people, Charles," she said openly.

"Thank you, my dear," Hillel said lightly. "I think we can do a great deal with you, Chuck, by diversionary camouflage. I can give you a tattoo that will not only cover the scar from the medchip removal but divert people's attention from the rest of you. I have some really outrageous choices available. And you'll have to shave your head, of course."

"I expected that," Charles said flatly.

"As for you, my dear—"

"I'm not shaving my hair, and no tattoos," said Cinnamon flatly.

"No, no. Not necessary. We're going to change your hair color, cut it, and fatten you up. Your figure's too perfect. It draws attention. Now let's see. What would you prefer? Larger hips perhaps? Larger bust? Flabby arms? If we had time I could really do a lot with your bone structure, but you did say no surgery. Still, perhaps a bit of a hawkish nose."

"Are you out of your mind? You're not messing with my nose!"

Hillel shook his head.

"Really, young lady, It's not permanent. It's a cosmetic prosthesis that you can remove any time. You're just too pretty to go unnoticed, that's all."

"Well..."

"Good. Hawk nose and wider hips. You don't want the extra weight up around your shoulders and chest raising your center of gravity if you have to get physical. We'll use pads around the thighs. No cellular injections. Besides, I don't have any on hand."

Cinnamon frowned and nodded. "That doesn't sound too bad."

"First things first, however, let's get those medchips out. Are you sure you don't want replacements? I think I can find a couple that are very close to your actual medical histories. Ah, yes. Here we are. A delightful couple from Denver who met an untimely demise while visiting Yosemite. The medchips were presumed lost in the fire."

To Cinnamon's look of questioning dismay, Charles said, "Don't ask."

Hillel invited them into another room outfitted as a medical facility and mechanics shop. There was an examining table and instrument tray at one end of the room. Cinnamon was surprised so much could be crammed into what appeared to be a rather small house.

He had Cinnamon sit and place her hand on a stainless steel table under ultraviolet light. He slipped on a pair of imaging glasses and examined her hand.

"Hmm. Yes. Good job. It's neatly imbedded in the carpel above the middle finger, just as it should be. I'll have it out in less than five seconds. Do you want an anesthetic?"

"No," she said, "I need to stay alert."

He grinned.

"Good, because I haven't got any anyway," he laughed. "Just kidding, my dear. Now put your hand down there, please."

He probed with an instrument that looked to be a cross between a hypodermic and a screwdriver. She felt only a prick as he injected the needle into her hand, and then a peculiar vibrating sensation as it spun inside the incision. He pulled it out after several seconds.

"Nice job, if I do say so myself," he said. He pushed the needle into a small vial and spun it again and then extracted it and set it aside.

"That should do it," he said. He placed the vial in a larger case and handed it to Cinnamon. "That's your medchip, my dear. Don't lose it."

Charles was next, but when he sat and put his hand under the light, Hillel hesitated.

"Problem, Stephen?"

"I know it's none of my business, Charles, but are you an orphan?"

Charles stared at the man and nearly withdrew his hand.

"What makes you ask that?"

"Are you?"

"As a matter of fact I am. How did you know?"

"The scar on your hand, I've only seen one other like it. He said he got it in an orphanage when he was a kid."

"Here in Atlanta?"

Hillel shook his head. "Actually, in Kansas City. It's been years though."

"Is it important?"

"No, not really. It's just a curiosity. You know how I am. Now hold still."

He repeated the procedure, handing Charles a case similar to Cinnamon's except that whereas hers was red, his was black. Charles slipped it in his pocket.

As painless as the removable of the medchip, the tattoo proved to be a different matter. Its creation was identical to an actual tattoo, but it used inks that responded to certain wavelengths of light by simply disappearing without scarring or damage to the skin. Charles was assured that there would be no trace of it once corrected and he was glad for the temporary artwork. It was a large illustration of an elaborate Celtic knot, done in bright reds and blacks, blues and yellows and shimmering green. He knew that human nature being what it was, it was probably the only thing anyone would remember about him physically if asked.

While Cinnamon dyed her hair a mousy brown, Charles first cut his hair and then shaved his head. He walked about the room, razor merrily humming away, and watched Stephen play with their two clipboards. Within two hours, Cinnamon had been completely 'uglified', as Stephen called it, with wide hips, very short mousy brown hair and a nose that spread around a central hump, as if it had been broken at a young age and never properly cared for. Fortunately, the full skirt that Cinnamon had bought meant that she could accommodate her new shape without a change of clothes. They had new identities, new identification cards, credit cards and new names. They were now Mr. and Mrs. G.W. Jones of Savannah, Georgia. As a final gesture, Stephen attached a prominent mole to Cinnamon's left cheek, just to the side of her new nose.

"I think that should do it," Stephen said, admiring his handy work. "I'm not sure I'd recognize either of you myself in a crowd. With that mole as a focus, people won't even be able to remember the proper dimensions of your face. I particularly like the fact that it's hairy, don't you? Nice effect. Now remember to waddle, my dear. Otherwise, it will look unnatural. Do you want me to hang onto the medchips for safe keeping or are you going to take them with you?"

"We'll take them," Charles said. "I don't want you involved in this mess anymore than you have to be. No evidence means no charges."

"I appreciate that," said Stephen.

"One final thing. Your medchips now show you both as dead, since they were removed. They will continue to broadcast for another ten minutes or so, which should alert anyone looking for you as to the location of the bodies. Fortunately, they'll be looking in the wrong place. The telemetry is being rebroadcast from here to an incineration unit near the Chattahoochee River twenty miles away. By the time they figure out what's happened, the medchips will have been deactivated and will be untraceable back to me. I've also done a bit of surgery on your clip boards. Tracers have been removed and ID codes scrambled. As of now, you are both ghosts."

"I thought you couldn't remove tracers," said Cinnamon.

Hillel looked at her and offered an almost apologetic smile.

"You can if you designed them in the first place."

"Jesus, you know some strange people, Charles."

"You said that before, and I'll thank you to leave my family out of this."

On the street, they noticed that the sounds from the festival across the street had diminished significantly. Apparently the concert was over and people were shutting down their booths. They crossed the street quickly, stayed with the crowds on the way to the parking lot, and made their way to the Arrow Marine.

"We'll have to ditch the car, you know," said Cinnamon.

"I know. It's much too conspicuous. We'll pick up mine. I keep it in a garage on the east side and we can drop this one off at the same time."

Cinnamon laughed.

"You have a car? I can't believe that!"

"Well, I do. Just because I like to fly doesn't mean I don't have a car. I haven't used it in almost three years."

"Oh that's just great. It probably has four flat tires and dead fuel cells, not to mention, no fluids. This is going to be fun."

Charles didn't comment. He directed the navigation unit to a location on the east side filled with warehouses and small manufacturing concerns. He leaned back and relaxed and was soon sleeping soundly. In no time, they were both sleeping soundly, recovering from the day's ordeal. The Arrow Marine sped effortlessly through traffic, weaving in and out, magically finding alternate routes and avoiding the snarls on the main roads. It wove its way through residential sections and districts slowing only long enough to navigate an antiquated railroad crossing near Agnes Scott College, and onto another section of warehouses two blocks off the main road. It came to a stop in front of a dark featureless metal frame building with no signage and no lights. By now it was well after midnight.

"We're here, wherever here is," Cinnamon said, shaking Charles roughly.

Charles stretched and yawned, taking in a great drought of air and rubbing his face. He made to run his fingers through his hair but stopped suddenly.

He chuckled.

"Habit," he said. "I always do that when I wake up. There's just nothing there to work with now."

"Are you sure we're in the right place?"

Charles looked around. "This is it. Wait here. I'll only be a moment."

He got out and looked around, trying to penetrate the shadows for any sign of movement. Satisfied that they were alone, he walked to a large door and punched in a code. In response, the door swung upward and lights came on inside. He then drove the car inside. The door closed behind them automatically.

Cinnamon looked around in amazement. She was in a large, well lit, open space containing two bays with lifts and perhaps a dozen cars, all neatly lined up at an angle, their noses perfectly aligned along a yellow strip on the floor. The vehicles included both vintage and newer models and two were modified sky cars. The place was immaculate. There was no dust, no grease on the floor and no telltale odor of gasoline or solvents in the air. She whistled.

"Nice place, Charles. You keep your car here?"

He went directly to an older plain black sedan and touched the door panel. It opened immediately. "Get in," he said.

When they were settled, he turned the key and the engine came to life with a roar.

"What the hell's that?! She said with a jump.

"It's the engine. This is a hybrid, vintage 2010. She's a real sweetheart."

"This thing runs on conventional gas?"

"It runs on electricity. The generator is driven by a gas turbine. Don't worry, Cin, it won't explode."

"But it's going to need gas!"

"They still sell the stuff. Besides, it has a full tank and a range of nearly a thousand miles before we need to refill it. I just had it overhauled."

"And you wanted inconspicuous!"

Charles just grabbed the wheel and pulled back on it and the car began to back out of the space.

"There are over thirty thousand hybrids just like this one, same color and same make, registered in the state of Georgia. This one is registered in the name of George Washington Jones, just like my ID says. Do you know how many George Washington Jones's there are in the United States? Well over three million. That's inconspicuous enough. And don't sell Isabel short. She was clocked at over one hundred sixty on the straight away. You be nice to her."

"Who's Isabel?"

"You're sitting in her."

Cinnamon let out a very loud unladylike snort and grinned at him. "You named your car? You actually named your car? I can't believe this."

"I need a Black Rock tea," he said to no one and turned the wheel toward the now open doors. "And we both need sleep. Let's find a room and crash."

TEN

WHEN CHARLES WOKE it was still dark and Cinnamon was already up and busily clacking away at her viewer. He looked over at the dark haired woman sitting at the com desk at the far end of the room. Her bed looked like it had never been slept in. He shook his head to clear the cobwebs and again tried to brush his hair back with his hand. The rough stubble on his naked pate finally brought him to reality.

"You been up all night?"

"Nope," she said, still looking at the viewer. "I got up about an hour ago. I've been trying to contact the others."

"Any luck?"

"Well, Sarah and Anton are okay. They're in Baja. If you're going to hide, it's not a bad choice. It's still pretty wild and woolly down there."

Charles sat up and looked around.

"They sure got there in a hurry. What time is it, anyway?"

"About seven thirty, I think. The sun's been up for about half an hour."

He rolled out of bed and slipped on his trousers. Pulling open the heavy curtain about four inches he looked out at an empty swimming pool and through the trees beyond it, a bright sun low on the horizon. He pulled the curtain close again.

"Gimme a minute to wake up," he said.

"There's tea on the counter next to the coffee pot."

"I hate tea!"

"Not this stuff, you don't."

Charles lifted the cup and inhaled deeply. The aroma was the unmistakable pungent bouquet of Black Rock. He moaned in pleasure and drank deeply.

"I can't believe you did this for me," he said.

Cinnamon looked up from the screen and grinned.

"Well, you said it made you sharp, and that stuff takes a good twenty years to kill you. I figure another day or two won't hurt."

"Um, just what do you mean another day or two?"

Cinnamon looked back at the screen and began cycling through information screens.

"Oh, nothing," she said. "I've also found Craig in Philadelphia, of all places, but Susanne, Bobby J. and Meg are all still off the leash. There's no telling where they are. None are answering coded calls."

"I hope they're all right. Got any ideas about what to do now?"

Cinnamon finally signed off and looked up.

"That's your department, boss, but if you want my opinion…"

"Please," he said feeling honestly at a loss.

"Well, I've been thinking about all this, and there are some obvious things we know and some obvious moves we could make."

Charles was splashing water in his face now, reaching for a towel.

"Like what?"

"Would you please put a shirt on, Charles? It's very distracting."

"Sorry," he said, grabbing his shirt and putting it on. "So like what?"

"I don't think there's much doubt that our friendly missing Vanderhoorst is involved in something sensitive and that the Pentagon's trying to shut us down to keep it quiet. That's one thing. Secondly, we still have a murder on our hands and a serious breech of security in the trace program, which is probably not connected to Vanderhoorst. I think our involvement with him was accidental. There was just a simple miss identification of the DNA analysis."

"You don't think Vanderhoorst is connected with the body?"

"I don't see how. I know his DNA says he is the dead body, but it's an obvious mistake. What we need to do is find and correct the security problem while avoiding Federal death squads in the process."

“Great,” Charles thought aloud. He took another long pull on the mug of tea and sat in a bedside chair. “Just what I wanted to hear. So how do we proceed?”

Cinnamon gave him a strange look and he offered her a mock frown.

“Think of it as a proficiency test, Cin. How would you proceed?”

“Well, first I’d have the DNA on our victim checked again by an independent laboratory. I’ve still got one shoe in my handbag, and an analysis of that white goo we found as well. Secondly, I’d try to get word to the Federals that we have no further interest in Vanderhoorst and would they please leave us alone. Next I’d start over with the Perry Mall surveillance tapes. If they haven’t been sanitized, they’re our only other lead. We have to find out who this character is before we can figure who would want to kill him.”

“Sounds good except for contacting the Federals. It’s an invitation to get ourselves killed. At this point, I don’t think they care if we’re interested in Vanderhoorst or not. The very fact that we know he’s working on some super sensitive project is enough to want us out of the way.”

“Damn paranoid Federals,” she groaned.

“Remember. Paranoia is what keeps us in a job.”

“Then damn the job too!”

Cinnamon was pacing now, which was not an easy task in the hotel room, and Charles retreated to the bathroom and turned on the shower. He stripped, stepped in, and received the hot water gratefully just as the Black Rock kicked in. He stood euphorically feeling the water flow down over his sore body, not daring to move. This was too good to disturb. Finally, he showered, rinsing with icy cold water and stepped out. By the time he had dried off he was feeling human again.

“Your turn,” he called from the bathroom. Cinnamon didn’t answer.

“Cin? You there?” He called louder. Still no response.

He stepped out of the bathroom and looked around. The room was empty. There was no sign of a struggle. He looked for a note and found one taped to the door. Where was she? Charles reached for his sidearm and pulled it from the holster. He checked the magazine and cracked the door enough to see out. The car was gone.

“Holy hell!” He muttered. “If she screws with my car, I’m gonna kill her!”

He opened the note and read it. She'd taken the other bloody shoe to a private laboratory near by and would be back soon. There was nothing he could do but wait.

Two hours passed which he spent checking news reports on the room's cable feed to no avail, and trying to formulate in his mind what to do next. The more he reviewed the events of the past several days, the more confusing it appeared. Finally, he heard footsteps outside. He again reached for his pistol and dropped to his knee just to one side of the door. Cinnamon walked in carrying a newspaper and a soda. She stopped dead in her tracks when she saw Charles and instinctively reached for her small automatic.

"Jesus, Charles. You scared the hell out of me," she said.

Charles slipped his pistol back in its holster. "Where the hell have you been? It's been two hours!"

"Having tea with the Queen," she quipped and brushed past him. She plopped herself down in the chair by the small table and opened the paper. "I dropped the sample off at a good lab that I've worked with before and picked up a paper. I thought I'd see what they're saying about the explosion. Who knows? Maybe I'm listed as dead."

"I hope we both are," Charles said and peeked out the door at Isabel, who was properly parked and had arrived without a scratch, then turned to finish dressing.

When he had finished dressing, he came out of the bathroom to find her in the same chair pouring over want ads in the paper. He knew what that meant.

"Any word?" He asked.

"Susan and Meg both coded in and they're okay. There's no word from Bobby J. as far as I can tell. Here. You try."

She threw the want ads section of the paper to him and stood, stretching. He watched her as she arched her back, her body forming a graceful curve that accentuated her bust line seductively. If he didn't know better, he'd have sworn it was on purpose.

"So are we dead?" He said reaching for the front page.

"Missing, actually. I'm presumed dead though, which probably means they think the explosion got me. It's you they're probably having fits about. After all, there's no telemetry signature on either of us now, is there?"

Charles said nothing. He looked at the lead story about the explosion, trying to glean something useful from the accompanying photo of the scene. Nothing looked out of place. He threw it to one side and gave the want ads a quick perusal. He found the two coded ads for Meg and Susan and agreed that Bobby J. hadn't reported in yet.

"I wonder where he is," he said to no one. Cinnamon was in the bathroom, taking a shower.

When she came out of the bathroom, Charles avoided turning her way just in case she'd decided to arrive au natural. That lasted for all of twenty seconds. He looked up and found her fully dressed, toweling her hair roughly. She looked back at him absently.

"What?" She said.

"Hmm?"

Cinnamon gave him a sly smile. "You look disappointed."

"'Don't know what you're talking about."

"I've got to call the lab. I'm going to use the hotel line in case there's a flag on any references to our corpse in the data base. We are checking out, aren't we?"

"In about twenty minutes," Charles said.

He was thinking how good it was to have a partner that could anticipate him and who thought along the same lines as he. It did save a world of discussion. Cinnamon dialed out through the room's com line and began receiving hard copy almost immediately. She read it as it arrived, frowning.

"Well?"

"Good news, bad news," she said.

"Does it matter which I get first?"

"Not really," she said, gathering the five page report together and scanning it again. "They're both the same."

"Specifics?"

"We didn't make a mistake. The DNA trace on the victim is definitely Peter Vanderhoorst. The white substance, by the way, is a synthetic clotting agent given to hemophiliacs. It stays liquid no matter what, which is why it was still oozing in the dried blood."

"Vanderhoorst's records didn't indicate he was a bleeder, did they?" asked Charles.

"Nope. No mention. It could have to do with his operation, but I've never heard of anything like that. Basically, we're back where we started from. We don't know anymore now than then."

"I wonder..."

"Hmm? Oh, I was thinking. Vanderhoorst is still the key. We didn't actually speak to him, did we? How do we know the recorded message hadn't been manufactured? He could have been the result of an imaging program for all we know. Considering how much money the man has, or had, it might benefit some people to keep him alive, at least on paper. I think we need to talk to his man Hodges again. Is your uniform still clean?"

"Excuse me?"

"Oh, never mind. Just put it on. We're going to go see our friendly neighborhood butler," he said. "Let's get out of here.

ELEVEN

THEIR SECOND VISIT TO MR. VANDERHOORST'S penthouse was far less cordial than the first. Cinnamon looked sharp as ever in her uniform, though she regretted having to leave the prosthetic 'thunder thighs' behind since her slacks would never accommodate their bulk. Still, with new nose, altered hair and a prominent mole, she was virtually unrecognizable. As for Charles, he wore his Homeland Security cap with the bill pulled down over his eyes, and between that and the very noticeable tattoo, he would pass. They arrived unannounced and approached the security guard at the front desk in their most intimidating official manner.

"We're here to speak with Mr. Peter Hans Vanderhoorst. Please tell him we are coming up," said Cinnamon in her 'don't mess with me' voice.

"I'm sorry, but Mr. Vanderhoorst has only just arrived from Europe. He's recuperating, and is not receiving..."

"You do recognize the uniforms?" asked Charles sharply.

"Of course, sir, but..."

"You are aware of the extent of our powers to investigate?"

The security guard hesitated and then said, "I'll call right away."

They waited as he spoke first to Hodges and then to someone claiming to be Vanderhoorst. The guard had slipped an ear bud into his left ear for privacy, so that they were privy to only his half of the conversation.

"Yes sir," he was saying. "No sir, these are two different Homeland Security investigators. Certainly, sir."

He swung his com screen in their direction so that those in the pent house could see them and then he swung it back around.

"Yes sir," the guard said. "Right away, sir," and to Charles and Cin, "He said to come right up. Please use the third elevator on the right and it will take you directly to the penthouse."

"Thank you."

Hodges answered the door as before, filling it with his bulk and blocking their way. He offered his usual salutation, introducing himself and then said, "I am afraid that Mr. Vanderhoorst is somewhat indisposed. He has just returned from Switzerland where he underwent a serious operation. However, if I can be of service, I would be glad to."

"We'd like to come in," Cinnamon said.

Hodges looked at her, his mind working wildly and for a moment they were both afraid that the huge man would recognize them. After a moment, he stepped aside, smiled and offered a slight bow, and said, "Certainly."

Once more in the living room, they waited while Hodges disappeared into the depths of the apartment. They settled into the awkward chairs they could find. There is no sense in sinking into an overstuffed monstrosity that could later be an impediment to their movements. They positioned themselves facing both the front door and the hallway down which Hodges had disappeared, with their backs to the wide expanse of windows.

"I was afraid he was going to recognize me," Cinnamon whispered.

"He may have. At the least he recognized the voice, whether he could place it or not. That disguise of yours is awfully good. You are just flat, butt ugly."

Before she could respond, Hodges was back. He bowed.

"Mr. Vanderhoorst has agreed to see you, though I would caution you that he was sedated for a very long time and is not totally recovered. Please be as brief as possible."

"Certainly," said Charles with a British clip and in a tone two octaves below his normal timbre.

They followed Hodges down a short hall into a room smaller than the one they had left. It appeared to be a study, though the billiard table at one end said that it was used for other activities as well. He signaled for them to wait and again disappeared down a hallway. Almost immediately, he was back, pushing an old fashioned non powered wheelchair occupied by Peter Vanderhoorst.

He was a small man, though his exact height was difficult to determine from his seated position. Charles estimated him to be no more than five foot seven or eight. He had thinning yellow grey hair and a sallow complexion and was wearing a richly embroidered black-on-black dressing gown, a blanket draped over him from the waist down. An oxygen tube was fitted around his neck and two small probes rested on his upper lip, just below the nostrils. Vanderhoorst really looked the part of the invalid patient.

"I am Peter Vanderhoorst," he said with a barely discernible accent. His voice seemed strong, though he spoke in small segments in between breaths. While they were talking, Hodges would adjust the tube from time to time to keep it properly distanced from the nose.

"We greatly appreciate your willingness to see us," Charles said.

"Of course, I hope you will excuse my rather informal appearance."

"Not at all, we're sorry to intrude on your convalescence. It was a serious operation?"

Vanderhoorst waved the inquiry aside with a sweep of his hand.

"Nothing really, just an inconvenience. I was undergoing a procedure to clear the plaque from my arteries surrounding the heart. It's more a nuisance than a hardship." He smiled disarmingly.

"I hope you will not be offended, but we do need to verify that. Could we see the incision?"

"Certainly," he said and pulled his dressing gown aside. Hodges leaned over and unbuttoned his shirt and pulled it back. He smiled pleasantly as they examined the sutured wound, a very neat incision just over the breast bone approximately seven inches long. Hodges pulled close his shirt again and buttoned it.

"Is this more about that poor unfortunate who was killed the other day? Two other investigators were here earlier to discuss it with me but, of course, I was out of town."

"Just clearing up some details," Cinnamon offered. "It's a follow up to the earlier inquiries. Have you any idea why you would be confused with a victim?"

Vanderhoorst shook his head. "I have no idea. I can't imagine where the error could be. I am unaware of any associate or friend who has recently disappeared. It's really quite beyond me."

"Hmm. We analyzed his blood for DNA and the results said that it was you."

Vanderhoorst looked puzzled.

"Is that possible?"

"It's not supposed to be, which is why we're here. By the way, are you a hemophiliac?"

Both Hodges and Vanderhoorst gave them a sharp look.

"What did you say?"

"The deceased was taking a synthetic blood clotting agent. It indicates hemophilia."

"No, I'm not a bleeder. I'm sure I'd know if I were."

"Undoubtedly. Well, perhaps the clotting agent is what is masking the DNA analysis accuracy. We found twelve out of twelve alleles identical to yours. Could it be a relative?"

"I am an only child and have no close relations. Sorry."

Charles nodded and looked at Cinnamon. She gave a brief signal with her eyes. Charles looked back at Vanderhoorst, smiling calmly from his chair and at Hodges, menacingly hovering beside the wheelchair, ready to stand between his employer and the two agents.

"Well, I suppose that does it for now. Thank you for your cooperation and we wish you a rapid recovery."

"Thank you very much," he said. "By the way, have you checked in with the agents who were here earlier? They may have more information, you know."

"They're both dead," Cinnamon said without emotion.

"Ah, I see. What a pity."

"It's a dangerous world, Mr.. Vanderhoorst, and we have a dangerous job. It happens."

"Yes. Still, such a pity. Hodges will see you to the door."

It was more of a dismissal than an invitation. The man was obviously used to being in charge. They said nothing and followed Hodges out.

On the street, they walked back toward the Homeland Security offices for several blocks, turning down a side street as soon as they were sure that they were not being followed. They turned back on their track and walked back toward the center of town. Charles cringed as Cinnamon led him across the concourse of the Five Points station, and they caught an east bound commuter heading for Augusta some hundred plus miles away.

Two stops further along, they left this train and returned on a west bound commuter that would take them within a few miles of their motel. Here they picked up Isabel and drove it back to their room. Neither of them spoke except for practicalities for the entire trip. By now it was well after noon.

"Well, that went well for a useless trip," Charles said when they'd entered the room.

"Useless?" said Cinnamon. "I thought it was most elucidating."

"Really? All we found out is that he really had an operation and was really out of town. I don't see how that helps."

"Did you see his sutures, Charles?"

He nodded.

"Looked damned real to me."

"Oh, they were, but the operation he said he had his micro-surgery. No one has cracked a chest to unplug arteries for a very long time. It's done with a probe."

Charles frowned.

"What are you saying?"

"I'm saying that they were in there for a different reason."

"But still, heart surgery?" Charles said more as a question than a statement.

"Not necessarily. The location of the incision could be for a number of possible procedures. We need expert advice on this one. Did you record it?"

Charles nodded.

"Of course. The only trouble is, we can't download it to the agency system without being detected, and our clipboards won't handle the load."

"What about Stephen?"

Charles thought for a long moment before answering.

"I don't want to get him in this any deeper than he already is."

"Well, then I guess we'll just have to depend on my memory. I'll see if I can reconstruct the image of the wound on the motel computer and render it. We can have someone who knows what they're talking about look at it later. Know any good surgeons?"

Charles didn't bother to answer. He just nodded toward the hotel's desk unit and went into the bathroom. Cinnamon slid into the seat at the desk and began sketching the wound from memory. Shortly she heard the sound of a razor as Charles shaved the stubble off of his naked pate.

He shaved carefully, completely denuding his head of whiskers and hair, leaving only the eyebrows in tact. After that he decided on another shower and a change back into his civilian clothes. When he finished, he would remind Cin to do the same. At length, satisfied with his transformation and freshly clean, he stepped out of the steaming bathroom.

Cinnamon was nowhere in sight. The console stood idle, the sharp, almost photographic, image of Vanderhoorst's mid section, wound and all, passively hovering on the screen. Cinnamon's uniform lay neatly folded on the bed and her civilian disguise was missing. He looked for a note, also to no avail.

Charles drew his machine pistol from its holster and crossed to the window, separating the curtains just enough to look outside. Isabel was gone as well.

"Damn!" He snarled. "She took Isabel! Again!"

He stepped back, finished dressing and returned to the console, which now indicated that a download to storage stick had been completed. He withdrew the small red cylinder from its driver and put it in the same case as his medchip. Charles was just finishing up when he heard a sound at the door.

"Probably her," he said. "Cinnamon, is that you?"

There was no answer.

He reached for his pistol again and padded to the door. Crouching, he put his ear to the door and listened. He couldn't hear any movement on the other side.

"Who's there?" He said sharply.

"A friend," a deep voice answered.

"I recognize my friend's voices, bud. I don't recognize yours."

"You have more friends than you think," the voice said with deep resonance.

Charles felt himself grow dizzy. He shook it off and knelt, his hand lightly resting on the door knob to see if anyone tried to turn it.

"I think you've got the wrong room, fella," he said standing again. "Move on."

"Let me in, Charles. Do you remember the Mona Lisa?"

"Yeah, Charles said, starting to feel a bit apprehensive. "She's the lady that's really DaVinci in drag! So are you in drag, fella? Take a hike."

An explosion of sound and movement burst through the doorway and threw him across the room to land between the two beds. Just as he landed, he saw two armed men dressed totally in black charge in, pistols at the ready. The weapons were AK military issue. Without thinking, he raised his own pistol and fired at their heads. The two lurched forward and down. Neither had fired a single round so far.

Charles was on his knees now, using the bed for cover. He crouched there, motionless, listening for any sound. He looked under the bed and saw a pair of blank eyes staring back at him but couldn't see the second man behind him. He lay perfectly still for some minutes, listening. Finally, he crawled around the foot of the bed and looked past the two bodies and out the door. Nothing moved. He stood and checked the two intruders. Both were dead with clean pinholes in the front of their skulls and an exploded mess at the back. He noted with satisfaction that both shots had hit the mark exactly where he had aimed them.

There was a sound of footsteps outside and he dove behind the bed again, readying himself for the next assault.

"Charles, what are you doing leaving the door open that...?" Cinnamon said, irritated.

He looked up to see her standing in the doorway, cylinder of groceries in one hand, the other holding her small automatic. It was pointed directly at him.

"It's me!' He cried. "It's just me!"

She lowered the gun and stepped over the two on the floor.

"If it hadn't been, you'd be dead already," she said. "Damn, you made a mess of them."

"Explosive cartridges. Not standard issue."

"I can see why. Have you searched them yet?"

"Just waiting for you, dear."

They each took a body and began going through pockets looking for any identification which, of course, they didn't' find. They stripped the bodies, checking labels and looking for tattoos, identifying marks or anything that would give them a clue as to whom the two were. There was nothing.

"We've got to get out of here now," Charles said. "There will be medtechs crawling all over this room in minutes."

"No there won't." Cinnamon said.

Charles stopped and looked intensely at his partner.

"They don't have medchips, Charles. Look at their hands. There's no insertion scar."

"Could have faded, it does that sometimes."

"Not that often, Charles, and not to two people together."

She rolled her corpse over onto its back and examined it further. She stepped back, moved to the other body and rolled it over as well.

"Look at their faces, Charles."

He did so.

"They're twins!" He said.

"That's bizarre," was all Cinnamon could say.

She studied them further. "It's more than that, Charles. These are the people at the Perry Mall that seemed to be everywhere at once. They're twins! No wonder they were picked up multiple times."

"Not twins, Cin. They were in four places at once, not two. They must be quads."

"Quadruplets? They would have to be unregistered and without medchips for us not to know about them. That's not possible. You might as well theorize myrmidons."

"Whichawhats?"

"Oh, you know. Things that are created in bunches."

"I'll stick to quads."

"It would explain why they didn't register at the Perry Mall. We just assumed that they must be a glitch in the program. Behold the impossibility or half of it anyway. There are two more out there just like them."

"Unregistered quads," she said. "Fascinating."

"Did you hear what I said, Cin? There are two more just like these floating around out there. We've got to get out of here as fast as we can. Grab everything that's ours and get in the car!"

Two minutes later they were in the car and driving toward the entrance. Clothes and other items were piled in a heap in Isabelle's back seat, and behind them, two bodies lay in an expanding pool of blood in the center of their motel room floor. Charles thought absurdly of how much trouble that mess was going to cause the maids.

They drove to the end of the parking area and turned right toward the entrance, picking up speed as they did. That's when they saw the van moving to block the entrance.

"Hold on!" Charles cried as he slammed on the brakes, turned the wheel and executed a perfect one-eighty while accelerating again. They were facing the way they had come. He swung back into the parking lot and he sped up, moving toward the dead end at the other end past their motel room. He never wavered.

In front of them was an old fence about four feet high and he prayed that it would give on impact. It gave easily as they crashed through it, crossed a narrow strip of grassy lawn and up a gentle slope, and found themselves airborne as they were launched over the edge. Isabelle emitted mechanical groans as they lifted into the air, then nosed over and crashed into a drainage ditch on the other side of the knoll, burying her grill and hood in the soft mud. Instantly air bags and foam deployed, locking them into their seats and cushioning the blow of the impact. Just as quickly, the bags deflated, and the foam powdered, falling around them like so much ash. Charles slapped his seat belt lock hard, releasing and turned to help Cinnamon. She was already free of the restraint and trying desperately to open her door.

"It's buckled!" He yelled. "Drop your window and crawl out!"

They were free of the car and scrambling up the far side of the ditch when they heard the whine of the van approaching on the side road in front of them. They slid back into the ditch and began crawling, making their way through the fetid sludge and fowl water of the ditch toward the right. Desperately they looked for some cover, some camouflage or an escape route. Settling for a large outgrowth of bushes along the margin of the ditch just ahead, they covered the ten meters separating them from this haven quickly and scurried up the ditch wall again and into the underbrush. Behind them, they could just make out a completely white, featureless automobile racing into the parking lot behind them.

"Time to go," Cinnamon said, and they launched themselves beyond the bushes and toward a low brick wall. They leapt over the wall and dropped to the ground behind it, coming to a halt.

In front of them stood two men, assault weapons at the ready, looking down at them and smiling pleasantly. Charles reached for his machine pistol.

"I really wish you wouldn't do that. Our employer would be most upset with us if either of you came to any harm. Besides, that hand gun couldn't penetrate our class 'C' armor and you'd never get your weapon high enough for a head shot."

Charles thought for a second and dropped his weapon. Cinnamon did the same. They collapsed against the wall and gulped in air, trying to catch their breath.

"Mr. Peavy," the larger of the two men said, "we have a question for you, and for you also, Miss Harper."

"Well?" snapped Cinnamon defiantly.

"You know a gentleman by the name of Stephen Hillel? He's quite worried about you both. He's asked if we could take you to a place of safety. Would that be all right with you? You see, things are never what they seem to be."

TWELVE

A PLACE OF SAFETY TURNED OUT to be more bizarre than Charles could imagine even Stephen coming up with. They were taken to the van where they were checked out and their scratches and contusions seen to by a very professional and very gentle medtech. From his massive size and military bearing, he was either a mercenary or a military operative. Either way, he was solicitous and kind in caring for them.

They traveled accompanied by a driver whom they could not see behind the wall separating the cab of the van from the cargo area, the medtech and two others, all armed to the teeth and well disciplined. No one spoke except in monosyllabic answers to their questions, and none volunteered any useful information. Reassuringly, their weapons were returned to them, but they were cautioned that for the moment, the para militaries were in charge. After a while they just sat and tried to catch their breath. The medtech gave each of them a shot, which he said was an antibiotic, but within minutes, they were both asleep. Exactly how long they slept they did not know, but when they awoke, Charles could feel the ache of sore muscles and a much bruised torso. He decided it must be from the car accident.

"Isabelle's dead," he said absently.

Cinnamon nodded. "I'm afraid so, Charles."

One of the guards was immediately alert.

"Who is Isabelle?"

"It's just my car. We crashed it into the ditch, you know."

The guard regarded them silently for a moment and said, "You named your car?"

"She was a good friend."

The guard simply continued to look at him, then turned away saying nothing.

They traveled for perhaps another half hour and then the van slowed, making several halting turns that felt like they were either pulling into a side road or a driveway. Shortly, it came to a complete stop.

The guards stood and helped their charges to their feet and the medic fired one last set of questions at them, looking for hidden aches and pains that he may have missed earlier. The back doors opened with a grating metal-on-metal sound that made Cinnamon cringe, and they squinted from the bright light now penetrating the cargo area. A single slender figure stood silhouetted against the light.

"Time to go," a very feminine voice said, and the guards urged them to step out.

They were in a parking area surrounded only by trees and underbrush. No buildings or any sign of civilization was evident with the exception of the tarmac on which they were standing. Without another word, the others climbed back into the van, the woman slid into the driver's seat, and they left. Charles and Cinnamon were alone.

"This is a place of safety?" Charles asked.

"We must be here for a reason, Charles. They wouldn't have gone to all that trouble just to dump us in the middle of nowhere."

They stood for a while, listening for any sounds of civilization or smells of the modern world they were used to. There were none. Around them, only the sounds they heard were of nature, a gentle breeze hissing through the upper branches of half naked trees, just coming to life with spring renewal, the sound of birds chirping in a territorial cacophony of calls and the background roar of open space. Wherever they were, they were not near civilization, and in this part of the country that was difficult.

"We're in the mountains, Charles, or at least the foothills."

"We must have slept for a long time."

"Almost five hours," she said, pointing to her watch. "I checked."

"So what do we do now?"

Cinnamon looked up at him and shrugged.

"You tell me, boss. I'm just your handy, dandy gopher, remember?"

"Yeah, right. Well, don't be alarmed. I'm a professional. I've got everything under control."

He reached into his pockets and pulled out everything for inspection. Taking the hint, Cinnamon did the same.

"Let's see what we have to work with," Charles said.

They spread their store of supplies out on the asphalt in front of them. There were keys to an apartment that no longer existed as well as a pass card to Isabelle, equally worthless on first inspection, two pocket knives, both Government Issue, two ID wallets, five sticks of gum, a magnifying glass, two hard candies, these last items from Cinnamon's skirt pocket, one book of matches and a pack of tissues. Of course, they also had two pistols with holsters and extra ammunition, but neither of them felt like trying to bring down a squirrel with a forty-five-caliber slug or her .38.

"Not much to work with, but we're resourceful," Charles said, grabbing a piece of chewing gum and plopping it in his mouth. "At least we won't starve to death."

"Nice," she said sarcastically, and looked around again.

They sat cross legged on the parking lot deck, soaking in the warmth of sunshine and asphalt. It was early afternoon by now and they were beginning to wonder what they would do when night fell. This was still early spring and the temperature was sure to drop by at least twenty degrees before morning, maybe more. They needed shelter and they needed to build a fire when the time came, and the time to do all that was not just before they needed it. It was time to start scrounging.

Cinnamon grabbed his arm as he made to stand and pulled hard.

"Do you hear something?"

Charles listened. There was a faint humming sound echoing off the surrounding woods, like a bee buzzing nearby. They sat listening and not moving for fear of losing the sound. Over time it became louder and eventually resolved itself into the rhythmic thumping of helicopter blades cutting their way through the air. They stood and cautiously stepped back off of the parking area back into the woods.

When it arrived, the helicopter proved to be a large one with a cargo deck in the rear and seating for probably six or eight people. Charles didn't recognize the profile and could only say that it was not military, not government issue, and not commercially available to the public. The public had long since foregone helicopters in favor of the small personal sky cars that now caused so much havoc around malls and sporting events.

The helicopter approached rapidly and descended with such a suddenness that Cinnamon recoiled. With a final dive, it leveled out just above the tarmac and settled gently on the ground. Charles and Cinnamon retreated as deep into the woods as they could and still see what was happening. As they watched, a lone figure stepped out, referencing his clipboard and looked directly at the two of them. He checked his clipboard again and looked up at them smiling and then signaled for them to come.

They stepped cautiously out into the open, Charles shielding Cinnamon as best he could, which was not easy as she continually tried to maneuver to stand beside him. Again the figure signaled for them to come, this time more urgently and they approached, keeping their eye on the open hatch for any sign of betrayal. The figure, anonymous behind his flight helmet and sunshades, ushered them into the helicopter still grinning and, motioned for them to sit and buckle themselves in. He closed the hatch and settled into a seat opposite them. They were airborne before they could finish locking themselves into the safety harnesses.

The cabin was surprisingly quiet with the hatch shut and the loud throbbing of the engines was no more than a whisper now. Their companion sat and buckled himself in as well, then pulled the helmet from his head and placed it on the seat beside him. He offered a pleasant smile.

"Sorry we're late," he said. "We got a late start, but we came as soon as we could."

He was a young man, no more than twenty, with short cropped shiny black hair and the broad features of a Polynesian. When he smiled, shining white teeth with a gap between the two front ones gleamed at him through a bright smile. Charles frowned and looked more closely.

"Do I know you?" He said.

The young man nodded.

"I'm surprised you recognized me. My name's Harry Kamahi. We grew up in the same orphanage."

Charles shook his head.

"That's not possible! You can't be more than twenty years old and I'm closer to forty, but you sure look like him."

"Chuck, it's really me," the young man said. "It's pretty miraculous, isn't it? It really is me, buddy."

"I don't understand," said Cinnamon. "How could you two have grown up in the same orphanage together and you look half his age?"

Kamahi shrugged.

"Good genes, I guess. Some people change, some don't. No matter. I'm here to get you two to a safe place and help you on your way with this investigation of yours."

"What do you know about it?" Cinnamon asked.

"Not many details, but that doesn't matter. I know the people who you're dealing with and that's enough."

"Specifics?" Charles said automatically.

Kamahi reached for two thermoses and looked at labels on the bottom. He handed one to each of them.

"That's Black Rock, Chuck. Stephen thought you might need it. The other one is broth, Miss Harper. It's laced with some pretty powerful nutrients. You know, buddy, someday that stuff is going to kill you."

"I've heard that," Charles said, accepting the thermos gratefully. They both opened the containers and poured the contents into their cups. Charles took a long pull on the Black Rock tea as usual while Cinnamon first sipped and then hungrily began drinking the broth. She poured her a second cup and drank it more slowly.

"Back to my original question, hairball, what do you know about all this?"

Cinnamon gave them both a confused look and in answer, Charles said, "It's a nickname. We used to call him the hairball when we were in the institute."

"It's better than Woodchuck, Charlie."

"Woodchuck?" Cinnamon said, chuckling.

"Please do not ever mention that again. I spent years living it down."

"In answer to your question, I really don't know much, but I think I can point you in the right direction. You've got some real predators on your ass, my friends, and they're not the type to give up. Those two that you encountered in that motel room were just the beginning. Frankly, I'm surprised they weren't the end. They're that good."

"We were lucky," said Charles.

"You were good," Cinnamon corrected.

Charles ignored it.

"So who are they and what are they after us for? It's just because we stepped into a local murder investigation?"

"You stepped in a lot more than that. Vanderhoorst is well connected and he's very important to the military."

"That we know, but important enough to try to kill an entire team of Homeland Security operatives? That's crazy. They can't hide something like that."

"Really?" asked Kamahi. "Tell me. How did they find you two in that motel?"

They looked at each other.

"We don't know. I don't think either of us has had time to think about it."

"Don't bother. It was the DNA analysis you ran."

"That was with a private concern," Cinnamon said.

"A private concern that had to access the national data base to match the DNA, right? As soon as it did, they traced you."

"But it was a blind search!"

"Using a Homeland Security clearance to expedite."

Cinnamon went very silent. Charles moaned.

"You used a priority clearance to expedite?"

"One little mistake," she whined. "How was I to know that they could trace our internal firewalls? They're supposed to be fool proof. "

"Actually, they are, but they can be traced from inside the agency."

A look of recognition crossed Charles' face.

"Rich," he said.

Kamahi nodded.

"As soon as that clearance was requested, he notified his friends and you were toast. The good news was that we were able to find you too. The bad news is that they got there first."

"Holy shit!" Charles mumbled.

"Which is pretty much what hit the fan, Chuck. By the way, we cleaned up the mess. The bodies are gone, the room is sanitized and you'll find your personal belongings along with three changes of clothes and your clipboards in the locker under your seats. When we get where we're going, we'll off-load everything you guys will need."

"This is a little fast, Harry. Everything we'll need for what?"

"To keep yourselves safe while you figure this out."

"Figure it out hell," Charles said. "I'm more at a loss than ever, and I've lost all my support, my team, my access to data... everything."

"You may be surprised," Kamahi said and looked out the window.

They were headed northwest, flying deeper into the Appalachians and away from the larger centers of population. Charles recalled his training on the area, of how vast it was and how easily someone could get themselves lost out here and never be heard from again. There had been several cases of fugitives escaping into these mountains and eluding the authorities for months or years. If they were going to hide, this was not a bad choice, though living in the woods like a primitive was an unappealing prospect.

Below them he watched the thick canopy of verdant evergreens that blocked any view of the earth below. It would take thermal and motion detectors if not surface search and targeting radar to spot anyone down there. For as far as he could see there were mountains and trees, valleys and trees, rivers or streams and more trees. It was hard to believe that nearly all of that forest was second or third growth, the original flora being completely removed over the past three centuries. There was a pristine majesty to the scene, even down to the sparkling quality of the light shining off water and rock. It was as remote as one could get on this side of the Mississippi.

They were descending now, the pitch of the engines slowing and their direction changing to the northeast as they did so. They made a slow, wide turn of maybe forty-five degrees and Charles looked out to see a small lake, shining brilliantly in the afternoon sunlight. There was no evidence of roads or even trails, and no highways or motor ways of any kind even in the distance. It felt more like Alaska than Georgia or North Carolina.

"Where are we?" Cinnamon asked.

"Where you'll be safe," Kamahi said.

Charles didn't care. Between the beauty of this wild country and the euphoric effects of the Black Rock tea, just now starting to wear off, he was quite happy to simply sit and wait for what happened next.

The helicopter began another rapid descent that sent everyone's stomach into their chests and their hearts into their throats.

Kamahi laughed. "That'll wake you, won't it?"

The feeling of weightlessness continued in spurts as the helicopter dropped, then leveled, then dropped again until it was hovering over the surface of the lake. Charles looked out windows on both sides of the cabin but could see no buildings or structures of any kind. Kamahi signaled for them to check their harnesses and did the same. With a sudden lurch, the machine sped for the shore to their right, aiming directly at a wall of majestic oaks and tall thin pines. Cinnamon put her hand to her mouth but made no sound. The helicopter reared, breaking its speed and then settled onto the water.

"This thing is amphibian? I didn't see any pontoons," said Charles.

"Doesn't have any. It's a land base vehicle only. Come on. Let's get out."

They released themselves from the harnesses and Kamahi slid back the hatch. Charles looked out. They were perhaps twenty feet from the shore, but the helicopter didn't pitch or drift at all. It was rock solid. Kamahi stepped out and splashed into the lake, where he stood, looking like Jesus upon the water.

"Come on out," he said. "There's only about four inches of water. We'll get your gear for you. Just follow that trail through the woods and you'll come to where you'll be staying."

Cinnamon pointed out a narrow separation in the underbrush to a very confused Charles, who stepped out into the water behind her and followed her across the shallows to the shore. She led him through the brush, picking her way carefully until they came to a clearing, covered overhead by a wide canopy of tall oaks. Trees surrounded the open space on three sides, and a wall of solid rock, some eight feet in height faced the fourth side, blending into the forest beyond it. There was no cabin or even a tent anywhere in sight.

"Well, if I've learned one thing from all this, it's that things aren't as they seem," she said, and sat down on a fallen log. Charles nodded knowingly and joined her.

"Remind me to tell you about that phrase later," he said.

Minutes later, Kamahi and three other men arrived by the same trail carrying two footlockers and an assortment of large canvas bags and crates. The fourth man in line was pulling a composite sled perhaps eight feet in length, filled with more equipment and boxes.

"This is as far as we go," Kamahi said. "You'll have to take the gear from here. The entrance is on the far side of those rocks. Sorry there's no elevator, but we wanted to minimize electromagnetic radiation emissions this close to the surface. I suggest you make three trips using the sled. It makes the going very easy."

With that he turned and walked with the others back the way they had come.'

"Hey, wait a minute! Where're you going? I thought you were gonna help us find out what's going on! Where's the help?"

"You've had it," he said grinning. "I'm surprised you didn't catch it, but I'll bet your partner did, didn't you, Cinnamon? You've got enough and it's as much as I'm allowed to tell you. If there's an emergency or you need anything, you'll find a contact code in the office. Good luck, buddy."

He left, ignoring Charles' protests. Kamahi and his companions disappeared into the forest again. Cinnamon began gathering supplies and moving them closer to the rocks. She disappeared briefly behind the wall and then emerged again and headed for the sled.

"There's a cave entrance back there big enough to drive a sky car through. I suggest we start with the sled, empty it wherever we end up and then come back for the rest."

"Now wait a minute..."

"Have you got a better idea, Chuck?"

"Damn it, Cin, don't call me Chuck!" He grabbed the lanyard to the sled and yanked at it, pulling it in the direction of the rocks. He was grumbling again.

They soon found that looks could be deceiving. Following the cave as it descended, they discovered that the further they went the more regular the sides and floor became until it was soon obvious that this was not a natural structure. Within two hundred feet it began to level off and followed a course that took them laterally along a straight passage ending in a heavy door. Inspection confirmed that it was some composite material, not metal. This portal was fitted with a one foot diameter wheel which, when turned, released the locking mechanism, and when they swung back the door they found themselves entering a fully furnished house, complete with three bedrooms, shower facilities and toilets, a large lounge, an office space, and a small kitchen. Lights came on everywhere as they entered and a soft thrumming signaled the activation of environmental controls. Charles whistled as they entered and did a quick tour of the house while Cinnamon emptied the sled.

"This is going to be incredibly comfortable, Cin. How the hell did this thing come about without anyone knowing about it?"

"And who did it?" She added.

"Somebody connected with Stephen Hillel, I'd say. The man's a wonder, even more so than I'd imagined."

"Well all my thanks to your strange friend, Chuckles."

Charles winced.

"You're just going to keep doing that, aren't you?"

"Only when we're alone," she said and gave him a very sensuous look.

"Well since I can't stop you, would you at least restrict your nicknames for me to Chuck? That's the one I grew up with."

"Done," she said, unloading the last packet from the sled. "Now let's go get the rest of the supplies."

THIRTEEN

OVER THE NEXT FEW HOURS they organized their supplies which included enough food for a month as well as other dry goods that would be needed: toilet paper, toothpaste, additional clothes, etc.. They were civilian but rugged, suitable to life in the country. They each took a bedroom to settle into, though there was an unspoken tension connected with this process. As soon as they had put everything away, they each opted for showers and a quick dinner. By evening, they were completely moved in and relaxing, lounging in bathrobes in the common room, tired, sore and feeling more secure.

"I'm turning in," Charles said at last.

"Chuck, I want to ask you something."

"Okay."

"It's a bit personal."

Charles slumped back down in the chair he had just gotten out of. He could feel a long conversation coming on.

"It's probably very personal if you feel the need to ask permission."

"You're making this difficult," she said.

"Sorry."

"I want to know what happened between you and Karen."

Charles didn't speak for a few minutes. Cinnamon started to say something several times but he put up his hand to silence her.

"We drifted apart," he said at last.

"Too simplistic," she said gently.

"I know. We'd weathered the usual storms that couples go through, I guess and we dealt with most of them pretty well. We had very different personalities, you know. With my training I tend to analyze everything, can't help it. She tended to let things come as they may. We used to drive each other crazy with that one, but finally came to an accommodation. She accepted my nit picking ways and I learned to love her.

"La-la land view of the world. Actually, the months after figuring out how to deal with that issue were wonderful. A lot of the tension went away. It was another issue that finally did us in."

"Okay," Cinnamon said softly.

"I'm sterile," he said flatly.

Cinnamon was silent, waiting for him to continue. When she didn't say anything, he went on.

In his mind he replayed the scene in their city apartment, after learning of his sterility. He remembered how silent she was, stunned at the news. They had often spoken of how he would not mind adopting a child, since he was an orphan himself, and how adamantly she had refused to even consider it. Discovering that he was sterile put a permanent pall over their lives from that day on.

"We'd been trying to have a baby for about three years before we decided to find out what was wrong. Karen kept saying that it had to be her fault, and frankly, I went along with it. She went in for the usual series of tests and they found nothing, so they tested me. I turned up fully functional as well."

"I don't understand. They found you were normal?"

He nodded.

"That's the hell of it. We went back to trying, but no matter what we did, Karen didn't turn up pregnant. In desperation we had more tests done."

"Um, what did they find, Chuck?"

"Well, believe it or not, my sperm's healthy but it won't penetrate the egg. It makes no sense. The way the doctor put it, I'm firing blanks."

"I'm so sorry," Cinnamon said.

"Anyway, since Karen wasn't willing to adopt and cloning is illegal, the only other alternative was a sperm donor, and I wasn't willing to go that route. That was a year before she died."

"You deformed freak!" She had said the night he found them together. "You damned eunuch! I can't believe how many years I wasted on you!

You knew it all along, didn't you? You knew it and you let me believe that I was the one! I hate you!" He left them there and never saw her again.

Charles wiped tears from his eyes and looked away. Cinnamon came to him and knelt at his side, taking his bowed head in her hands. She kissed him gently on his cheek and cradled him in her arms. Charles slid forward and knelt beside her, allowing her to hold him while he sobbed openly. It was the first time he had shown any emotion since Karen's death. He simply couldn't stop. She held him for a very long time, letting him sob, his shoulders heaving with the pain. Tears filled her eyes as she silently tried to comfort him. Some time later, when he had calmed down, she stroked his hair and pulled him to her.

"Let's go to bed," she whispered and she led him to her bedroom.

They didn't make love that night. Cinnamon held him in her arms the whole time while he slept the sleep of the dead. There must have been years of pent up sorrow in him for this to happen. It was as if he was resting, truly resting, for the first time in a very long time. In the morning, she slipped away and took a quick shower, then made coffee and set the round dining table for two. She then awakened him gently and fixed a simple meal of fruit and biscuits while he showered. Neither of them spoke of the night before. At first Charles couldn't bring himself to look her in the eye, but over time he relaxed, as much from her refusal to treat him any differently as anything. After breakfast he washed the dishes and settled in to see what news he could find. There was no reference of any kind to them or the incident at the motel. Even the explosion of the day before was relegated to a single comment buried near the end of the news broadcast, stating that the police were still investigating the accident and no new facts were available. By tomorrow, most people would have totally forgotten the incident.

"Kamahi said that he'd given all the hints that he could and that if I didn't catch it then you probably did. Have any idea what he's talking about?" Charles said.

Cinnamon shook her head.

"No idea at all. Something niggling at my mind and I keep going over the details of the conversations with him, but I get nothing. How about you?"

"Nothing. I don't know what he's talking about."

She thought for a moment.

"Well, there's the connection that you two have from the orphanage. You were there at the same time?"

"We grew up together. Actually we were best friends for about two years. He was adopted by someone when he was twelve. I seem to remember people coming to the orphanage and interviewing four or five of us. They adopted Harry and another kid. After that, I didn't see him again until yesterday."

"And he works for your friend Hillel?"

"I guess so. I'm not even sure of that."

"Hmm," she said.

"What?"

"Well, Chuck, there's something else."

"Oh?"

"He has a scar on his left hand identical to yours. I saw it when he handed us the thermoses."

"He does?"

"Hmm. Where'd you get that scar, Chuck?"

"I don't remember. I was pretty small, though. I've had it as long as I can remember. Funny. I never thought anything about it, but the other kid they adopted when they took Harry had one too. I haven't thought about that in years."

"I think we need to find out everything we can about that orphanage," she said. "How long were you there?"

"Until I was seventeen. I joined the Marines that year and haven't been back since."

Cinnamon was already in the office alcove, bringing up the search apparatus on the com unit.

"What was it called?"

Charles said nothing.

"Chuck? What was it called?"

"Do we have to do this? I don't think I have a lot of good memories about that place."

"We have to do it. Name, please."

Charles glanced at her, taking in her beauty as if he was seeing her for the first time. He suddenly realized what a large part of his life this woman really was.

"Furguson Academy of Lansing," he said.

"Michigan?"

"Yeah, which I always found strange it was located in eastern Tennessee. Go figure."

Cinnamon played with the keyboard for a moment. When she stopped, she ordered a hard copy and came to sit beside Charles.

"It'll take a minute. There are several files on them, most of them legal paper work, but one or two news items as well. So what was it like being there?"

Charles was frowning, thinking hard.

"It's hard to say, Cin. I mean, at the time I didn't think anything of it, but it was a very strange place. I've put it all so far out of my consciousness for so many years that I had forgotten just how strange it was."

"Like?"

"Well, on the surface, it was what you'd expect from an orphanage. We had dormitories for the younger kids and for the older ones, from age thirteen on, rooms that held four people. School was held on site. No contact with public school systems or other kids. They said they'd make fun of us because they didn't understand what it was like to be an orphan. The education was funny, too."

"How do you mean?" asked Cinnamon.

"I don't know. We had the usual classes, but then there were classes in logic and puzzle solving. Chemistry was taught beginning at age eleven, and physics at twelve. All of it was practical application. It was like engineering."

"I don't understand," she said.

"Okay. Take chemistry for instance. We learned all the usual stuff about chemical bonds and equations and valences and all that stuff, but the labs were designed to teach us how to put all that into practice."

"But isn't that normal in a chemistry lab?"

"They taught us how to make exotic compounds, like a kind of match that would spontaneously catch on fire after a given number of hours. They taught us to create medicinal ointments out of plants and minerals and how to manufacture highly toxic acids from household items. They even taught us to cook, and each dish was different in some way. Some were toxic except in small quantities while others boosted energy production in the body to almost superhuman levels."

"Not your usual high school chemistry class. Anything else?"

"Well, there was the physical training. We had that for two to four hours every day, the argument being that we needed physical skills if we were going to survive in the world. Like I said, I haven't thought of this in years. It sounds so weird now. I wonder why."

Cinnamon stepped back into the office alcove and retrieved the hard copy. The Furguson Home of Lansing had been incorporated in Michigan some forty years ago. It had moved south to Tennessee five years later, and had remained there ever since. The average occupation of the campus was one hundred twenty students and a staff of fifty. There were no records in the public files about its funding or who actually owned it. Both inquiries had met with brick wall resistance. One public source flatly stated that such information was not for public distribution and would not be provided under any circumstances. A second document, tax and licensing records from the town of Brewster and the state of Tennessee were equally uninformative. The only additional fact was that the school received substantial grants from a private foundation with the initials, CFWE, whatever that meant. Apparently the State of Tennessee found that to be sufficient for their purposes.

It was the third printed document that Cinnamon found to be most revealing. It was a group photo of the student body in the school in the year 2025, which would have been when Charles was there. He would have been eleven at the time. She studied it carefully, noting the names of each student, locating them in the seven rows of faces. ‘

"You and Harry are both here. What was the other boy's name?"

"Um, I don't remember."

She handed him the picture and pointed out him and Harry standing side by side on the fifth row from the bottom.

"Look at the names in the legend," she said.

Charles scanned the names and then matched them with faces in the picture. He noted several people that he recognized, sometimes frowning and at other times, smiling at the memory of friends.

"I don't see the other kid here," he said.

"Okay," Cinnamon said, retrieving another hard copy from the alcove. "Here's a picture of the following year when you would have been twelve. Let's see who is missing."

Immediately they were struck by the absence of Harry and on further inspection several others. None of them looked familiar to Charles.

"Chuck," Cinnamon said, examining the photo more closely, "Look at these two on the end of the middle row. Who are they?"

Charles looked but didn't recognize either of them.

"They're twins," Cinnamon said.

"Funny. I don't remember any twins from when I was there."

Cinnamon eyed him curiously.

"I see," she said.

She scanned the images again. Finally she returned to the alcove and after some manipulation, requested more hard copies. While she waited, she came back to sit beside Charles. She looked concerned.

"I want you to listen carefully," she said. "I want you to answer some questions about your years at the orphanage."

Charles squirmed but finally settled and said, "I've been doing that, haven't I?"

"This is different. Who did you live with, in the four person rooms?"

He thought for a moment.

"I don't remember," he answered.

"What was the name of the meanest kid in the school?"

"I, um, I couldn't tell you."

"This was an all male institution, right?"

"Um, yes."

"Then who are these two girls on the end of the first row?"

Charles looked at the picture again.

"I didn't see them before. Why didn't I see them before? They're as plain as the nose on your face."

Cinnamon set the pictures aside and said, "There were no girls on the end of the first row. I made that up."

"But...I just saw them!"

"Of course you did. You saw them because I suggested to you that they were there. Chuck, you've been manipulated. Somebody's planted false memories in your mind about this period of your life. Oh, it's not all a lie. That would be too easy to detect, but crucial memories have been blocked and other false memories inserted. The question is how much and why."

Charles' eyes glazed over. He had a sudden metallic taste in his mouth and the odd sensation of being suspended in space.

"What's happening now, Chuck?"

"I taste copper and smell fried chicken. I feel like I'm floating."

"Jeez!" She exclaimed. "Behavioral manipulation techniques and very sophisticated ones."

"I... I don't understand," he said, confused.

"We're leaving. Call for transportation and I'll explain on the way."

FOURTEEN

HARRY KAMAHI ARRIVED NEARLY TWO HOURS after they asked for transport. When they made the call, he had not seemed the least disturbed by their sudden desire to leave. They were waiting for him at the edge of the water when he arrived, dressed in heavy khakis and bush shirts, their side arms strapped openly at their hips, and wearing their Department of Homeland Security caps. Cinnamon had shed her thunder thighs, which as it happened was necessary just to fit into the khaki pants she was wearing. Charles maintained his bald head and had started growing a mustache, though for the moment it just looked like he had forgotten to shave his upper lip.

They were reassured by the sound of the rotors on the helicopter as it came into view. There was no mistaking that sound. It had to be the same one that had brought them. It settled into the water, kicking up a fine spray that wet them down like heavy fog. When they waded the short distance to the craft and climbed in, it lifted off almost before they were aboard. There was no one on the bird but Kamahi and the pilot.

"That didn't take long," he said. "Is he starting to remember?"

Cinnamon nodded.

"Bits and pieces mostly. After I finally convinced him that some of his memories were fabricated it got easier. The question is what's real and what's been planted."

"Same question I had when I figured it out," said Harry, "but I had help remembering, and it's been years."

"I don't have years!" said Charles, obviously irritated by the way the two of them were talking as if he weren't even there.

"Sure you do," Kamahi said grinning. "All you need right now are the important pieces, and that's what we'll work on."

"Well get to it, Harry. What am I missing that I need to figure out?"

Kamahi shook his head.

"It doesn't work that way. It won't do any good for me to tell you what's missing and what's not true. You have to come to it yourself or it will just be my word against your memories, but going back to the institution is a good start. That'll shake a lot of it loose."

"I hope so," Charles said sadly. "I really hope so."

"Well it shouldn't take too long for the process to pick up speed. It's already started, thanks to you, Cinnamon. That's the important part."

"How did you know I'd be able to figure out what was going on?" She asked.

Harry shrugged.

"Truth is, I didn't. It was Stephen Hillel that came up with that part. He said you were smart, that you had a background in social dynamics and an eidetic memory, whatever that is, and that you would be the perfect one to make it happen since this guy's in love with you."

Cinnamon turned red, a most atypical response for her and Charles just looked at his friend, dumbfounded.

"Sorry," Kamahi said. "I thought you two knew. The old man says all the signs are there."

Cin coughed and mumbled, "Um, I'm not sure..."

"He's probably right, you know," said Charles. "I'm not too good at dealing with my own feelings. Don't let it bother you."

Cinnamon turned and looked at him, more in shock than anything else. She looked away again and said nothing.

"That guy's never wrong," Kamahi said grinning.

They flew northwest, no one speaking for fear of being the first to break the silence. All three of them felt awkward, like three adolescents at their first dance. They just pretended that nothing had happened.

After an hour, the helicopter turned sharply to the left and began a slow circling descent. Below them Charles and Cinnamon watched the apparently abandoned air strip as they dropped closer and closer to the ground. At about five hundred feet, the helicopter stopped spiraling and settled onto the tarmac some twenty yards from a dilapidated hangar. Harry reached into the compartments beneath their feet and handed them each a day pack and shouldered a third one for himself. He stepped out behind them.

"You're going with us?" Charles yelled above the roar of the helicopter.

"Wouldn't miss it for the world!" Kamahi yelled back and they stepped away from the bird. It took off vertically and disappeared to the south.

Kamahi led them into the hangar where there was a sky car waiting. Without comment he helped them store their packs in the cargo hold and motioned for them to get in. They flew due west and just above the treetops and were circling for a landing in a small alfalfa field twenty minutes later. Kamahi explained that the sky car was necessary for the short trip because of the lack of good roads in the area and the possibility of detection. Charles filed all this away and made a mental note to ask later why detection was even an issue. After all, they were just going to visit his old orphanage, weren't they?

The field lay at the foot of a ridge, nestled in a valley surrounded by gentle hills covered with pine and hard wood forest. There were no buildings or any indication of habitation to be seen. The only evidence of life was the black car parked on the gravel road leading out through the woods and, of course, the alfalfa just beginning to ripen. When they had pulled their day packs from the sky car, Harry knelt and opened his, extracted a compact electronic device of some sort, all dials and protrusions, like something out of a bad science fiction movie. Toggling a single switch on the side of the case, he checked the readouts on the small screen.

"That's for the security network. I've just neutralized their surveillance. It's frozen to give the same readout continuously until I deactivate the unit. We'll leave this here with the sky car."

"They need a security net around an orphanage?" asked Charles.

"They do around this one," Harry replied. "Let's get going."

He led them up the ridge until they were near the summit and again stopped to delve into his day pack. He signaled them to do the same. From his pack he produced a small toy sound detector with a collapsible parabolic dish.

"Doesn't look like much, does it? Looks can be deceiving. This little toy has been modified to the point where the only part of the original that remains is the case. It saves questions if I'm ever searched by local police," he said.

In their own packs, they found Homeland Security field jackets, comlink buttons for their lapels and one very advanced needle gun. Charles' eyes lit up when he saw the weapons. Cinnamon automatically checked the charge, turned it over in her hands and inspected it, and exchanged it for her pistol, slipping it into her holster.

"No serial numbers, I see. This is experimental stuff, isn't it?"

Harry grinned.

"Not if you developed it."

Cinnamon gave Charlie a look of surprise as she remembered Stephen Hillel saying the same thing.

"You've got strange friends, Charlie," she said sarcastically again.

Their day packs also contained rations, three pillows of water and a lock blade knife. All of these fit nicely in a very official looking waist pack, marked Homeland Security.

"The comlink buttons are on an odd frequency and they are synchronized to change frequency every fifteen minutes," Harry said. "It helps to keep our conversations private and if they're monitoring with a normal scan, they can't keep up with the changes. If it's a really sophisticated scan, we're dead anyway, so don't worry about it."

"Are we infiltrating a military base or visiting an orphanage?"

"Yes," was all Harry would say.

They crawled to the top of the ridge and Harry held a penlight camera up over the crest, sweeping it back and forth until he found what he wanted. On their clipboards they viewed the feed, looking down on a set of white frame buildings surrounded by a high fence. Except for the fence, it looked like a typical campus. In the center of the compound there was the main building, a late 19th century country revival large enough for administrative purposes and perhaps five or six classrooms. To the right of this building was what appeared to be a mess hall and to its left, a large dormitory building, two stories high. Behind the main building was a small gymnasium, obvious from its design and jogging track. In front of the main building was a playground, lawn and small parking lot, now containing six ground cars and two sky cars. The sky cars were of an old military design typical of those purchased as surplus by private companies and foreign governments.

"Does it look familiar?" Cinnamon asked.

"Sort of," answered Charlie, somewhat vaguely. "I recognize the buildings, but the fence doesn't fit, and we didn't have a gymnasium like that when I was here."

"Actually we did," Harry said. "You and I just didn't notice it."

Charles frowned.

"That's possible?"

"It is with them," Cinnamon said. "They selected your memories, remember?"

"So what do we do now?" said Charles.

"Now, my friends, you two go down there by the road and interview the director. You're investigating a possible terrorist threat, one of your suspects may have been housed here in his childhood and you want to see his records. You will not be willing to tell them who the suspect is or why you think he was here, but since you're Homeland Security, you can ask damn near anything, and short of violence, they can't stop you. How's that for a scenario?"

"Simple, to the point and daring," said Cinnamon. "It's just oddball enough to be true. Just the way we work."

"Exactly!" Harry said.

"And what are you going to be doing while we're in the lion's den?"

"Me? I'm going roost right here and monitor the situation. You'll be able to hear anything I need to tell you, and I can hear everything that's going on the same way."

"Sounds simple," said Charles. "Won't they recognize me?"

"I don't think so. They probably don't even have the same people there as they did when you and I were here. Not only that, but you have no medchips They can't run a trace on you either."

"Won't that create suspicion?"

"Probably, but they'll think it's their equipment rather than you two. If they do figure out you have no medchips, I guarantee they'll be more frightened of you than of the anomaly," said Kamahi.

"I don't understand," said Charles.

"Later. Right now, you need to access their records and see who was really here when we were. Query our names and any others you might be interested in."

Charles and Cinnamon slipped back down from the crest of the ridge and followed Harry's directions, driving to the main road to the home. It was a rough drive through the trees to reach it and they pulled out, turning left onto the pavement, both aware of the warmth of the surface in the morning light. It was later than they had thought if the roadway was already heating up in the sun. Spring was definitely on its way. Absently, Charles looked out the window and scanned the sky for any telltale clouds or fronts moving in that might give them trouble if they had to leave in a hurry. There wasn't a cloud in the sky. At least the weather was on their side.

They drove around the bend in the road and down the two-mile straight of way to the main entrance of the home. Some twenty children ranging in age from six to perhaps ten were playing on the playground in front, apparently unsupervised. From the far side of the compound they heard what sounded like orders being barked inside the gymnasium. There was also the sound of singing coming from the classroom building. A large sign over the gate announced FURGUSON ACADEMY FOR CHILDREN in large block letters. They found the speaker box on a post to one side and pushed the button.

"Yes? May I help you?" said a pleasantly feminine voice.

"Homeland Security. This is official business. Please open the gate."

There was a moment of silence and then the voice said, "May we see some identification?"

"You may not," Cinnamon said forcefully. "If you do not open the gate, there will be a team here in twenty minutes to open it for you. Please do not waste our time."

Charles cringed slightly, sure that the bluff would never work. To his surprise, there was a loud click and the iron gates swung back into the compound. They drove through, looking as official and on purpose as they could. They pulled the ground car up in front of the main entrance and stepped out, taking in the scene. Three steps led up to a wide front porch, complete with white rockers and potted plants like something from a hundred and fifty years ago. Actual sash windows flanked the large glass paneled doors which sported a brass lever handle and stained-glass transom overhead. It was all very comfortable, very homey and very Victorian in feel. They could hear footsteps on the hard wooden floor inside.

The woman who came to the door was a pleasant middle-aged teacher type, well groomed and very attractive. She moved with the confidence of someone who took care of herself physically and someone who was bright and knew it. She smiled pleasantly and said, "How can I help you?"

They recognized her voice as the woman who had spoken to them at the gate.

"We're very sorry to disturb you," Cinnamon began, "but we're involved in an investigation that may include one of your former students. We need to see your records of students to verify this, or eliminate it as a possibility. May we please come in?"

The woman stepped aside and invited them in with a nod of the head. She continued to smile, apparently not the least perturbed by their request.

"If you'll give me the name of the person you're interested in, I can bring up the records for you immediately," she said.

Cinnamon smiled sweetly.

"Unfortunately we're not at liberty to divulge that information at this time. Federal investigation regulations, you know. If you would just give us access to your records, we can find it quite well for ourselves."

The woman frowned.

"I don't know. We have a complicated system. You'll probably need some help navigating the database. There are a lot of names in that database. Remember the Mona Lisa. There must be hundreds of those on file in databases around the world."

"Well I can tell you categorically that it's not a Mona Lisa that we're looking for. What system base are you using?"

"Um, Quigley Hypercube," she said, still smiling.

"I am qualified in QH up to version seven, which I believe is the latest one. We will have no problem."

"I don't know. Shouldn't you have a warrant or something? I mean, I don't mind you looking, but I have to cover myself legally, you know. The foundation that funds us might not approve."

"We're Homeland Security, ma'am," said Charles. "We don't need a warrant."

"Well we wouldn't want to cause you any trouble. What is the name of your foundation, and I can contact them about what we're doing. That should satisfy them as to your part in this. I'm sure it will be fine," said Cinnamon. She was smiling a bit too sweetly now.

"The Furguson Academy is wholly funded by the Quaker Lansing Foundation, a charitable not-for-profit organization," the woman said. She was no longer smiling.

"In Lansing, Michigan?"

"Yes," she said flatly.

Cinnamon punched her comlink button and spoke for a moment, asking that the Quaker Lansing Foundation be notified, assuring them that local personnel are cooperating and not to be held responsible for any breech of security. When she finished, she looked back at the woman and said, "By the way, you are..?"

"Mrs. Tuttle," she said tersely.

"Thank you, Mrs. Tuttle," Cinnamon said. "Now if you would show us to your records?"

Mrs. Tuttle turned and signaled for them to follow her, which Cinnamon did immediately. Charles just stood in place, staring.

"Charles?" Cinnamon said, but he didn't move. She reached out her arm and grabbed his wrist. "Charles? Are you okay?"

Charles shook himself and focused on her.

"Fine," he said. Let's go.

The woman led them down the main hall to a room in the rear of the building and ushered them in. It was modern and well appointed inside, with five com units arranged in a semicircle at one end of the room. They thanked her and asked her to leave. As soon as she was gone, Cinnamon sat at one of the com units and typed in some short commands. She turned to Charles and began using sign language.

"We shouldn't say anything. The room is probably wired, but I doubt if they have visual on us, and if they do, what are the odds they understand sign language? I've just isolated this com unit. No one can eavesdrop or monitor what we're bringing up."

It took Charles a minute to translate in his head what she was signing. He hadn't had occasion to use the visual language since his initial training with the department.

"I beep" he replied, keeping it simple and hoping he'd used the right signs. Cinnamon chuckled and turned back to the computer. She brought up Charles' name. Immediately the screen presented an information page including date of arrival, date of departure, vital statistics, source of placement and other facts. They scanned the information together. Charles pointed to the 'Source of Placement' entry which said simply, Quaker Project. Cinnamon nodded. Her memory would store the information along with the rest of the screen, which meant that they didn't need to transfer it or make a hard copy, either of which would have alerted those in the school to what they were doing. She ran her finger down the screen, noting each entry and stopped, pointing to another entry. It said, 'Final Disposition'. The entry was filled in with "conditioned and released into general population. Not retrievable." They looked at each other questioningly. She pointed to another category entitled 'Implantation' followed by the entry, August 25, 2026.

Excitedly, Cinnamon signed, "That's where the scar came from! Your medchip was implanted August 25, 2026, when you were twelve years old!"

"Eleven," he signed back. "I didn't turn twelve until December."

"Why did they wait so long to implant you? Why so late?"

"Maybe it wasn't. Maybe they removed my original one and implanted a new one to change my identity. See what it says about Harry."

She closed the record and opened the one for Harry Kamahi. An identical form popped up. None of this information was particularly revealing except that Kamahi and Charles were the same age, Kamahi being senior by two months, and that he too had an entry for 'Implantation' and on the same date as Charles. Both of them received medchips on the same day. "Why doesn't he remember?" thought Charles.

Finally, on a lark, she punched in the name Peter Vanderhoorst. Again the screen changed, this time to a new form. Cinnamon and Charles gave each other a surprised questioning look. Neither of them expected this. The page now listed three files to be accessed and directed the user to choose one. Cinnamon chose the first option. The screen went blank for three seconds and then came back to life with a standard form. The name on the form was '010743927'. A review of the other information revealed standard data except that there was no origin of placement, no date of implantation and in the slot for 'Final Disposition', it said, Facility Zed.

"Strange," she said aloud and returned to the previous screen. For each of the other two options they discovered that the forms were identical to the first. Apparently all three of these 'students' were now at Facility Zed, whatever that may be.

"Let's go," she said and stood, closing out the screens and returning the com unit to normal control.

"Positive. We have what we need. Apparently this was a dead end lead."

Charles nodded, understanding that this last statement was for the benefit of anyone who might be listening in. They left the room and started down the hall, intending to stop at the main office at the front of the building, but before they had gotten that far, Mrs. Tuttle emerged from her office and walked toward them.

"Did you find what you needed?" She asked.

"Yes and no," said Charles. "We found that the individual we're investigating was never here. In that sense, we found what we needed to know. You have a fine institution here, Mrs. Tuttle. I'm impressed with the physical facilities and with your record keeping. It's all very thorough and very much in order. Thank you for your cooperation."

"You're very welcome. If you give me some warning if you come again, I can arrange lunch and a tour for you."

"Um, thanks very much. We'll keep it in mind. We can find our own way out."

With that they moved past her and out onto the front porch. Clouds were gathering in the east, a sure sign of trouble ahead. If the weather was building in that direction, it meant counter winds and heavy rain. They needed to get airborne soon or they'd be grounded until it was over. Charles pointed to the clouds and Cinnamon nodded. She slipped into the driver's seat without discussion and started the car. Charles sat in the passenger seat and closed the door. As they were heading for the gate, their ear buds came to life and Harry began giving orders rapidly.

"Listen carefully," he said. "They've placed a device under your car. From the size and shape I very much doubt if it's an explosive device. It's not even near the gas tank. It means that you're under surveillance though. Not to worry. Leave the compound and return here. When you parallel the field, the bug will simply cease to function and you'll become invisible. Just to be sure, don't slow down when you get to the side road. Keep going about a hundred feet, then back up, that way they won't notice the reduced speed. The weather's closing in pretty fast here and we need to get airborne. Someone will pick up the car later. Do you read me?"

"I beep," they said in unison.

When they arrived, Harry reached under the car just forward of the front seat and retrieved a small black cube. He put it on the ground and burned it with his needle gun, leaving only melted plastic and fused circuits behind. Harry then signaled them to follow him back up to the ridge.

"We'd better get going, Harry," Charles said, looking at the gathering storm.

"In a minute. I want to show you something."

The settled in just below the ridge where they had been before and looked at the monitor, the penlight camera still being trained on the school below. Nothing appeared to be any different, and Charles started to mention it when he caught some movement on the edge of the screen. Another ground car, obviously Federal issue, was pulling up to the gate. The gate opened immediately and the car pulled up in front of the main building. The back doors opened and three men stepped out, two typical security goons, the other dressed in a long hooded robe. He looked like some kind of a monk.

"Now what the hell is going on?" Cinnamon said.

"I'd say you've made someone very nervous. It didn't take long for someone to show up to talk about your visit. I'm glad you left when you did."

"Charles, do those two bodyguards look familiar to you?" said Cinnamon, alarmed.

Harry adjusted the camera to bring the image closer and when Charles looked more closely, he released a huffing sound. "I thought we killed them!" He said.

"You mean the two at the motel?"

"It's them!" Charles yelped.

"So there were four of them. I wonder if there's any more."

"That doesn't make any sense! How can there be four?"

"Why not," said Cinnamon. "There were four unidentifiables at the mall. They must be quads after all. So what's with the monk?"

"That's not a monk, Cin," Charles said. "Whoever it is, they're wearing the robe to keep from being recognized from satellite surveillance. If they're going to that much trouble, they must really think Homeland Security is involved and they're afraid of the implications."

"I'd say that's about right," said Harry.

The sound of booming thunder crashed down on them from the east. That was all they needed to make up their minds. They scrambled down the hill and headed for the sky car. After Harry deactivated the surveillance blocking device and packed it along with the penlight camera and monitor, they climbed aboard. Now airborne they flew low over the hills to the south, trying to side step the storm before it arrived and twenty minutes later were winging back to the east at top speed. They didn't gain any altitude for nearly half an hour.

FIFTEEN

THEIR PROGRESS WAS SERIOUSLY hampered by the rain and the wind of the storm that had swept so swiftly over the southern Appalachians. It was not until much later that they were to discover that this was no ordinary storm. It would prove to be a powerful weather system that would rage for the next five days, causing extensive damage from Baltimore to Mobile to Tampa. None of this mattered to those in the sky car, of course, nor would it have mattered to Charles if he had known what was happening. All he knew was that the sky car was being buffeted by extreme winds and that he was busy remembering events from his past.

He sat silently, running the events of the past few hours over in his head again and again. Vaguely, he recalled pain, exhaustion and regimented recitations in classes that bordered on insanity. Faces appeared in his mind, some insignificant and others somehow important, though why they were important was beyond him for the moment. He heard rhythmic chants in his head, lessons to be repeated again and again until they formed imbedded mantras in the minds of the students. Smiling, he remembered rebelling against that regimentation of ideas, and of being punished for his refusal to follow the 'party line'; the details eluded him. All he knew for certain was that whatever they were being taught to believe, he saw flaws in the logic and refused to believe it. On more than one occasion he could recall being called 'stupid', 'incorrigible', or evil. He felt the pain of those epithets, but not the reason for them or for the unspeakable fear he had felt during that part of his life.

"Harry," he said at last, "What do you remember about our schooling at the orphanage?"

Harry didn't answer. He was very busy attempting to keep the sky car in a level glide, but he smiled slightly at the question. Cinnamon signaled him to keep quiet and watched the terrain below them. They were skimming along a deep valley between high steep ridges at about three hundred feet, and in the country side that was a dangerous thing to do. Somehow Charles simply didn't care. He just looked away and returned to his thoughts. A particular chant kept trying to fight its way to his consciousness, and the more he tried to remember it, the more it eluded him.

In desperation, he brought his legs up against his chest, assuming fetal position and began to rock. What was going on? His lucid mind noted the significance of his actions, like a child hiding from ghosts under the bed, but he had no idea what he was afraid of, feeling helpless, paralyzed by his own past and his inability to remember it, the tune kept playing over and over in his head.

She was a large woman, and severe in every respect. Her heavy orthopedic shoes of black leather, tied in a simple bow across the instep matched her straight black dress, shapeless and hanging like poorly designed drapes. Her hair was pulled back in a tight bun and her wire rimmed glasses cut into her fleshy nose as if they were in the process of growing into her face. She was looking down at a very small and very scared Charles Peavy, though that wasn't the name he was using back then. Beside him stood Harry, sucking his thumb and staring at the floor, swaying nervously from side to side.

"You will sing the school anthem with the rest of the class and that's all there is to it!" She was saying. Charles was too frightened to tell her that he had never heard it and that he was new. Shouldn't she know that already? And what about the kid beside him? He hadn't said much the whole week Charles had been here, but shouldn't he know the song?

She reached out with a twelve-inch ruler and struck Harry across the face, sending him whimpering to the floor.

"Now sing, damn it! Sing!"

"But I don't know...," was all Charles was able to utter before the ruler came down across his face as well. The brass edge cut deeply and he began to bleed.

"You will sing, not speak! Do you understand?"

Charles looked up at her helplessly and tried to think. In desperation, he sang the only song he could remember; one from the nursery he had been in before coming here.

"Jesus loves me, this I know, 'cause..."

Again she slapped him across face with the ruler, screaming uncontrollably.

"You'll go to the head mistress' office immediately, do you hear me? Well? What are you waiting for?"

They ran. He remembered that they ran, but he no more knew the location of the head mistress' office than he did the school song, so he just followed Harry. The beating he received there stayed with him for a long time, and the friendship between these two was cemented for a life time.

"Harry, I'm remembering more now. You and I were always there together, weren't we?"

"Hmm? Um, yeah, buddy, but don't bother me now. We're landing," Harry said sharply. "I can't hold her much longer in this weather. If the winds don't get us, the lightning probably will. I see a parking lot over there to the right next to that office complex. We're landing there to wait this storm out."

He took control of the craft and turned sharply to the right, lifted the nose of the sky car until he was at five hundred feet, then began a slow descent, gliding directly into the nearly deserted parking lot below. They came at high speed over a narrow field on the edge of the tarmac and he waited until the last minute before braking. It seemed crazy to Charles, but when they finally slowed and the nose of the sky car tried to lift in the high wind, he understood the necessity of maintaining speed. Harry was one hell of a driver.

They rolled toward the nearest building and under the shelter of an overhang at the main door. Without a word, the three of them stepped out and through the doors of the building into the foyer.

"Well that really sucked, didn't it?" Harry said.

"Hell of a storm," Cinnamon added, shaking the rain from her hair.

Charles looked around. The foyer was fairly large with an information desk in the center, now unmanned, and a series of uncomfortable looking sitting areas situated equally around the walls. The entire front of the building was glassed in and the other three walls were of some pinkish polished stone. Charles speculated that they were probably marble or marble composite.

"Where are we? This place looks familiar," Charles said.

"'Damned if I know, but it's dry and it's safe for the moment. I suppose we should tell someone we're here, don't you think?" replied Cinnamon.

As if on cue, a party of three men appeared at the far end of the room, one moving to enter the information booth, the other two coming forward to meet the three visitors. It was obvious that the smaller of the two men, balding, probably in his mid fifties wearing a very expensive silk suit, was in charge. His companion, bulkier and dull of eye was most likely security.

"Good afternoon," he said as he approached. "I am Ian McShea, director of the center. How can I help you?"

He extended his hand, which Harry took briefly, smiling. "I'm afraid we've arrived quite unintentionally and unannounced. We were forced down by the storm and needed a bit of shelter until it blew over. I hope we're not too disruptive to your work."

McShea nodded, continuing to smile. "Not at all, not at all. I hoped that this visit from Homeland Security wasn't official," he said, nodding to Charles and Cinnamon.

Harry laughed softly and shook his head.

"Totally coincidental, I assure you. There's no known threat to you or your facility that I know of," Cinnamon said pleasantly. "Our driver just chose the nearest shelter in the storm."

"Ahh," said McShea. "In that case, let me offer you our hospitality rather than official cooperation."

It was an odd comment that sent all three of them to thinking, trying to figure out exactly what the man had meant by it, but they also all did their best to pretend that they understood.

"If you'll excuse me asking, exactly what is it that you do here?" Charles said.

"This is a private funding operation, actually. We handle a number of charitable organizations and distribute monies for their support. At last count, I believe we are working with nearly one hundred fifty-separate charitable operations. The name of our corporation is CFWE, Incorporated."

They were silent for a long moment.

"The initials stand for something?" Cinnamon prodded.

"Goodness yes. It stands for Charles Furguson World Endowments. One of our clients is close by here, actually. It's the Furguson Academy not more than forty miles from here."

"An academy of science?" Cinnamon asked.

McShea looked at her quizzically. "Why no, not exactly. It's a school for orphaned and abandoned children."

"A noble cause," said Harry.

"But do come and sit, my friends. I'll have some refreshments brought out and you can wait out the storm here in the waiting room." He signaled to the security type with him as he said this and the man walked away.

"We wouldn't want to trouble you."

"No trouble. No trouble at all. We don't see many visitors here. But tell me. Why are you in this area anyway?"

"Official investigation," both Charles and Cinnamon said together. He seemed somewhat startled by their sudden pronouncement. That was exactly what it was a pronouncement.

"Very official, it would seem," he said. "I'll ask no more. May I know your names?"

"Harry Whiting," Harry offered.

"Bill Williams," Charles said. "This is my partner, Naomi Haggard."

"Delighted to meet you all. Do come and sit."

They followed their host to one of the chair groupings near the front entrance and as they walked, Cinnamon frowned at Charles.

"Naomi?" She mouthed silently. Charles chuckled but said no more.

No sooner had they been seated than an attractive young woman approached pushing a tea cart. On it were small sandwiches and glasses of lemonade. The cart appeared to be real wood, perhaps mahogany or a dark stained cherry. Whatever else this facility was, it was rich.

After she had gone, Charles said, "I couldn't help but notice a family resemblance between that young woman and yourself. Are you related?"

McShea never missed a beat.

"My niece," he said, then gave them a rather sheepish look. "It's nepotistic, I know, but I promised my sister that I'd take care of her, and she is extremely capable. She's my personal assistant and occasional hostess. I appreciate your not mentioning it in front of her. She's rather sensitive about working for a relative."

"If a person's good at their job, who cares how they got it? That's what I always say," offered Harry.

"Tell me about the center here," Cinnamon said, more to change the subject than anything. "Is this where you do the accounting?"

"We do everything here: hiring, processing applications from charities, accounting, distribution of funds and security."

"Security?"

McShea almost puffed up as he continued.

"Oh yes. Think about it. We have very rich endowments and do a great deal of philanthropic work, yet you've probably never heard of us. That's no accident, Miss... Haggard was it? If we were well known, we'd be inundated with requests for funding by every organization in the world. We keep a low profile. Actually, most of our endowments are not from a charity's solicitation but rather from their selection. We seek out worthy causes and that requires a great deal of investigation and security. It all comes from here."

"We must compare notes on methodology sometime."

"I think not, Agent Williams. Just as you have your secret ways we have our proprietary methods. I dare say some are as sophisticated as your agency's."

There was an awkward moment of silence while they all sipped their lemonade. The director looked up and out the front wall of glass at the parking lot.

"It seems the storm has abated," he said. "I'm glad we were able to offer you shelter. Please keep up the good work. I'm sure the lack of terrorist attacks in recent years is largely due to your efforts. Now I must leave you. I trust you can see yourselves out."

There had been an edge in his voice when he said this, and he abruptly rose and walked away without further conversation. The three of them looked at each other, Harry raising one eyebrow and shrugging.

They rose and walked out to the parking lot and back into their sky car. In less than a minute, they were airborne again.

Initially, no one spoke. Harry busied himself monitoring the controls and vectoring them to a new destination while Cinnamon tapped away at the virtual keys on her clip board and Charles sat quietly frowning.

"I think it's obvious that we need to check out CFWE a bit more closely," Charles said.

"Already on it," Cinnamon said, navigating through screen after screen in a financial markets search.

"Odd that we should have to put down there of all places," he said looking at Harry. Harry didn't even seem to notice.

"Kismet, maybe. Coincidences do occur, you know."

"Okay, Cin, so coincidences occur, but this one's beyond belief."

"Just be grateful that we found them. Without the full name it would have been a lot harder to find any information on them. We knew the academy was funded by CFWE but I couldn't find out who they were. Now I think I can."

The sky car followed the storm track well behind the rapidly moving system which was traveling north east on a relatively normal weather track. Below them they could follow its passing from the debris and flooded areas that dominated the landscape now. They then turned southwest and headed back to the safe house in the mountains. The sky car had extreme range and they were able to take it all the way back to the lake and their hideaway. Harry dropped them off, this time closer to shore so that they barely got their feet wet, then lifted and sped off to the north. He made a wide arc before heading back to where they had left the helicopter.

As they walked back along the path, Charles said, "I want to get the team together again. We need to contact them and see if we can meet up somewhere."

"Where do you suggest? We can't bring them here. This is Hillel's turf, you know, not ours."

"I think I know of a place," he said cryptically.

The rest of that day and the next were spent signaling the team and working on what information they had. Most of it led to dead ends. There was no record of an Ian McShea or his niece, either in U.S. records or worldwide. The same was true when they ran the name of the head of the Furguson Academy, Mrs. Tuttle. Either they were obvious aliases or someone with the capacity to do so had gone to a great deal of trouble to expunge their identities from the record.

CFWE turned out to be a different matter. Cinnamon was sitting quietly at a terminal after lunch on the second day when she suddenly pumped her arm and said, "Yes! Eureka!"

"Whatcha got?" Charles said.

"It seems that CFWE is wholly funded by the Beckwith Corporation who is represented by Chandlar, Taylor and Woolcott of Boston, Mass."

"That's nice," Charles said sarcastically.

"No, no. That's not the point. Chandlar, Taylor and Woolcott, LLC of Boston, Mass has only two clients. One is CFWE and the other is…?"

"Um, could it be Vanderhoorst?"

"You got it!"

"It all comes back to him, doesn't it?"

"So it would seem," she said.

"So let's see what we have. We have the CFWE, a foundation that funds charities, including the Furguson Academy where I grew up and where people are apparently indoctrinated or, if they fail to be, have their memories wiped and tossed out when they hit eighteen or so. We have Vanderhoorst who funds said CFWE yet hides his connections with it. We have quadruplet assassins, two of which are probably still alive and kicking and who want to do you and me in because we're investigating a murder at the Perry Mall, where there is a corpse that the records indicate is Vanderhoorst himself, though the man is very much alive and was in Switzerland having an operation at the time of the murder. Have I got it so far?"

"Don't forget the disappearing ambulance, attendants and corpse and the missing forensic evidence," Cinnamon added.

"Right. I think it's time we see what Ben Delano's come up with. If we can directly tie Vanderhoorst to the Perry Mall murder, we may be able to piece some of this together. Let's get in touch with Delano. How's it coming with the team?"

"I've sent a call to everyone but Bobby J. He's still missing. I think we can assume that he's either so far undercover that even we can't find him, or they've gotten to him. I don't know what else to believe."

"Well, he's got to come up for air sometime. We'll find him. I'm wiped out. I'm going to crash as soon as I finish contacting Ben. I suggest you do the same. Tonight will to be a long night."

SIXTEEN

HE HAD BEEN IN A DEEP sleep for two hours or more when Charles felt her hand on his back. She was caressing it softly, stroking up and down his spine with her fingertips. At first he thought it was Karen who used to rub his back when she came to bed, but, of course, that was impossible. He lay perfectly still, pretending to be asleep, and just enjoyed the pleasure of her touch.

Finally he stretched and rolled over to face Cinnamon. "If you keep doing that, I won't be held responsible for what happens next."

"That's the plan," she said.

Without thinking, he reached out and pulled her to him, feeling her body beneath the T-shirt she had raided from his dresser. He felt himself stirring uncontrollably and kissed her deeply and long.

"That's the way things start," she said.

"Are you warning me or inviting me?"

Cinnamon smiled.

"If you don't know an invitation by now, mister, I don't know what to think."

He kissed her again, this time slipping his hand up under the T-shirt and caressing her from shoulders to buttocks. She pulled away and knelt over him, pulling the shirt up over her head and slowly reaching for his belt buckle. He rolled onto his back and relaxed, folding his arms behind his head looking at her. She was amazing. Her body was firm and yet supple, shapely with perfect breasts and a flat hard stomach. Even her navel was beautiful.

There was urgency about her movements that nearly equaled his. He tried to help, but except for arching his back to make it easier for her to pull down his trousers, she wouldn't allow it.

Cinnamon straddled him without comment and settled down over him as if it was something she'd done many times before. She let out three quick little breaths as she guided him into her and then moaned softly. For Charles, it was almost more than he could bear. He was briefly afraid that he might ejaculate prematurely, but soon he was into the rhythm of the moment and just relaxed.

"Chucky, you've been holding out on me," she said. "Where've you been hiding that?"

"Don't spoil it," he said.

"Was that too raunchy for you?"

"Hell no! Just don't call me Chucky!"

Cinnamon threw back her head and laughed and began a new series of movements, at first slow and then increasing in speed and rhythm, a look in her eyes he had never seen before. It was magical. They made love as if they were meant for each other; as if God had crafted each of them for the pleasure of the other. To his amazement, when he finally reached his peak, so did she. The crescendo lasted for a full minute and then she collapsed on top of him, nestling in against his chest and panting.

"Wow," she said.

"Yeah," he panted. He couldn't think of anything else to say.

A half hour more passed before either of them moved. Charles slipped out of the bed and turned on the water in the shower. He returned to the bedroom to find Cinnamon gone. He took a moment to straighten the bed and then headed for the bathroom only to find her waiting for him, hair sleeked back and dripping, the water flowing over her body like a fountain. Immediately he was aroused once more and joined her.

"Making up for lost time?" She whispered.

"Shut up," he said, and pressed her against the wall. There was almost a violence to their passion this time but she wasn't afraid. She was as hungry for this as he, and as he lifted her by the buttocks, she slipped her legs around his waist and clawed at his back. It only served to increase his passion. This time, it lasted longer, and by the time they'd finished, the shower was running cold. She melted into him toward the end and began to sob softly, her tears mingling with the water and warming it. Charles knew that he could never experience another woman without comparing them to Cinnamon and be found wanting.

"I'm sorry," he said softly.

She pulled away from him slightly and said, "What for?"

"For taking so long to come to this."

They held each other for a long time before turning off the water and stepping out of the shower stall, shivering. He started to towel her off but she stopped him.

"Nope," she said. "You'll rub me raw. I need to pat dry, thank you. A girl's got to think about her complexion–all of it."

Charles stepped across the bathroom and stood by the door watching her. Every movement she made only served to arouse him again. With an effort, he backed into the doorway, grabbing another towel from the shelf and began drying his back.

"Damn, Chuck. You're insatiable!" She said, looking down at his nearly erect penis.

"Only for you, darlin'. Only for you."

"Well I'm clean and dry now, and I'm not about to hop back in that cold shower, so you'll just have to take me on the bed!"

With that, she bounded playfully out of the bathroom and through his bedroom, shedding water from her hair everywhere as she went. He watched her run away, following every movement of her hips as she did. Cinnamon toweled her hair quickly and lay across the bed, inviting him to join her. He lay beside her and caressed her body, tracing an imaginary curve from her throat to her thigh with his fingers.

"My God, you're beautiful," he whispered. She lifted and straddled him, looking down at him with penetrating eyes as she guided him gently into her. Then she closed her eyes and uttered a quiet groan.

Later, as they sat on the sofa in the common area, Charles realized how free he felt; how liberated this woman had allowed him to be. He started to mention it but changed his mind, not wanting to spoil the moment with talking–too much possibility for rationalizing what he had experienced. It was then that the com unit signaled and she walked, gracefully and quite naked to the unit to check it.

She hovered over the clipboard screen for a moment and then whispered, "Oh my God."

"What's up?"

She turned and looked at Charles in horror.

"It's about Ben Delano, Chuck. He's dead. It happened the same night you got the car from him. They say it was a heart attack."

Charles was on his feet and looking at the screen. He read the short message from Harry over and over again. The man was dead, and he doubted very much if it was a heart attack.

"They're tying up loose ends. They must still think we're dead and now they've killed Ben. They'll be after the rest of the team next. If Rich isn't involved, he'll be on their list too. We've got to get the team back together. As soon as they contact us, give them this information." He began scribbling notes on a pad beside the clip board. "It's instructions on where to meet us and when. Send it in the clear but in a micro burst. Unless they've been monitoring this unit, they won't have enough time to record the message. In fact, if they were monitoring this unit, they'd have been here for us by now. I'm going to start packing."

"Shall I call for Harry to get us some transportation?"

Charles thought for a moment.

"Hold off on that for now. Let me think a bit."

Cinnamon was already busying herself on the virtual keyboard when he left.

Over the next several hours they were too busy to think about their new relationship, Cinnamon pouring over the com unit trying to contact team members and to find out what was going on in the world, Charles busying himself with packing and, more importantly, thinking. He played the last week over in his mind again and again, trying to find that illusive connection that seemed to hover at the corner of his consciousness and would begin to tie all this together. Occasionally Cinnamon would walk by, distracting him momentarily, but he was pleased to find that she was not a major distraction. It wasn't that he didn't notice or didn't care. It was more a matter of confident comfort in their dynamic, as if they had been a couple for years and were completely comfortable with each other. There would be time to explore their love for each other later. For the moment, they had serious problems to deal with.

The more time passed, the darker Charles' mood became, as some pieces began to slide into place. He did not like the picture they were creating at all. Slowly he came to conclusions that he did not like to think about, which only made him more subdued and more remote, a condition that Cinnamon was quick to notice. She was wise enough to leave it alone, but the darker his mood, the more she worried. Finally, after a brief discussion of what they would need from here on out and how to proceed, Charles gathered the equipment they would take with them and began sledding it to the entrance of the cave. After the third load, he stopped and stood in the middle of the clearing on the other side of the rocky entrance, looking up at the stars. It was there that she found him.

"I've been in contact with everyone but Bobby J.," she said. "They've all received instructions and all have acknowledged. They should be there by this time tomorrow. Remember that we have a couple coming all the way from Baja, and that means taking the Transcontinental Tube. The terminal delays will keep them from arriving much before tomorrow evening."

Charles nodded and said nothing.

"I've also been able to find out more about Ben Delano."

Charles looked at her with a combination of pain and rapt attention.

"He was found in his car outside his townhouse, slumped over the wheel. They moved quickly on his case because of who he was and his connection to you and me. It seems that the locals are taking a very dim view of having a Federal agent blown up in their city. The autopsy was immediate and thorough and they have stated for the record that it was definitely a heart attack."

"Were you able to get a look at the blood work? Did they do a tox screen?"

She nodded.

"All the usual tests and a couple I've never even heard of."

Charles raised an eyebrow.

"Unusual, considering your forensics studies."

"They're coming up with new methods all the time. There's no way I could be up on all of it unless I want to become one of them. Anyway, it all proved negative. If he was killed, they must have used voodoo."

"Hmm," Charles said and frowned.

"So is there anything untraceable that could have been used?"

Cinnamon thought for a moment.

"Actually, I can think of two that could cause the same symptoms and are untraceable, but both are only deliverable by aerosol. Unless he was gassed, and that would have left traces in the car and on his clothes, we can rule them out."

Charles tensed.

"Can you get a list of his effects when he was brought in?"

She nodded and smiled.

"I already thought of that. I checked just to be sure but there was nothing out of the ordinary. He just had the usual personal belongings on him plus his official police gear."

"No nasal spray or other medications?"

"Not a one. It was one of the first things I checked when the tox screen came up negative."

Charles thought back to the last time he'd seen Ben, how he'd been nursing his cold and spraying meds up his nose. How better to introduce the poison?

"He was definitely murdered," he said.

Cinnamon said nothing.

"Call Harry now," he said after another moment. "Tell him what's happened and to bring any additional equipment he thinks we may need. We've got to leave stat. I want to be there when the others arrive."

"Okay," she said and disappeared around the rock shelf that hid the entrance to the tunnel.

They heard the helicopter approaching an hour later, traveling in the night without lights of any kind, producing a deep whomping sound from the rotors that sent shock waves through the air. The closer the vehicle came, the more they could hear the accompanying high-pitched whine that told them extremely powerful electric motors were busily supplying power to the blades. That could only mean a large equipment transport was on the way. Harry had arrived with the equipment.

As it came in across the lake, its black on black outline in the sky made it nearly invisible and they stepped back a good fifty feet in an attempt to escape the spray that was about to be kicked up by the massive machine. When it landed, it created a rain for fifty yards in every direction, soaking them on the spot.

"He could have warned us," Cinnamon said.

"Not Harry. That wouldn't be as much fun."

Cinnamon gave him a questioning look.

"It's a stray memory. Things are starting to come back to me."

Harry hopped down from the cargo door on the side of the long cigar like craft and grinned, ignoring the spray that was covering him with sheets of water as well. He signaled and called uselessly through the din. Charles and Cinnamon grabbed the lanyards on the overloaded sled and trotted off toward him. Loading the sled took all three of them and they all made another trip to retrieve the rest of the gear. Back inside the craft, which lifted off immediately, they accepted towels and the three of them tried to dry out as much as they could.

"Nice entrance," Cinnamon said with obvious irritation.

Harry laughed loudly, throwing his head back, hands on hips, looking like something from an old Sinbad movie.

"Well, you didn't give me much to go on as far as the equipment was concerned, so I decided to err on the side of caution. It takes a big machine to haul all this stuff!"

They looked around them for the first time. Along with the usual array of crates and container packs, there were two vehicles toward the rear of the beast, one, a small two person skimmer of military design, the other, a heavier hover craft, armored and armed. Charles whistled.

"What'd you do, rob an armory?"

"Let's just say I was able to borrow some interesting equipment on short notice. Hillel says he'll have to charge you for all this, but you and I both know he won't. The man's got more money than God, and he has to spend it on something."

"Well," mused Charles, "I guess we could use a little overkill right about now anyway."

"How big's your team?" Harry asked.

"Five more. There were eight of us all together, but it looks like they've already taken out one of them. We lost contact with an operative as soon as we scattered."

"There's still eight," Harry said, still grinning. "I'm going along, and where are we going anyway?"

"You sure you want to do that, buddy?"

"Are you kidding? I wouldn't miss this for the world. Besides, who's going to pull your asses out of the fire when you screw up?"

"Okay then, but remember who's in charge."

Harry gave them an unfathomable look.

"I know it better than you my friend. Things are never what they seem to be."

"That was you?" Charles nearly shouted.

"What was me? What are you talking about?" Harry seemed to honestly not know.

"Where... did you hear that phrase?"

"From Hillel. He says it all the time. Why?"

"Um, nothing, just another small mystery solved. At least, I think it is."

SEVENTEEN

CHARLES VECTORED THEM TO the rendezvous point and with the help of the two vehicles they were able to unload everything in a matter of minutes. They erected two tents for themselves, strange contraptions resembling snail shells that pulled over to accordion out into a semicircular tube. They covered the other supplies and equipment with tarps since they would soon be moving it again, and then settled down to wait. Cinnamon and Harry were fascinated by where they were. Charles had led them deep into the wilderness in the TAG area, where Tennessee, Alabama and Georgia all come together. It was a very wild and very primordial landscape, completely covered with pine, hardwoods and scrub brush surrounding the valley into which the transport had delivered them.

Actually, valley was not exactly an accurate term for their location. They were actually in what could more accurately be described as a gigantic sinkhole, some five miles across and nearly six hundred feet deep. The eroded walls sloped inward, a mixture of rock and soil, covered with vegetation as was the valley floor. A single narrow fire trail cut into one wall by the forestry department led from the edge to the valley floor but was totally invisible from the rim or from the air. It was as if they had been swallowed by the earth. They would be completely invisible to all but the most sophisticated thermal imaging equipment here.

"How'd you find this place?" Harry asked.

"By accident. In one of my military training exercises we were dropped into the mountains to survive on our own for a week. We were sent out with no equipment at all, no orientation maps or instructions, and only light clothing. No one was within five miles of anyone else and we had to find our way out."

"Sounds like standard survival training to me," said Cinnamon. If he didn't know better, Charles would swear she was just a little jealous. She had never done any Federal service but Homeland Security.

"Well it became very un-standard in a hurry. We were dropped in early April and one of those freak blizzards popped up. This was before we could predict those things the way we do now. At any rate, I found myself freezing to death, starving and desperate for a place out of the weather. I decided that this was not a planned part of the exercise and started heading south to find civilization. I found this valley instead."

"So did they ever extract you?"

Charles shook his head.

"The storm screwed up the telemetry on our tracers and they couldn't locate anyone for days. Of the twenty-seven who started the exercise, five died. Three others lost limbs to frost bite. We were out here for more than four weeks, but in the end those who didn't die simply walked out. It's a testament to our training."

"How'd you survive?" asked Cinnamon.

"Well, I don't want to go into it too much, but I found this valley and a cave on the lower wall to the east where I set up housekeeping. I started a fire using flint and a knife blade and once I thawed out, I lived on roasted roots and rabbits while I waited out the storm."

"I thought you said you were out here without any equipment."

Charles grinned. "I said that's how they sent us. I'm afraid I cheated."

"You what?"

"I cheated. I smuggled in a pocket knife and it's a damned good thing I did too, or I'd be dead now. You'll never find me without some sort of small edged blade and a magnifying glass now. The rest can all be improvised."

Cinnamon and Harry just looked at each other. Harry shook his head.

"I'm surprised they didn't catch you."

"Oh, they did," Charles said passively. "It cost me my commission and a discharge from the Marines. The Corps was my life, but they didn't have much choice. You can't have your people going around screwing with the training, you know. I'm not very good with authority. Anyway, they made an example of me and gave me an honorable discharge. My C.O. was really pissed. He said I was a survivor, in spite of directly disobeying orders."

After that, no one spoke. They turned in and slept soundly until morning.

They were up at dawn, loading supplies and equipment into the two vehicles in preparation for moving their base to the caves on the eastern edge of the valley. Once loaded, they made their way along the stream bed of the creek that meandered east and west through the valley floor and then began cutting their way up the shallow slopes leading to Charles' old hideaway. He worried about the path they were cutting through the underbrush, but it was unavoidable, and the overhanging canopy of water oaks and Georgia pines would hide most of the route from prying eyes. One would have to be looking specifically for them in specifically this spot to see anything out of the ordinary.

By noon, they had established the new camp and hidden most of their crates and boxes in the back of the cave where they would not be seen. A small bit of cutting and stacking underbrush completed the job, covering both the entrance to the cave and the vehicles outside. They looked over their handy work, trying to find blatant errors in their attempts to cloak their location from view and found none. Beyond that, there was nothing to do but wait for twilight and the trip up the trail to the top of the ridge above. They would be meeting the others there, assuming the other team members were able to secure transportation and that their GPS systems were working properly.

While they waited, Charles talked to Harry about their childhood together, finding that most of his memories were accurate until about the age of ten. It was then that the intense indoctrination began and those who were found 'wanting,' were culled from the rest of the students. He particularly remembered an incident just before he was shifted out of the advanced training into something called 'corrective indoctrination'.

"It was in the fall, as I remember," he told Harry. "They had been talking about blind loyalty and how one always obeyed their superiors. I asked who was supposed to be my superior and they said they were. When I asked what made them superior, they beat me."

"Physically beat you?" Cinnamon asked in surprise.

"Oh, it happened a lot, at least to me."

Harry nodded assent and motioned for Cinnamon to be silent.

"Anyway, they beat me and told me that if I had no loyalty to those who guided me that I was useless to the collective society. As I remember, my response was something like 'screw the collective'. After that, I was pretty much ignored by those I'd been studying with. A week later, I switched to another class. My God, Harry! You were in there too, weren't you?"

"Right along side of you."

A flood of memories flew through Charles' head, mostly vignettes of alternating violence and isolation. In his mind's eye he could see a constant barrage of yelling and chanting by the instructors battering at him for days. He began to weep.

"You're remembering, aren't you?"

Charles nodded.

"They talked us into forgetting what we had been learning before. They talked us into denying that any of it ever happened."

"Yep," said Harry. "I remembered that four months of hell after more than ten years of being plagued by blank spaces in my memories. It took Hillel and a lot of medtherapy to bring it back. You've come to it pretty quickly. You're stronger than I am, Charles."

"I thought it was longer than that."

Harry looked sadly out the entrance to the cave at the landscape beyond. "For you it was longer. I was sent to live with a farming family in Ohio, of all places, right after I'd been 'de-programmed'. I was too old to be adopted, but they found a family willing to take me in as unpaid labor, and I stayed with them for three years. When I was nineteen, I left and made my way to Chicago."

"But you, my friend, were the stubborn one. Your course in de-programming lasted for most of your sixteenth year. I found out later that you'd been at it for nearly ten months before they let you go. By your next birthday, they'd found a way to shove you out the door too."

"Hmm. The Marines. At least it was my own idea."

"Was it?" Harry asked.

Charles stared at him for a long moment and then sighed.

"Things are never what they seem to be, are they?"

Harry smiled sympathetically.

"Not as true now as then," he said.

Charles held his head in his hands and softly allowed tears to flow. Cinnamon reached for him and pulled him closer, holding his head against her chest and stroking his hair. Harry stood and stepped outside, ostensibly to relieve himself but in truth to just give Charles time.

An hour before sunset Harry made them coffee and they drank it quickly. Cinnamon was pleased that Charles opted for the coffee though the Black Rock tea was there for the taking. When they'd finished, they boarded the skimmer and started up the trail for the rim. The trail was not well kept, with large rocks the size of watermelons protruding from the midst of the roadbed along the way, particularly near the two switchbacks near the top. They were glad they had taken the skimmer. The heavier vehicle could have made the run, but it would have been a near thing, and they preferred to put it in harm's way on these walls only once, when they left the valley for some new destination.

At the rim, they slipped the vehicle neatly beneath a grove of large maples, the branches forming a thick canopy over head. They dismounted and waited, hunkered down by the roadway, awaiting the arrival of the other crew members.

By nine they were becoming discouraged. It had been dark for an hour and the others were expected to start drifting in hours earlier.

"Something's very wrong," Charles said.

He and Harry scanned the horizon for signs of incoming fliers and all three of them listened in silence for the thrum of diesel motors or the whine of electric cars. There was nothing.

"Maybe we don't all need to be waiting. We're pretty vulnerable here," Harry observed.

Charles considered this for a moment and shook his head.

"If they trace us this far, they can trace us to the floor of the valley. Let's stay a little longer."

"I hear something," said Cinnamon. Charles and Harry strained to listen but heard nothing. They remained silent for several minutes and then began to hear the faint hum of a flier in the distance.

"How'd you do that?" Harry whispered.

"I don't know. I've just got good ears, I guess."

The sound became louder, approaching from the southeast in the direction of civilization. Several more minutes passed before they could make out a single flier, low on the horizon but just above the trees, approaching them.

"The pilot's either in trouble or not very experienced," Harry said. "Look at that wobble."

The flier was wobbling badly. The closer it came, the more pronounced its instability seemed. Charles was beginning to wonder if it would be able to stabilize well enough to carry out a vertical landing in the small patch of ground where they stood. One miscalculation here could send it over the rim and into the valley below. Instinctively, they moved back toward the trees as the flier slowed and hovered tentatively over the clearing. It began its descent, each side of the roughly circular craft dipping in turn as it tried to come down. In the end, at a height of about eight feet, it simply fell, landing hard and flat on the rock strewn ground. Immediately the engine shut down and it was silent.

The three waited another few minutes, but when no one emerged from the cabin, they clambered over the wing and pulled the emergency hatch release. It gave reluctantly. They looked at each other, wondering whether to go in, but in the end, Cinnamon pushed them aside and climbed into the darkened interior.

"Wait here," she said sharply as she entered.

They could hear her moving around inside, pushing objects aside, like a dog rummaging through a garbage pile. From what they heard, she was making her way toward the control station and the pilot.

"I need help!" She shouted and the two men rushed the hatch, initially jamming themselves in the entrance, trying to squeeze through at the same time. Inside, the cabin was a wreck. Seats and overhead doors were scattered around the aisle and piled up on each other making it difficult to move forward, but with a series of tosses, pitches and a final leap over a pile of debris in the aisle, they made their way to the cockpit. Cinnamon was kneeling over the pilot, busily unbuckling the harness and checking for injuries. One look at the red hair told them that it was Sarah.

"Anyone else aboard?" Harry asked.

"Not that I've been able to find. You might look around, though."

Harry turned and began making his way back through the flotsam toward the cargo hold. This was a big flier, a commercial unit that could hold up to a dozen people. He thought to himself that it was no wonder the woman had trouble handling it. Even with auto controls and servos these were a beast for anyone but an experienced pilot.

Cinnamon pronounced Sarah free of internal injuries or broken bones, at least as far as she could tell, and checked the bandage on her left hand to be sure it was secure and clean. They lifted the now moaning woman from the seat, carrying her back toward the hatch. By the time they'd made it to the door, Harry had joined them. He answered their silent question with a shake of the head. No one else was aboard.

They lowered her gently into their own skimmer and descended the rim to their refuge. Sarah was coming back to life, distressed, angry and confused, but still, she seemed to be all right.

"She's a pretty little thing, isn't she?" Harry said as they were bringing her into the cave. "I wonder how she feels about Polynesians."

"She's not a thing!" snapped Cinnamon, "And you stay away from her!"

Harry shrugged. "Just thinking out loud," he said passively.

"Harry, you get on back up to the rim, if you're willing," Charles said calmly. "There may be more of our people coming. We'll take care of Sarah."

"I'm willing," he said and was off.

Sarah slept. The two of them satisfied themselves that they hadn't missed any injuries and Cinnamon cleaned the scratches on her face and forearm and then they left her to heal. There would be time enough to talk when she awakened, and if anyone had followed her, they'd have known it by now. For the moment, they could assume that they were safe. Harry joined them an hour later. He had nudged the flier over the edge into the valley with the skimmer. It landed to the south of their cave, and Charles and Cinnamon noted with satisfaction that it had knifed its way down among the trees and was immediately covered by the overhanging canopy of pine and oak limbs. When no one appeared at the rim for more than an hour, he returned to the cave. By the time he had settled in, Sarah was awake.

It took her a moment to realize where she was. Unfortunately, the first person she saw was Harry, smiling down at her from beside the cot; a total stranger with a wide grin, a two-day growth of a beard and a large hunting knife strapped to his chest. Before he could move, she'd sat up, reached up and pulled the knife and was holding it to his throat when Cinnamon grabbed her arm.

"Sarah!" She yelled. "You're safe!"

Sarah looked around, lowering the knife, but still keeping her eyes on the stranger, calming herself, forcing herself to breathe in a more normal cadence and then cautiously looked quickly at Cinnamon.

"He doesn't look safe to me," she said.

The three of them laughed and she flopped back down on the cot letting go of the knife. Cinnamon let go of her wrist.

"Let's just say that I'm safe when it comes to you. Hi. I'm Harry. Sorry if I frightened you. You've got quick reflexes. Another few seconds and I'd be bleeding like a stuck pig."

"Well," she said sheepishly. "That was the idea. Sorry."

"I beep. We're clear."

"Sarah, what happened?" Charles asked. She looked up at him and shook her head.

"Hard to say. I got word that Craig and Susan were going to meet me and Bobby J. at the airlift in Philadelphia and we'd all come together, but when I got there, no Bobby J. Susan was there, but she signaled me to make no sign of knowing her and I followed her through the main concourse to the restrooms. I waited five minutes before going in, just to be sure that she wasn't being followed. No one went in or came out, but when I did go in, I found her dead. Her throat had been slit." She shuttered. "There was blood on the walls, on the floor, on the doors to the stalls..."

"Never mind that now. What happened next?"

Sarah shook off the memory and took a deep breath.

"I called the locals and left."

"You called the locals?" Cinnamon said.

"I wasn't going to just leave her there! Don't worry. I used a public line, blanked the local scan and covered my face. If they ever figure out who I am they'll have to use voice recognition and you know how those public coms are. I don't think it'll matter."

"Bobby J. never showed?"

She shook her head.

"Not a sign of him. I made my way to a flier bay and stole that flier." She looked up at him. "That thing's hard as hell to fly!"

"You're sure they didn't trace you here?"

She shook her head again.

"I scrambled the code on the flight telemetry unit and flew by hand."

Harry whistled.

"Damn, girl! You must be one hell of a pilot!"

"Um, I guess so. I don't know. Survival instinct will do strange things, you know."

"How'd you know how to scramble the flight telemetry unit?" Charles pressed.

"Oh, that. I looked it up."

"You what?"

"I looked it up. The flier had a maintenance manual in the on-flight, and I just read it. Once I'd looked at the schematics I just figured it out."

Charles just shook his head and smiled.

"Well I'm glad you did."

"Hmm," she said. "The flight net thinks I'm on the way to Thule, Greenland. That should give them a few hours of grief."

Now Harry was laughing again.

"And a national emergency search from here to the North Pole, too, I'll bet!"

Sarah smiled and then chuckled.

"Hadn't thought of that," she said.

"What about the others?" Cinnamon asked. "You were in Baja with Anton, weren't you?"

"They got him, Cinnamon," she said seriously. "And they got Meg. She'd joined us when she couldn't make contact with Bobby J. and while we were waiting for him to catch up with us, they sent their people. I am the only one that's still alive." She offered a grim look. "But there are six bad guys that won't do any more damage."

"Is that when you got that wound on your left hand?"

Sarah looked at her left hand, tightly bandaged, like she was wearing a white boxing glove. "No. That's where I cut out my medchip. We all did, I think."

"Dear God," Cinnamon said. "You'd have to take out the whole middle finger."

Sarah smiled weakly, "Better than being dead," she said.

Harry was grinning again.

"This is my kind of woman," he said admiringly.

"You...don't happen to have any record of all this, do you?"

"You don't believe me?"

"It's not that. I want to study it if you have it to see if we can learn anything about them. It would be helpful."

"Um, yes. I think so. My cap-camera was on the whole time. It's in the flier."

Cinnamon and Harry groaned simultaneously. Sarah looked at them, confused.

"What's wrong?"

Charles smiled.

"Not much. We just have a salvage job at first light, that's all. I'll have Harry tell you about it later."

Harry just said, "Hmph!" and turned away.

EIGHTEEN

BY ELEVEN A.M. THEY HAD RECOVERED the cap and Cinnamon was helping the one-handed Sarah rig one of the clipboards to take the download. A search of the public information sources and as many of the classified ones that they were able to scan showed no unusual activity or suspicious messaging. Apparently, the official net wasn't looking for them. There was an article about a massacre in Baja by bandits and a search was underway for a lost stolen flier over Labrador, but other than that, all seemed secure.

The download was bloody but not very informative. The part they were interested in lasted forty eight seconds, the entire length of the battle, and in that space of time, six assassins as well as two of their friends were killed one by one. Charles thought of how much it looked like a two-dimensional video game, something he had seen in a technology display at World Trap Games last year. The game had been rather boring because of its operation in only two dimensions, but this was not. When it was over, he was sick to his stomach and he wasn't alone.

"Destroy it," he said.

Cinnamon stared at him.

"It's evidence."

"We don't need it. We have an eye witness and we've seen it. Destroy it. I don't want anyone seeing our people go through that."

"Charlie..."

"Do it!" He snapped and left the cave.

Cinnamon followed him, keeping her distance as he found a large rock to sit on and then settled in beside him. She put her arm around his shoulder and rested her head on his arm.

"I'm sorry," she said. "They were my friends too. You're right to erase it. That's no fit memorial to who they were."

Charles said nothing, just sat staring at the ground. Cinnamon hugged him and said nothing further. They stayed like that for nearly an hour before Charles finally released a great heaving sigh and turned to her.

"Come on," he said. "We've got to get this done."

In the cave, Sarah and Harry were talking quietly and gathering the equipment for packing.

"What are you two up to?" Cinnamon said.

"We're leaving, aren't we?" said Harry. Sarah looked at the two in the entrance, sharp eyed and alert.

"How'd you know?"

Harry turned back to what he was doing, stuffing the last of the blankets into a duffle bag and stacking it with the other supplies ready for loading.

"Don't be ridiculous," he said. "What do you need?"

"Can you get a strike team together? A good one?"

"Are we going after Vanderhoorst or the orphanage?"

"The orphanage first, I think. There'll be hell to pay with Homeland Security over this."

Harry looked at Sarah, who nodded.

"We thought the orphanage first too. Don't worry about Homeland Security. Things aren't..."

"Always what they seem," Charles finished. "Okay. Let's get going."

Harry was his usual efficient self and within an hour they were on their way by skimmer to rendezvous with the strike team. They approached the school as they had before, settling into the nearby valley. They off-loaded quickly, Harry busily stacking equipment on the ground beside the cargo hold while Sarah, Cinnamon and Charles fanned out and looked around. The lack of company told them they arrived undetected. Harry called them in after a few moments.

"What kind of weaponry do you want?" He asked.

"Whatcha got?" asked Sarah.

"For you a K-19," he said, producing a small automatic weapon and bandolier from a crate on the ground. "It's light, accurate and has almost no kick. For your weight and size it's the best there is."

Sarah took it and hefted it expertly, bringing it to her shoulder and aiming off into the distance.

"You don't happen to have..."

"A scope?" Harry said, producing a short telescopic site from the same crate and handing it to her. She clipped it onto the weapon and aimed it again. She smiled and nodded.

"Impressive," he said.

"I'll settle for my standard issue," said Cinnamon. "I'll be busy with the computers once we're in while the rest of you play cowboy."

Harry handed her a bandolier of clips for her sidearm.

"How about you, chief?"

"Something a bit heavier, if you please. I intend to do some damage," Charles said.

Harry pulled an odd looking contraption from another case, all tubes and optics, and handed it to Charles.

"This is just the thing. It's a chemical laser. The electronics are for aiming and tactics. It carries a hell of a punch, but only in short bursts. This one pulses, so don't expect to sweep the area with it. Just aim and pull the trigger. Think of it as an electronic shot gun. It'll cut a hole in anything about three feet in diameter."

"Harry, this thing... "

"Shouldn't exist. It doesn't officially. Consider it a gift from Hillel; he said it needs field testing anyway."

Charles took the chemical laser. Its weight was manageable. After looking it over, he smiled grimly.

"This'll do."

The four of them donned armored vests and proceeded by foot to the top of the ridge separating their valley from their destination.

Below them, the school had changed radically. The fence around the compound had been doubled and there were military vehicles parked to one side just outside the fence. Four Bradley Nine tanks bristling with weaponry were inside the fencing, one in each quadrant of the area. Two were hovering while the other two rested on the ground. Soldiers walked about pursuing various tasks while a cluster of three officer types conversed with the school's director on the front porch of the administration building.

"Well, that tears it," said Charles.

"Getting cold feet?"

"I'm just not willing to go up against our own military. I'm not a terrorist you know. If the U.S. Military is defending this place, I'll not be involved in a fire fight."

"Neither will I. Look closer, Charlie. Do you see any rank or insignias? These aren't Army or Marine, my friend. They're either mercenaries or belong to some group that's not supposed to exist. Either way, I'd say they're fair game. Personally, I think they're a threat to internal security and well within the purview of Homeland Security operations."

Harry was almost chuckling at this last statement, seeming quite pleased with himself.

Charles looked again, scanning the quad with his monocular. Harry was right. There were no indications of rank or of what unit they belonged to, and their weapons were not standard issue. They were definitely paramilitary; someone's private army perhaps?

"Okay. I guess we wait for the strike team and hope they're not detected."

Harry emitted another sinister chuckle and nodded.

"They're already here and obviously not detected."

Charles scanned the ridge on the far side of the valley and then worked his way around to the left and the right as far as he could. He saw nothing.

"You're sure they're here?"

"And in place. Trust me on this one."

"So what now?"

"Your call, Charlie. All we need to do is give my men final instructions and launch the attack. I suggest we wait about a quarter hour. The sun will be in their eyes as it comes over the rim of the valley. You can target all four of those Bradleys. The weapon will do the rest. Just aim and plot them in and when you fire it will take out each target in turn. Aim for the motors in back. The hydrogen makes one hell of an explosion."

Charles was beyond being amazed at anything his old school mate said at this point. He sighted in on the four hover tanks and looked around. There was still no sign of the strike force, but if Harry said they were there, he was sure they were. They quickly determined to use the destruction of the four Bradleys as the signal for a coordinated assault on the compound. Once Charles opened up, they would converge on the target from four directions, firing from above to avoid friendly casualties and then mopping up afterward. Everyone was to be warned to avoid killing students or directing fire into the dorms and other buildings. If they received fire from a building, surgical strikes were to take out the defenders. Charles was sure they'd thought of everything, and equally sure that as soon as the action started, all their plans would be in the garbage. They'd just have to do the best they could.

Harry sent out the instructions by line of site beam communications and received confirmation from the team leaders around the rim. Another four or five minutes, and they'd start the show. It was then that they heard the sound of a ground car motor coming from the direction of the road to the front gate. Charles and Harry looked at each other and then at the girls. Sarah had a look of determination that sent chills down Charles' back, while Cinnamon seemed nervous, frustrated at the delay. They waited.

Just as the sun began to peek over the edge of the valley, a black limousine drove into view and proceeded to the front gate, which opened without hesitation, and entered the compound. The same robed figure that they'd seen before stepped out of the back of the vehicle and walked toward the group on the veranda. He had a commanding gate.

"Bonus," said. Harry.

"Maybe we'll get them all?"

Harry's com unit began flashing rapidly and he checked the readout.

"Look behind you," he said when he had read it.

Charles rolled over far enough to look over his shoulder. A dense fog was rolling in over the rim behind them. It cascaded past them, covering them with dew, the breeze passing over them chilled and rapid.

"Shit!" Snapped Charles.

"No, no. This could work to our advantage! We can get in there a lot faster under cover of the fog. I didn't see any infrared goggles on those guys down there."

"That's fine Harry, but I can't aim this thing in the fog!"

"Not to worry," said Harry. "You've already targeted the Bradleys. As long as you're facing the compound, it'll find 'em. Once targeted, it zeros in on their location using a combination of infrared and electromagnetic emissions from their bodies. They're like signatures."

They waited for the fog to fill the valley. If it was a typical bank, it would clear itself out in less than an hour, burning off in the rising sun. By that time, they should be in complete control of the camp.

They waited another five minutes, until the fog was deep and soupy, totally obscuring the school compound from their view. Harry tapped Charles on the shoulder and he fired, waited for the 'ping' that announced it was ready again and fired a second time. He hesitated on the third shot as a dull WHOMP came from the direction of the first Bradley, followed by a loud explosion and a concussion wave that swept a hole in the fog. They could clearly see what remained of the Bradley, burning where it stood. As he fired a third and fourth time, the second Bradley exploded creating a second clearing in the fog which formed a billowing donut around it. A third explosion followed as the third Bradley met its fate, but there was no fourth explosion.

"Now we're screwed!" Charles growled.

"Can't be helped. If the team keeps its head down, they can keep clear of the armor and still fire into the crowd. Let's hope it's enough."

Automatic weapon fire could be heard all around the rim of the valley. Brief flashes dotted the landscape, not only at the rim but down the inside slopes as well. Charles was more than a little impressed. There must have been close to five hundred men out there, and he hadn't seen one of them.

To their right they heard a loud report and an area of the hillside erupted into a shower of earth and rocks. It was accompanied by rapid machine gun fire and smaller explosive charges from the same location. The fourth Bradley had moved into action.

"There's your target!" Harry shouted, pointing to the source of the canon flashes.

Charles lined up his sights just behind the muzzle blast and fired. Again there was the familiar WHOMP but no accompanying explosion.

"Aim further back!" Harry said. "You're too far forward!"

Charles fired again, shifted his aim slightly and fired again. This time, the muffled concussion sounds were followed almost immediately by a loud explosion and shock wave. The fourth Bradley was burning and a number of bodies dotted the ground around it.

The fog was beginning to lift. The combined infernos from the armored vehicles were causing an updraft, drawing the covering mist into the sky and dissipating it. Targets appeared everywhere, milling around in confusion. Sarah joined the fight, firing off short bursts one after another, and each time she did, another mercenary fell. Harry joined her while Charles looked for more large targets and Cinnamon remained still having nothing to do until they entered the camp. Frustrated, Charles finally settled on the limousine as a target and cut it in two just as the robed figure ran from the administration building. He retreated immediately back inside. Charles followed up with an attack on the row of trucks outside the compound wall, systematically destroying the engines of each from nearest to farthest away. In less than two minutes, all ten vehicles were ablaze or scattered around the parkway.

Harry signaled and they started down the slopes to the compound below. He put out an arm, slowing his companions so that the strike team could enter first. They were crack troops, and definitely U.S. military trained shock troops. They worked their way through the fences and advanced on the buildings, performing with professional efficiency and thoroughness. Once they were engaged below, Harry signaled the other three forward.

Sporadic shots rang out as the security force mopped up the last of the resistance, checking each building for mercenaries or non-students. Inside of fifteen minutes, they had gathered the surviving mercenaries and school officials into the center of the compound where they sat, hands on the back of their heads. The team was already beginning to process them for interrogation.

"I don't see Mrs. Tuttle or that hooded figure," said Cinnamon.

"They might still be in the admin building. For all we know, our robe wearer is out there with the staff in the middle of the quad."

Cinnamon scanned the three dozen prisoners sitting on the ground.

"Not there," she said.

"How can you be that sure?" Harry asked.

"He wore wool slacks and black shoes. He wouldn't have had time to change that much. Besides, none of these are tall enough to fit his description."

Harry just stared at her.

"Perfect memory," she said smiling and headed for the computer room.

Sarah was busily going from dormitory to dormitory, trying to calm the panicked students and reassure them that they weren't going to be hurt. She started with the youngest and worked her way up. In the fourth building, she found the oldest students ranging in age from sixteen to eighteen. Telling them to relax and come out into the quad, as she turned, a single shot rang out and she pitched through the door into the compound.

With the exception of six guards, everyone turned in her direction and brought their weapons to bear. The students began filing out into the compound in orderly fashion, moving alternately to the left and the right of the doorway with military precision. They were all armed. Not one of them looked at the moaning Sarah, now crawling away from the building toward her companions. A tall young man of about eighteen, the last of those to leave the building, stood in the doorway with an automatic pistol in his hand. He was smiling.

Harry raised his weapon, but Charles called out, "Wait!"

He took several steps toward the assembled group and yelled, "Remember the Mona Lisa!"

Instantly, all but the young man in the center dropped their arms to their sides.

"Recall!" screamed their young leader and they resumed aiming at the team.

"Nice try, Chuck," Harry yelled. "Drop them all!"

The strike team opened up on them. The students returned fire momentarily until they had been silenced by the automatic weapons fire from more than three hundred angry troops. More shots were fired from the second floor, killing five of the troopers and sending seven more to the ground, bleeding. Charles raised his weapon and fired at the second story windows in turn, creating a virtual firestorm in the building. The firing stopped, but in a minute four, stout, young students emerged through the front door, weapons blazing. They were dropped as they emerged.

"What the hell were they doing?" Cinnamon yelled. "What were they thinking?"

Charles gave Harry a glance of recognition.

"That's right, Charlie. That would have been you and me if they'd kept us and trained us. These others are probably fine upstanding graduates of the program."

Charles allowed his weapon to slump beside him, finally letting go as it clattered to the ground. He flopped onto the ground and stared at the bodies in front of the dormitory. Looking up at Harry, who just looked back blankly, he then noticed Cinnamon walking toward the administration building. Sarah cried out and his gaze swung in her direction, where two medtechs were working on her. There was nothing he could do there, he decided, and as Harry rushed over to check on her, he stood, strapped on his weapon and followed Cinnamon through the doors and down the hall.

When he approached the computer room, he saw her standing inside, staring at someone or some thing on the far side of the room. She looked frightened and confused. Charles swung his weapon around and aimed it at the wall, approximately where whomever or whatever she was looking at would be located.

"How could you?" She was yelling. "How could you do this?"

A muffled voice uttered something unintelligible and Cinnamon dropped her weapon to the floor. That was all the incentive Charles needed. He fired from the hip, blasting a hole approximately three feet in diameter through the hall wall and on through the outer wall of the computer room. Through the opening, he saw the lower half of a robed figure crumple to the floor. The top half, from the waist up, had simply disappeared. Instinctively, when Charles fired, Cinnamon had dropped to the floor and rolled, retrieving her weapon and now pointed it directly at Charles. She looked puzzled and dazed. For a full minute, they stared at each other and finally he said, "Cinnamon, it's me. It's okay now. What was that all about?"

She slumped forward and lowered her weapon, panting deeply as she sank to the floor.

NINETEEN

CINNAMON WAS HEAVILY SEDATED for the return trip. After the incident in the computer room, Harry turned over analysis to his own men and rushed the Homeland Security team away by skimmer. Sarah was awake but groggy, her left shoulder bandaged and her left arm in a sling. That coupled with her still bandaged hand, she was quite a mess. Sarah was on heavy pain killers that relaxed her to the point that she didn't even seem to be herself, resembling more an innocent teenager than the woman who felled more than a dozen mercenaries only hours ago. The medtechs pronounced her in good condition and on the way to recovery.

As for Harry and Charles, they rode silently, allowing the skimmer to find its own way home. They had considered a visit to the CFWE to see how they would react to the destruction of the school but let it pass. There would be plenty of time for that later and they had the ladies to care for. For the moment, they were more concerned with the fate of the children in the orphanage and what to do with them now. The facility was secure but the children would have to be moved.

"They're probably going to have to be reprogrammed, you know," said Harry. "It's not going to be easy."

Charles nodded.

"At least I remembered the trigger phrase that they used on me. They used it that day we went to use their computers, and I was as helpless as a baby until Cin, pulled me back. I figured it'd work on them too."

"Yeah, Chuck, but not on their leader."

"You mean the dead one," Charles said flatly. He could still see the students going down like a picket fence in the hale of fire from his own men.

"Well, it almost worked. At least it broke the spell it had on you."

Charles nodded.

"Maybe."

They thought it over and decided that it was time to inform Homeland Security. Even if Rich was part of all this, he'd have to handle an official report, particularly one forwarded to the Secretary of Homeland Security himself. Still, Charles wondered how high this conspiracy went and what it was all about.

"What the hell do you think they were doing there?"

"Building assassins, probably," answered Harry.

"Or a secret army?"

"Not likely. There weren't enough for that. My money's on assassination teams. The question remains whose assassination teams were they?"

"Whomever they were, they were fanatical. Did you see the way those boys just calmly came out shooting? They had to know that they couldn't win."

"Like robots," Harry said.

"Maybe we'll know more after we talk to Cinnamon." He looked down at her, peacefully sleeping in her seat as if the world was perfect. Casually he reached out and brushed a few strands of hair from her cheek.

"You do love her, don't you?" asked Harry.

"More than I imagined possible."

Harry shifted in his seat and looked out of the window, saying nothing more. Charles decided it was the best his friend could do to give him some privacy.

Back at the underground safe house, Charles carried Cinnamon by sled down the tunnel and put her to bed. Harry helped Sarah navigate the rock face and tunnel, sitting her on the sofa in the common room and preparing tea for all. He was genuinely solicitous to the fiery red head's needs, an act of kindness Charles found out of character with what he remembered from their school days. For a time, the three of them sat sipping tea quietly; Sarah was becoming more and more coherent as the pain killers wore off. Harry prepared a hypodermic to ease the pain without the grogginess and dosed her with it.

"What now?" Harry asked abruptly.

"Dunno. Got any ideas?"

"Well, it all comes back to Vanderhoorst, doesn't it?"

"Seems like it to me."

"Why don't we just arrest him?" asked Sarah.

Charles shook his head. "Can't do it. He's too well connected and he's too powerful. Any attempt at that would just get us in even more trouble and he'd be free by the next morning."

"We can always just kill him," Harry said, taking a long pull on his tea.

Charles and Sarah stared at their companion and said nothing. He looked up at them and shrugged.

"Okay. I guess not."

"What we need is to understand exactly what's going on here and make it so public that it can't be denied any longer."

"Maybe I can help."

It was Cinnamon. She stood at the door to the bedroom, hair uncharacteristically askew, still wearing the same wrinkled clothing she had on the raid. There were blood spatters and mud stains on the legs and shoulder and she had a large bruise forming on her left arm where she had fallen. Charles thought she had never looked so beautiful. She entered the room, grabbed a mug of tea from the tray and slipped it into the food service. In ten seconds, she pulled it and sat beside Charles on the sofa.

"Well, don't you want to know how?"

"When you're ready," Charles said.

"To start with, the robed man was Bobby J., which explains the way the bad guys always knew what we were up to and how to find us. He sold us out, Charlie. I don't know how long he's been working against us or why, but there it is. That's one problem we won't have to worry about any more. The other thing has to do with the students."

"The ones at the school, right?" said Harry.

She nodded.

"More specifically the ones that decided to fight. I looked them over when they came out and something bothered me about them. When I woke up a little while ago, I kept playing the scene over and over in my mind trying to figure out what was bothering me. What I found explains a great deal."

"Well?" said Sarah with some irritation.

"There were two sets of twins, two sets of triplets, and a set of quads among them."

"Now that's weird," offered Charles. "Why would they have so many multiple births? Maybe Harry's right. Maybe they're growing assassins, which would explain how one person can be in four places at once on the mall tapes. They were another set of quads, but where did they find them all?"

"They're not multiple births, Charlie," she continued. "They're clones."

"Clones! That can't be! They proved that it can't be done successfully in humans years ago. Even research on the subject is forbidden by law after so many failures in the attempt!"

"Vanderhoorst," Harry said softly. "He's got the money, he's got the connections and he's got the immunity of government sponsorship. He's been building clones."

"But why?" asked Sarah.

"For assassins," Harry said.

Charles grunted and shook his head.

"That's a lot of trouble to go to just to develop a crew of assassins. There are enough government agents available who would do the job willingly. It doesn't wash, Harry. Sorry."

"Well they're doing it for some reason."

"Okay. So, the clone idea makes a great deal more sense than the thought of them getting their hands on that many multiple births and being able to orphan them, isolate them, and train them. Clones make sense. There are no family members to contend with, no records of birth, no need for medchips, and no great loss if one of them is killed. The question remains why do it? It's incredibly difficult, it's costly and it's risky."

"Only Vanderhoorst can tell us that," said Cinnamon. "We need to pay him another visit."

" I'm calling Rich," Charles said.

"Are you sure you want to do that, Charlie?" asked Cinnamon.

"I don't think we have a choice. We're going to need all the help we can get if we go after Vanderhoorst and he's the only one that can give it to us. If he's part of the scheme, we'll find that out too. I think we found our leak with Bobby J. I'm hoping that's all there is. It's time, folks, to come back to the land of the living."

Charles looked at Harry to see what his reaction would be. He smiled and said nothing.

TWENTY

THE PARTY RETURNED TO HILLEL'S cottage next to the park to have their medchips re-implanted. Hillel was not there, but a small, somewhat weasel-like woman greeted them before they reached the porch and silently ushered them in. She led them into the back rooms without a word and proceeded to reinsert the devices, moving with mechanical efficiency.

"I see they expected us," Charles said, hoping for some response, but he was ignored.

When Sarah's turn came, the technician acted as if there was nothing unusual about her four fingered hand, first examining the wound and satisfying herself that it was not infected. She then chose a medchip from her stock that she initialized and inserted.

"This is in your own name, Miss Duncan. I have an ID for you as well." Within minutes they were back on the street and into the skimmer which was very illegally resting in the side yard. In less than five minutes they were landing in the transportation bay at Homeland Security.

The three agents, Harry Kamahi in tow, went directly to Rich's office and past his secretary. When they entered, he was not alone. Charles and the others looked around the room, recognizing two agents from his section and three others whom he had never seen before. All were tall, heavily muscled and standing in a crescent around the walls of the room.

"Hello, Darren," Cinnamon said. "I see you were expecting us."

Rich's mouth dropped open and he stared in spite of himself.

"I… was expecting Charles Peavey, but not you or Sarah. Who's your friend?"

"Harry Kamahi, meet Darren Rich. He used to be my boss before I died."

"Jesus, Charles. Why aren't you dead? And why aren't Agents Harper and Duncan dead too? All three of your medchips were reporting you deceased. In your case I knew better, but the other two?"

"Uh, can we lose the audience, Darren?" Charles said, looking at the other agents. Rich signaled with a nod of his head and the others left, closing the door behind them.

"It's a long story, Darren, one I'll tell you when we have time. Look, I'm sorry, but I thought you were part of this mess until it dawned on me if you were, we'd never have gotten as far as we did. We've been way out on a limb and we need your help. Are you going to do something about all this or are you just going to have your… the gentlemen outside, make us disappear?"

Rich somehow knew better than to play the angry boss right now. He eyed his guests silently, just long enough to consider his options and then said, "What do you need?"

"Who was the man who left your office as I came in that morning? He went to a great deal of trouble to hide his identity."

"I'm not sure, actually, and that's the truth. He came with all sorts of credentials and briefed me to kill the investigation of that murder at the Perry Mall. He said it was a matter of national security and that I'd be briefed by National Intelligence in due course. You should have seen the list of signatories to his credentials. Everybody from the New Pentagon to the FBI had signed off on him. I just did what he told me or thought I had until you decided to go rogue."

"Rogue?" Charles said with an innocent smile. "I went rogue? I was just doing what you told me to and finishing up the case until people started trying to kill us!"

"Don't kid a kidder, Charles. You went rogue."

"Well, that's a discussion for another day. Have you been able to find out anything about Ben Delano's death and missing ambulances?"

"Old news," said Rich. He finally turned to the security team and signaled them to relax. "We found the real ambulance with its locator burned out down around Peachtree City as originally reported. After looking over your case records, I started looking for the one you suspected to be up around Tate and found it too. It was a shell. No engine, no transmission, just a body and four wheels. Someone went to a lot of trouble to send us off on false leads. Forensics found nothing, and before you ask, I isolated the forensic studies from the main center and had everything sent directly to me on sticks."

Charles nodded, impressed.

"Maybe you earned your job after all."

"And maybe I can put your little group of zombies on ice, my friend. Watch your mouth!"

"Sorry. Old habit. Always pull the chain of authority and all that. So what about Ben?"

"Your friend died of a real live heart attack."

"No drugs? No shock or other contributing factors?"

"None that we could find. The autopsy showed a congenital condition. He had heart disease and it just gave out."

"That makes no sense, Boss. I've known him for almost ten years. We started together at Homeland before he went civilian. How could he pass his physical with a heart defect?"

Rich just shrugged.

For the next half hour, the four of them provided Rich with a synopsis of what had come to pass over the last week. They were careful to exclude any reference to Hillel or his activities. Harry became the helpful friend with connections unnamed who was able to help them. By the time they finished, Rich was up and pacing the wall behind his desk.

"Peavy, you'd better be telling me the truth about all this," he finally said.

"Every word, Darren. It's all real. I'm surprised you didn't find the bodies we left behind. Homeland ought to be sharper than that."

"Hmm," Rich mumbled. "With our tracking systems all fowled up we don't know what telemetry to believe anymore. No telling how much has passed by unnoticed. Did you know we're overhauling the whole system? Tech support is in an uproar. The joint agencies are busy arguing among themselves as to who let the bugs in, and local support swears that it's all your fault. One thing's clear. This Vanderhoorst is the key."

"We're going after him."

"You're damn right we are. I'll clear it all the way to the President if I have to."

"Um, I wouldn't do that. Vanderhoorst has connections everywhere. The only way to catch the S.O.B. is in the moment and before he has time to find out what's going on."

Rich thought for a moment.

"Okay. Here's what we can do. I'll notify everyone concerned about your going to pick up Mr. Vanderhoorst for interrogation at the same moment you're entering his place. There won't be enough time for anyone to warn him. Fair enough?"

"Fair enough."

"How many men do you need?" Rich said, reaching for the com console.

"Just what we have here. Your five can cover exits while my team goes in."

"Even Sarah?" said Rich with surprise.

"Especially Sarah."

Twelve was a long walk or a very short ride from Homeland Security. They opted for the very short ride. Cinnamon, Harry, Sarah and Charles arrived in a motor pool unit, the other five agents right behind them in a Homeland Security van. The five in the van pulled into the underground parking facilities and posted themselves at both parking exits and at the three outside doors. Sarah entered the lobby first, her arm in a large cast and carried in a sling. Her other hand was freshly bandaged and looked more than ever like she was wearing a boxing glove. As Charles had expected, there was a rent-a-cop at the desk in front of the elevators. She sauntered up to the desk, swivel hipped and doing her best to emphasize her ample cleavage. She smiled at the guard.

"Perhaps ya'll can help me," she said in a deep southern drawl. "I'm lookin' for my old room mate from college. I was told she has an apartment here."

The guard remained stone faced and professional.

"Yes ma'am?" He said.

"Her name's Melanie, Melanie Harris? I think she's on the eighteenth floor."

"Sorry, ma'am," the guard said, consulting his listing. "No Harris', Melanie or otherwise anywhere in the building."

Sarah rolled her eyes and gave him an exasperated look. "Maybe she's under her maiden name. Is there a Merriweather in your list?"

The guard seemed irritated and after a moment shook his head.

"No Merriweather either. Sorry."

Sarah leaned over the desk as far as she could to look at the screen. She pressed her breasts against the counter, pushing them even farther out, much to the delight of the rent-a-cop.

"Are you sure?" She said. "Could you check again?"

The guard typed in the name again slowly, dividing his attention between the screen and Sarah's obvious charms. Just as he finished, she reached over the desk and sprayed him from a small atomizer. He slumped forward and then slid to the floor. The other three joined her, handing her the regulation armor vest and headed for the elevators. Sarah was almost squealing with delight at her performance.

"I gotta remember you can do that," Harry said, smiling with a boyish Polynesian grin.

"Don't worry about it, stud. I only use it in the line of duty."

As usual, it took almost two minutes for the elevator to make its way to the top floor and then begin its horizontal journey.

"Something's wrong," Cinnamon said.

"Yeah, I noticed," answered Charles. "We've shifted to the left instead of to the right. Either the elevator's been rerouted to a more secure entrance or we're expected."

Weapons were drawn and Cinnamon pulled a flash grenade from her outside jacket pocket. She depressed the plunger and kept it there. If it were a false alarm, she could always reset it before deployment. All four of them were now wearing dark goggles. The door opened slowly and they could see shadows on the other side. There were two of them, one on each side of the opening in the blind spot, hugging the wall. Cinnamon didn't hesitate. The grenade rolled slowly through the door and exploded, emitting a brilliant flash of light and a brief puff of dense grey smoke. Both men screamed and began choking. The team poured out through the elevator and bent over the now fallen guards, strapping them while Sarah gave each of them a burst of her atomizer. Looking around, they found themselves in a dead end corridor that led nowhere. To the right was a window and to the left a blank wall. In front of them was a panel much like the sunburst bronze door to Vanderhoorst's penthouse, but it was solid.

"Now what?" asked Harry.

"How the hell do I know?" said Charles stepping back into the elevator to examine the panel. Sarah stepped in beside him and began scanning the walls. Before Cinnamon and Harry could react, the door closed and the elevator began its trip back toward the core of the building.

"Shit!" snapped Sarah. "Now what?"

"Now we ride. Cin and Harry will have to figure this out for themselves."

When the elevator reached the central core, instead of descending it continued to the right, following the path it had on Charles' last visit. They readied themselves as it slowed and then came to a complete stop. Sarah and Charles pressed themselves against the walls on either side of the doors and waited, again a flash grenade at the ready. The doors opened. No one was there. Charles looked down the corridor in Sarah's direction while she did the same in his. No one was about.

"What do you think?"

"I think we don't have much choice. You want high or low?"

Sarah pointed toward the ceiling with her eyes. "I don't fancy crawling with this cast on my hand."

"Ready?" He asked.

She nodded.

Charles dove through the door, facing down the hall toward the entrance, while Sarah leapt a good three feet in the air and launched herself toward the opposite wall, facing the opposite direction. There was no one around. Charles came to his knees, reset the flash grenade and slipped it back into its holster on his armor jacket. Sarah took a deep breath and gently nursed her shoulder with her good hand.

They settled down for a moment and walked the hall to the huge sunburst doors to Vanderhoorst's apartment. Charles found a hiding place behind a large urn and Sarah, now once more composed and looking pristine, pressed the intercom.

"Yes? May I help you?" said a familiar voice from the speaker.

"Hello. My name is Yolanda Mertz. I'm here to see Mr. Vanderhoorst, if he's in."

There was a short silence followed by an irritated Hodges saying, "I did not receive word from the front desk that anyone was on the way up."

"Well, I'm sorry, but there wasn't anyone in the lobby when I came in. I just took the elevator directly to this floor."

Again there was a short silence.

"State the nature of your business with Mr. Vanderhoorst."

"I am acquainted with a Charles Peavy, whom I understand Mr. Vanderhoorst is looking for. For a reasonable consideration, I can lead him directly to the man."

"One moment," Hodges said and the speaker went dead.

There was a metallic rumbling in the door and slowly it began to open. Hodges stood in the doorway dressed as before, complete with velvet collared black coat and ascot.

"Mr. Vanderhoorst will see you, Ms. Mertz, and you may inform Mr. Peavy that he can come out of hiding. No harm will come to him from either myself or Mr. Vanderhoorst. Really, this attempt at intrigue is quite unnecessary."

Charles stood up and again pocketed the flash grenade. He slipped his assault pistol back in the holster and smiled at Hodges.

"Good to see you again," he said.

Hodges led them into the drawing room, where Charles and Cinnamon had been brought before. They sat with their backs to the wall on the left, sitting forward in the chairs ready to move in a hurry if necessary.

When Vanderhoorst appeared he was walking, albeit assisted by a fine silver handled cane and the pleasant smile of their earlier meetings was gone entirely. He looked both annoyed and threatening as he walked through the door to the living room and seated himself in a large wing chair.

"Let's not play more games," he said. "What is it you want?"

"I want you," Charles said, "and I want to know what's been going on?"

"You have questions for me?"

"Many," Charles hissed.

"Very well. I will answer them truthfully, since neither of you are leaving the premises alive anyway."

Charles felt a heavy hand grab his arms and pin them in a vice like grip. He was completely unable to move. With little or no effort, Hodges pulled his wrists together and held them with one huge hand while he removed Charles' assault pistol from its holster with the other. Tossing it aside, he retrieved the flash grenade and expertly reached over and down to Charles' ankle, where he pulled the small back-up weapon from its holster. When he had finished, he released him.

Sarah stood and reached for her own weapon but Vanderhoorst had produced a large caliber pistol from his smoking jacket and pointed at her. She re-holstered her weapon and raised her hand as Hodges crossed to her and retrieved her weapon, tossing it aside. He leaned purposely over her as he did it, his putrid breath gagging her, his grinning face staring at her cleavage.

"I think he likes you," Vanderhoorst said.

"Forget it, Vanderhoorst," Charles said. "We didn't exactly come alone."

"Yes, I know. There are five men downstairs and those other two are being taken care of in the dummy hall as we speak. Pity really. My men seemed very surprised when you found them. I must remember to confiscate your spray device, young lady. I'm intrigued."

"If you've hurt those two..."

"I haven't hurt them, Agent Peavey. I've killed them, or more precisely my men will have killed them by now. Now ask your questions."

Charles said nothing.

"Speechless, are we? You must have been very fond of them. Well, no matter. I'll do the talking. You want to know what my connection is with that poor unfortunate who was murdered and mutilated. True? And you'd like to know why we've been breeding genetically identical people and training them at the school. It's all quite simple, actually. I'm very surprised that you haven't already guessed."

"I've got a pretty good idea," Charles growled.

"Yes. No doubt you do. Well, the multiples are agents of the United States Government. I've been breeding them for years now. They are indeed clones, engineered to have certain characteristics necessary for clandestine operations carried out by various agencies. Now that's certainly not a new idea, but my multiples are different. You see, they are not truly identical. In appearance they are often indistinguishable, but at the cellular level, either by chance or by design, they differ in significant ways. Some are incredibly strong, like Hodges here, and have unwavering loyalty to whomever they serve. Others have a...what should I call it...a moral flexibility that makes them ideal for assassination and sacrifice. Still others are designed for replacement parts for their host."

"Which is what the Perry Mall murder was all about?"

Vanderhoorst nodded.

"Precisely. You will note that you discovered the gentleman was a hemophiliac. That was genetically engineered into him to insure his loyalty to me. You see the synthetic blood that he injects is very expensive and there are limited sources. In fact, my companies are the only sources. It was unfortunate for him that what I needed was a replacement heart. If it had been an eye or a kidney, he might still be alive today."

"Did he...know his circumstance?"

"Oh, dear no. He knew me only as his benefactor, and since we never met, he had no idea that he was my identical twin.'

"The mutilations, removal of hands and feet, the eyes and ears and all that. Were you harvesting or just trying to put us off the track?"

"Put you off the track, though at least his left hand had to go to eliminate the medchip."

"And the medchip tracers? How did you manipulate our software?"

"You mean the Marginal Resource Provider's Group software? The software produced by MRPG which is a subsidiary of Callidon Tech Medical, LLC, which is a subsidiary of... ah well. That's boring. Suffice it to say that I am the one that originally produced the software in the first place.'

"And the medchips?"

Vanderhoorst frowned and fidgeted, twirling his cane in small circles. "No," he said studying a spot on the floor. "Your friend Hillel did that. He's a nuisance I must deal with some day."

"All that may be, Vanderhoorst, but why murder the man and dump his body at the mall? Why not just have him brought in and do it in one of your facilities? I assume you have facilities for that."

"Ah, yes. Very good. We had to do it on sight because you see, my multiple was not too keen on donating his heart in the first place. When my men were picking him up he resisted and they were forced to kill him. I believe they broke his neck, as I remember. After that, it was necessary to save the heart quickly and leave the body behind."

Charles smiled.

"You know, the more bodies you leave around, the more difficult it becomes to cover all this up. Homeland Security is already involved and they know where we are and what we're doing. You might as well let us go."

"No doubt you think I should just turn myself over to the authorities? Even you must realize that my connections would allow me to be back in my home before evening. No, Agent Peavey. The reason I have to kill you and your team is that if I don't, you'll have to kill me. It's the only way to be sure I don't continue my activities. You do see that, don't you?"

Charles glared at him darkly. His eyes had been shifting, looking for some out but with this last exchange, he concentrated on his captor.

"I see it," he said.

"If this was a melodrama, now is the time I would say how much I regret disposing of such a worthy adversary, but it's not a melodrama, is it? The truth is ridding myself of you and your fellow gadflies will be nothing but a relief. I really don't have time for all this. I have too much to do, and now that I've got my new heart, I've got the energy for it, so I hope you'll excuse me."

Vanderhoorst leaned forward and grasped the top of his cane. He stood up and turned away, leaving the room.

"Dispose of them, Hodges," he said over his shoulder as he left.

Hodges walked around to face the two. Grinning maliciously, he considered his two captives, obviously more interested in Sarah than in Charles.

"Forget it, asshole," she said coldly. "I doubt if you've got anything I'm interested in anyway."

Hodges' visage turned dark as he leered as her.

"Is that so?" He said as he began undoing his belt.

"Oh, please. If you're going to kill me, do it now, but don't expect me to offer an exchange of sexual favors for my life. We both know it won't happen. Quite frankly, I don't think you've got what it takes."

In response, Hodges dropped his fly and unhooked his pants with one hand while pointing his weapon at Charles. He let the trousers fall to the floor and stood there, naked from the waist down.

"Oh my," she said with real appreciation. She started to reach out for him but he swung the weapon around and pointed it at her forehead.

"Now don't get jumpy, my friend. I just want to admire it,' she said, and leaned forward.

He kept the pistol pointed directly at her forehead but allowed her to adjust her position in the chair to better come to him. Charles was becoming sick at the sight of the huge man's erection. It was, he had to admit, extraordinarily large, but the thought of Sarah's touching it produced waves of nausea in his gut.

She stroked the penis underneath, moaning slightly and readjusted her position again, bringing her bandaged arm forward to balance herself. In one swift move, she opened her mouth, steadied herself against him with her bandaged arm and fired. The end of the cast exploded, leaving a large ragged hole where Hodges' crotch had once been. He looked down at her, his eyes bulging, his mouth open and slack-jawed in his astonishment. It lasted for only a second and then he pitched backwards onto the floor. Sarah followed up with a second shot to the head, sending pieces of skull flying toward the piano.

"The things I do for my job," she said in disgust, wiping her free hand on her blouse.

"Jeez, Sarah," Charles said. "That was disgusting. Remind me to never get you mad at me."

She offered a sardonic smile.

"Remind me to never wrap my arm in a cast with a sawed off shotgun again. That thing hurts!"

Charles stood and crossed the room to retrieve their weapons.

"If we're lucky, Vanderhoorst will think those two shots were Hodges doing us in."

"Unless he knows the difference between a pistol shot and a shotgun blast, or has cameras, or is listening, or all three," she said. "Will you please get me out of this damn cast?"

Charles handed Sarah her side arm and reached to the back of the cast, just below her elbow. He grasped a small tab and pulled it forward quickly, virtually unzipping the bottom of the cast and then he spread it, throwing it aside. Sarah replaced her arm in the sling and rubbed her shoulder. "Is it bleeding again?" She asked.

Charles checked her shoulder and found a few spots of blood. "Not much," he said. "You'll be fine, but you may have pulled a stitch or two."

"So what do we do now?"

"You sit your asses back down and shut up," said a familiar voice from the doorway, "and drop the weapons. That means the one in your pant's leg too, Charlie."

TWENTY ONE

CHARLES DID AS HE WAS TOLD and dropped the weapons. He was fumbling with the ankle holster while Sarah unwrapped the shotgun from her wrist and forearm. Charles could see the dark powder stains on her fingers where the weapon had discharged close to her hand. His head was spinning, trying to make sense of what was happening. Sarah grumbled to herself as she finally released the restraints and the shotgun dropped heavily to the floor.

"You seem confused, Chuck."

"You could say that," Charles said, flopping back into the chair. "I thought you were dead."

Ben Delano grinned broadly and gave a slight bow, being careful to keep the assault rifle he was carrying carefully aimed at the two of them the whole time.

"Nice piece of work, huh? Actually, I am dead. You could find my body at Masterson's Funeral Home if you hurried. They won't bury me until tomorrow."

"You want to explain that?" asked Sarah, somewhat disgusted at once again being someone's captive.

"Ask your boss," Delano said. "I'll bet he's figured it out."

"It was your multiple."

"Right. It was my multiple. He was engineered to have a congenital heart condition and when I needed to die, we simply helped him along the way."

"You were part of this all along, weren't you?"

"Absolutely," Delano said. "I believe you were wondering who it was that kept asking for help from FEMA and Homeland Security, weren't you? It was me. I'm the one that called. I was pretty sure they'd send you and that was important."

Charles nodded. "Okay, Ben. So why me?"

"Not too hard to determine, really. Vanderhoorst asked me to clean up the mess, and since we needed to get rid of you anyway, I thought it was a good opportunity to get you involved. I knew you couldn't resist a good mystery. You got sucked in good, didn't you buddy?"

"None of this makes sense. If you'd left it a local matter, there would have been no problem. Why involve me?"

"As I said. We had to get rid of you. Vanderhoorst knew you'd be a problem some day and he's very good at heading off trouble before it starts."

Charles shifted in his seat and noticed how carefully Delano followed the move, always keeping his weapon on the two of them.

"I still don't understand why I would be a problem. I didn't even know that Vanderhoorst existed or that he was involved with cloning assassins, and apparently others as well."

"Actually, there are only a small number of assassins. Most are simply agents. There's an inordinate amount of dirty business connected with Vanderhoorst's operations, what with government contracts, competition and foreign industrial espionage. We just counteract any attempts to rock the boat."

Charles shook his head, jerking it as if to clear the cobwebs. His head was spinning.

"That doesn't explain why you wanted to kill Charles," said Sarah. "Is he that good?"

"He's that dangerous," Delano replied. "You see, it's not his ability as an agent that's important, it's who he is. It's where he came from."

"The orphanage," Charles said, starting to realize it. "I was at the orphanage and sooner or later, your boss was afraid I'd remember the way Harry did. Then I'd be on that place like fur on a, um, rabbit." This last he said with a brief look of embarrassment toward Sarah.

"Man, you are dense, Chuck. You still don't get it."

"Get what?" He said with genuine frustration.

"It's who and what you are! You just didn't see what was going on, you were a part of it! Damn it, man. Why do you think you have such an affinity for Black Rock tea? That stuff is caustic as hell. It kills people eventually. You think that was an accident? You were engineered that way!"

Charles and Sarah both stared at Delano, speechless.

"Well damn," Sarah said.

"You mean..." Charles said, but he was unable to finish.

"That's right, buddy. You a multiple, a clone! You're not an original. He works for Vanderhoorst and he's as good at your job as you are. Every move you made, we could counter because you're so much alike, but after Karen's death, you became a loose canon, unpredictable and suddenly in exactly the jobs we didn't want you in."

"I'm a...what?"

"Oh, get over yourself. You're a multiple. You are what you've been fighting! We've been playing you from the first, my friend, but we had to do it in a way that would not create suspicion when you died. All well and good, but you went to Hillel, something your original would never have done, you fell in love with your partner..."

"You're in love with Cinnamon?" said a surprised Sarah.

Delano ignored it.

"And through him you found Harry."

"Is he, um..."

"Nope. He's an original. He had two multiples because he was so promising, but they were both killed in an operation in Singapore."

"Unhuh," was all Charles could say. He was now totally disoriented.

"Gotcha, didn't I?" Ben said, grinning wider than ever. "Gotcha, you sucker, and now it's the end game. You were never good at the end game, were you, Charlie? That's where you always lost it, you know. Take a look at your marriage. Look at your military career. You just never could finish up your games, could you?"

Charles looked up at his old friend pathetically.

"Was that engineered, too?"

Ben laughed.

"Nah. That was just stupidity on your part. We can chuck that one up to your wife. No matter. You're on the way out anyway. Vanderhoorst's gone, on the way to Switzerland or somewhere and we're shutting down the operations in the city. You haven't done too much damage, you know. We've lost the school and may lose the Charles Furguson World

Endowment front, but Vanderhoorst doesn't seem to mind. He can afford it. Anyway, the only loose ends to tie up are you two and Rich. He may be a problem since there are no multiples of him, but we'll manage. There are lots of ways to make murder look accidental or natural Now if you would please, stand and close your eyes."

They both rose carefully, looking for some opening, but there wasn't any this time.

"Keep them closed and you'll live a little longer," he said flatly.

They did as they were told. Charles heard a hissing sound and that of Sarah collapsing on the floor. Before he could react, he smelled a strangely sweet yet savory aroma and the room went blank.

When he came too, he found himself in the back of a transport skimmer, trussed up like a Christmas turkey and gagged. It was a full ten minutes before his eyes adjusted to the light and his head was pounding. His mouth was dry to the point of burning as were his eyes, and he reminded himself to talk to Sarah later about her magical knockout spray, that is, if there was a later. When finally he focused, he was staring into the bloodshot eyes of his red headed companion, also tied up tightly and also gagged. She looked back at him with a mixture of anger, panic and hurt in her eyes. He blinked as calmly as he could, trying to bring her out of the panic. This was no time for that.

Slowly he looked around. It was a smaller skimmer, bare of any other cargo with no separation between the cargo area and the passenger area. The back tier of seats were empty and the only other person he could see in the machine was Ben Delano, the back of his head unmistakable balding pattern and a long scar which he had obtained during their training at the academy. Delano was casually propped up in the driver's area, looking out the window at the passing terrain as the transport guided itself.

He turned and looked back at them. Charles shut his eyes a split second before Delano had turned totally around.

"Awake, I see. That's good. We'll be at the drop off point in a few minutes. You know, it really is a blessing that you removed your medchips. It makes it easier. There won't be any telltale alarms when your body hits the water. Did I mention that? I'm dropping you off about ten miles off the coast of Savannah. Don't worry. You won't drown. From two thousand feet I doubt if you'll even feel it. Now that's what I call considerate."

Charles looked around frantically, wriggling imperceptibly in his bonds to test the possibility of getting himself free. At least if he was going to die, he'd rather do it fighting than packaged like fifty pounds of potatoes or a side of beef. The bonds were too tight; there was no play in them at all. In fact, he wondered why he still had feeling in his arms and legs at all. When he finally gave up, he looked over at Sarah questioningly. She shook her head in answer to his unspoken question. There was evidently nothing they could do.

They flew on for what seemed like forever, but eventually, Delano decided that it was time to take care of them and he rose from his seat at the controls. He reached down behind the seat to his right and withdrew a slab of lead, elongated with a channel down the middle of its underside and a loop and chain in the center of its top. It required two hands to lift it. Just as he was beginning to move toward the two of them, the vehicle lurched and he pitched forward, dropping the heavy weight.

"What the hell!?" He snapped, rolling over and trying to stand.

Another jolt hit the craft, this time accompanied by a large report, like that of a canon going off. Delano crawled forward, making his way to the driver's seat and slid in, buckling himself in. He scanned the horizon and then checked his instruments. All Charles could see were a few blurry red shapes on the heads up display that told him nothing. A third jolt rocked the craft, this time causing it to pitch to the left and begin a descent.

"Ah, shit!" Delano said as he scanned the controls frantically.

Releasing the automatic navigation unit he grabbed the wheel, fighting it to keep level. This went on for several minutes before it became apparent that staying in the air was not an option. Delano decided that a plunge from two thousand feet was not a good option either, and began a slow turn and descent to the left. Currents buffeted the craft as it fell more and more quickly toward the water. The engines began to make a deep grating sound and one shut down completely, emitting billowing smoke into the cargo area and cockpit. Having only one functioning engine just served to increase the speed of their descent and tighten the spiral that they were in.

Charles had to give him credit. Delano was apparently a very good driver. He manhandled the controls like an expert, compensating for each jolt and countering the skimmer's tendency to side slip. The wind was whipping by them loudly now, not a good sign. It could only serve as a warning that the hull had been breached and that the tear, wherever it was, was getting larger. Toward the end, a loud groaning sound overhead announced the opening of a huge gash in the skin of the skimmer, allowing sunshine and a vicious wind to enter. It flipped the skimmer on its back as it settled roughly into the sea.

Charles looked at Sarah as the water began to pour in through the gap and the skimmer tilted on its nose. He chanced a glance at the control area only to find Delano, head against the window, laying sideways with a crushed skull and protruding vertebrae from where his neck should have been. His cold lifeless eyes stared back at him just before it sank beneath the rising water.

Sarah wriggled sideways and wormed her way toward the rear of the craft. Charles followed suit, fighting the upward path that they had to take as the ship stopped its tilt and settled at a thirty degree angle. The gaping tear in the ceiling turned floor was now completely submerged, and like an over turned bucket, they bobbed about caught in the air pocket in the rear of the vehicle.

Somewhere along the way, salt water had worked its way under the edge of the tape across Charles' mouth and with all his strength, he opened his mouth, pulling it away from the gag. Sarah actually smiled and did the same.

Charles looked at her quizzically and she said in a hoarse, breathy voice, "You look like you've got the nastiest mustache I've ever seen."

"We're drowning and that's all you can think to say?"

"We're breathing," she answered, "and I'd rather go out with a laugh than a whimper!"

"Hysteria," Charles thought, "pure hysteria."

Suddenly there was a bumping sound and the vehicle lurched again, turning completely over on its back and soaking them with the wave of water that rushed toward them from the front of the vessel. Another bump and the ship had turned completely over so that the gash in the roof was once more above them. They began bobbing again, awash with sea water but alive and breathing fresh air. Both began to laugh with abandon. It was a ludicrous way to die. Either they drowned or they died of exposure, their bones picked by passing gulls or perhaps some fish trapped in the interior of the vessel with them. As if in answer to this thought, Charles felt a small something swim past him, brushing against his body as it glided by. He was about to verbalize his extreme displeasure at the situation when a shadow crossed his view from above.

He blinked, trying to focus. Looking up he saw a silhouette leaning over the edge of the gaping hole overhead. It was either the creature from the black lagoon, he decided, or someone in a wet suit. Again he began to laugh, this time hysterically as this last thought seemed too funny to him to contain.

"Yes!" cried Sarah. "Oh, yes!" and she began to cry.

"Hi, guys," said a cheery voice.

"Harry? Is that you?"

"I hope so, but you never can tell, really. I might be my multiple in disguise."

"You don't have any multiples, damn it, and if you were I wouldn't care. Get us out of here."

"Half a mo'," he said and disappeared from view.

The skimmer shifted again, but this time it stabilized rather than increasing its roll. Harry reappeared and carefully lowered himself over the edge into the ship, landing between the two immobile agents.

"May I be of service?" He said.

Suddenly it dawned on Charles that Harry was alive; he was really alive.

"Cinnamon! Is she alright? Is she alive?"

"Relax, buddy," Harry said, cutting through the polymer bonds that held Sarah tightly bound. "Cinnamon's fine. She's waiting topside for you. But it's ladies first, as they say, and Sarah's infinitely prettier than you."

He looked down at her face, tape still stuck to her upper lip, blackening bruises over both eyes and a cut on her left cheek.

"Though I bet she's seen better days."

"Just get me out of this!" She snapped, wriggling in her loosening bonds.

Harry looked her over appreciatively.

"Damn, you're sexy when you're bondage," he said.

"Damn it, Harry Kamahi, if you don't get me out of this thing, you'll never have anything but fantasies in your old age. Now cut the damn straps.!"

Harry cut the rest of the bonds, smiling and humming to himself. He helped her to her feet and gave her a boost as she crawled out of the opening in the roof.

Charles was quickly freed and he too crawled out the overhead hole, rolling to one side and landing in the deck of another skimmer tied along side. Harry followed moments later and helped them both to the luggage hatch. They dove into the interior and through the open door into the main cabin. Cinnamon grabbed Charles and hugged him, grinning from ear to ear. She kissed him hard and pulled him into a seat along with herself, lifting the dividing arm rest in the process.

"I thought I'd lost you," he said.

"Me too you," she answered.

Harry closed the hatch, slipped into the cabin and slammed the luggage compartment door behind him. He stood, bent over in the cramped cabin and signaled the man in the driver's seat to go. They pulled away, rose into the air at a steep angle and turned west, increasing speed as they flew back toward the coast.

Charles collapsed into Cinnamon's arms, breathing deeply. She stroked his forehead, pushing aside the matted hair and kissing him over and over again.

"Don't ever scare me like that again," she whispered.

"I really didn't want to do it this time, you know. How the hell…I thought you two were dead! Vanderhoorst said his men were taking care of you when we were in the penthouse. How did you…?"

"We damn near were," she said. "He did send two men, Charles, but we took care of them instead of the other way around."

"Cinnamon, there's something I have to tell you."

"Not now, darling. Rest."

"No, now. I need to tell you now. I'm a multiple, Cinnamon. I'm a clone. Vanderhoorst told me!"

"I know," she said, smiling gently.

"You what?"

"Your, um, I guess your original for lack of a better term was one of the two men Vanderhoorst sent to kill us. When they showed up in the elevator, I thought it was you coming back for us. It took only a split second to realize it must be your multiple, and I dropped them both without a word."

Charles swallowed hard.

"How did you know? What if it was really me? I mean, Me me? You might have killed me."

"I knew."

"How?" He said again.

She reached out and touched his forehead just over his left eye.

"Ow!" He exclaimed. "That hurt!"

"Of course it did, Charlie. It's the cut you got in the raid at the Furguson School. It's healing badly. I'm afraid it's infected. Anyway, the other you didn't have that cut and that could only mean one thing."

"That it wasn't Me me?"

"Right, and quit saying that. He was not the Charlie I love, and that's all I needed to know."

"Well, damn," Charles said, "just damn!"

EPILOGUE

VANDERHOORST WAS NEVER FOUND. As expected, the New Pentagon and other agencies refused cooperation and informed the Office of Homeland Security that by Presidential order, they were to stand down on the search for the man. His holdings were transferred to a new board of directors drawn from some of the leading CEO's in the country and continued to function unabated as they had before. This was with the exception of the Charles Furguson World Endowments, which was dissolved, its primary officers and executives receiving light and unpublicized sentences for various civil crimes. Hillel was able to replace the software programs that surveilled the public with an even better version that was virtually guaranteed to thwart any attempts at tampering, that is unless one had created the program. This was something that Charles and Cinnamon never bothered to tell authorities.

When next they saw their mysterious mentor, it was at the wedding of Sarah and Harry Kamahi, held on a beach on the 'big island' of Hawaii. Charles and Cinnamon had flown in from their home in up state New York among the finger lakes. When they arrived, they were two white ghosts among a host of well tanned and naturally swarthy guests, all of whom were either local or had been attending marriage celebrations for the past two weeks. All this was funded, of course, by Stephen Hillel, who stood by Harry's side at the wedding, dressed in old shorts and a bright Hawaiian shirt and looking more like a beach bum than a recluse genius. As for Charles and Cinnamon, she was the maid of honor and Charles was honored by being asked to give the bride away.

All through the ceremony, partially traditional and partially what Charles found to be the most incomprehensible combination of Hawaiian mysticism and New Age chant, he shifted from foot to foot, scraping sand fleas off his ankles and suffering from serious hay fever. He sorely wished he was back in the frozen north, even if he was a southern boy at heart.

The shaman who accompanied the minister performing the ceremony circled each of the participants in turn, chanting and waving a broken paddle as if it were a religious icon. When he began his circumnavigation of Charles, he hesitated, looking him in the eye and chanting a sing-song string of alliterations full of 'ka's and 'hi's' and then passed on. As he finished, several of the onlookers drew in their breath in surprise. The rhythm of the chant was mesmerizing, and Charlie suddenly realized that he was staggering, about to pass out. He shook himself and regained his composure.

The ceremony ended with a great cry and Harry scooped up his bride in his arms, carrying her off to the luau nearby, followed by a cheering crowd. Cinnamon and Charlie joined them, doing their best to imitate the sounds of the Hawaiian songs being sung. They located their assigned places at the luau and sat on mats on the sand, pleased to find Stephen Hillel seated beside them.

"Well, now," Hillel asked as the roast pig and *poi*, the yams and steamed fish and great bowls of rice were being passed around, "How have you two been?"

"Couldn't be happier," Cinnamon said. "Retiring from the agency is the best thing either of us ever did. Besides, the private sector pays better, right partner?"

Charles nodded absently.

"Right, partner," he said.

Both Hillel and Cinnamon studied him, and never the one to be shy about expressing an opinion, Stephen said, "Something's bothering you. Get it out. This is no place for dark secrets."

"Uh?" said Charles. "Sorry. I was just wondering what that shaman said. I didn't understand any of it, of course, but it seemed different than what he said to the others."

"It was," Hillel said.

"You could tell?"

"Certainly. I can even tell you what he said."

Charles and Cinnamon gave him equally astonished looks.

"What was it?"

"He said you're both about to have your lives changed by a quest you've been on in your hearts but not in your minds. He said you are destined to confront a great evil, one that you've encountered before, and that you will prevail, though not without pain and difficulty."

"He said that?" Cinnamon asked.

Hillel nodded and began devouring pig voraciously.

The two of them fell silent, thinking about what Hillel had said. At length, Charles said quietly, "It can't be Vanderhoorst. He's done."

Cinnamon nodded.

"I was thinking the same thing. You know, Hillel, I never would have suspected you spoke Hawaiian."

"I don't," he said, examining the remains of a large bone that he had been gnawing. He pitched it over his shoulder like a medieval knight and dipped two fingers into the purplish starchy *poi* in front of him. He plopped the mass in his mouth noisily slurping and licked his fingers.

"If you don't speak Hawaiian, how do you know what he said?" Charles said evenly.

"Simple. I paid him to say it."

Cinnamon laughed loudly, throwing her head back and actually snorting. She sat up, putting her hand over her mouth in apology.

"Things are never what they seem to be," she said.

Charles just stared.

"I don't see why you're so surprised, you know. Am I the only one who sees Vanderhoorst as just the beginning? You two wanted him so badly you couldn't stand it. Now that he's behind bars, you're left without a *raison d'etre.* Why do you suppose you quit the agency and became private operatives? Homeland Security just isn't enough anymore, but as private citizens, you can chase bad guys to the ends of the earth. Hell, everybody that knows you two knows it's true."

"We...that is...," Harry started.

"What he's trying to say, Stephen, is that we know you're right, but we have to make a living, you know. We're meeting with a new client in New York next week and he promises to be a very lucrative source of funds. Assuming we take the job, it could set us up for a good many years, and then maybe we'll think about other things. Charlie's got a wife now and that's a responsibility that his wife is not about to let him forget."

"Right back at you," Charlie said feigning annoyance.

"No need to wait. You can start immediately. You're being hired to set up a new security net to replace one that was seriously compromised recently. It's a very big job. 'Should keep you two busy for some time."

"Oh?" said Cinnamon suspiciously.

Hillel nodded.

"I'm the client."

He gave them a conspiratorial smile that widened into a raucous grin and resumed his meal.

The two of them looked at each other and said simultaneously, "Ahh."

Sneak Peek Chapter

Rhoedraegon

Hans Rhoedraegon and Clarion Skeelar sat together, watching intently as events unfolded in the streets of the capitol. Security forces surrounding the governmental complex were being hard pressed by the mobs of rioters pushing at their lines. Here and there a breach would appear whereupon sonic cannon would momentarily stun the knot of angry people until the breach could be closed. Shots occasionally rang out and even naked firebrands tossed over the heads of the troops would land harmlessly in the plaza where they would explode with a loud report and little damage. Clarion and Hans were far removed from the crowds and the chaos, huddled with their families on the Skeelar estate outside Second York, where both of them had substantial business interests. On the com display, a mob was surging toward the Congressional Complex while a second horde of protesters slowly made its way toward them from the opposite direction. Neither man spoke, though their looks of utter despair reflected their thoughts. As the crowd met in Freedom Square, squads of police, far too few to stem the tide of violence erupting around them, tried desperately to push back the surging masses, wishing the security troops were available to them. Clarion and Hans watched transfixed as the two groups quickly engulfed the police and once the police were swept aside, clashed violently. Hans Rhoedraegon looked away in disgust. As if on cue, Skeelar killed the transmission and sat for a moment in silence.

"It's begun, hasn't it?" said Hans sadly.

Clarion frowned and nodded, not bothering to look over at his friend.

"We knew it would come eventually," he said.

"But to happen so soon? It's only been ten months since the institution of pure Democracy."

Clarion Skeelar sighed.

"And this is what you get with Democracy; one man, one vote, no representatives, no councils or parliaments, just mass voting on every issue. Everybody gets an equal say in government. Well, it's what they wanted and it's what they've got."

"There could be billions of deaths," Hans noted solemnly.

Skeelar looked over at his friend now and smiled.

"And there would be, if it were not for your plan."

"I hope it works. Still, millions may die before things are brought under control."

At that moment, the doors behind them opened and the huge chamber was alive with the echoes of children rushing into the room. Two boys and two girls, all under the age of ten, ran across the polished floors, clattering and laughing as they rushed the two men seated before the console. Behind them, two women followed at a more leisurely pace.

Hans looked up at the women smiling while his companion frowned at the unruly antics of the four children, now busily climbing onto the laps of the two patriarchs.

"Elisa, can't you control these two?" Clarion said, shifting to accommodate the two girls, one on each knee. He smiled at them in spite of himself, never able to maintain a scowl in the presence of his twin daughters.

His wife approached unsteadily. Hans could tell that the medications were not doing the job as they should. Elisa was thinner than he had ever seen her, and her sunken eyes stared almost blankly out at her husband. Close behind her came Beatrice, Hans Rhoedraegon's own precious wife, reaching out to steady her companion gently but firmly as she swayed beside Clarion Skeelar's chair.

"Rest yourself, Elisa," she said in a soft melodic voice. "Here. Sit beside me on the hearth."

She lowered Elisa to a sitting position on the great stone bench surrounding the fireplace, now cold in the summer heat, and sat beside her. Hans watched Beatrice for a moment with deep affection. He was so glad that she was in his life. She had given him two fine sons and a third, he had been assured, was on the way. She steadied Elisa Skeelar with one hand while resting her other on the growing belly where their third child now grew.

"Hans," Beatrice said, once she had settled Elisa into a comfortable position, "how is it going?"

"As expected," he said simply.

"Then the world government is really going to collapse."

"It collapsed long ago, my love. This is just the final death throes of a deeply wounded animal. The New Order has failed."

"How could it happen? Why did it have to be this way?"

"We both know the answer to that," Hans answered. "Sometimes the best way to save a situation is to just let it collapse and then pick up the pieces."

"Yes, but all those people..."

"...would still die if we had tried to fight the movement toward forced economic equality. The only difference is that we would have died with them. The people would have devoured the producers in their greed and then destroyed themselves picking over the bones of a once great technological world. This way there will be someone around to put things aright when the chaos has run its course."

"Are we going to die, Daddy?" asked Peter, Hans's eight-year-old son.

"Some day we'll all die, of course. Everyone does, but not from this madness. We're going to survive to restructure the Seven Worlds into a new order, one that works, based on productivity and free will choice and rewarding those who can create what the society needs for its growth and its survival. Oh, we'll still take care of those who can't fend for themselves, but those who want to take wealth away from others won't be in control, sucking us dry."

The boy Peter simply nodded, not understanding a word of it, except, of course, that he was going to die, but just not right now. Absently, he played with his toy systems cruiser, all fins and windows and bristling on three sides with stubby weapon pods, and wondered what it was like to die. He decided he'd have to think on that later. It was more than he could handle for his five years on the planet.

"It's all your faults, you two and the others!," said Elisa. "None of this would have happened if you'd just agreed to keep producing for everyone!"

"We should become the slaves of a welfare state? We should produce at no profit and no reward for our work? Without compensation for inventing, developing and creating the machines and businesses that keep the Seven Worlds alive? I'm sorry, my dear, but we've been through all this before. I'll not work for others while they do no work for themselves. I'll not be a slave to anyone, most of all them."

"Men of ability owe it to the rest of humanity to carry them. Everyone knows that!" She said.

"What a wonderful idea. From each according to his abilities and to each according to his needs. It failed in Russia in the twentieth century, it failed in the Americas in the twenty-first, and it failed in China after the second Cultural Revolution eighty years later. When will people learn?

"I owe it to the rest of humanity to take care of them? I owe nothing to any man," Hans said a bit too sharply, "and no man owes me anything. What I do I do freely because I choose to, not because others tell me I owe it to them! I'll give a man the shirt off my back if he needs it, Elisa, but if he tries to take it away from me, no matter what his excuse, I'll fight him to the death!"

"Hans," Beatrice whispered. "Be kind. Elisa doesn't understand."

Hans pointed to the com unit.

"Neither do they, and that is why they blindly go about the process of destroying each other, every one of them sure that their needs are greatest and someone else should satisfy them! That's why every one of us who supply the wealth of the human race chose to simply stop producing eleven months ago. Let them play their idiot games! We refuse to be involved!"

"You're an evil man, Hans Rhoedraegon," growled Elisa and choked out the last words in a fit of coughing and gasping for breath.

He thought for a moment, frowning.

"Hard, perhaps, but I'm not as cruel as those who would have such utter contempt for another human being as to believe that we are all equally capable of all things, or that they know better how I should live my life than I do. Such a view only serves to drag us all down, to reduce the whole race to the lowest common denominator and destroy the talented. Thank God I have the choice of producing or not producing and that others understand and agree with me."

"If you don't make the things, Daddy, then where will they come from?" asked Hans's second son.

"That, James, is the point. If we don't make things, then there will be none. No one else will do it. They're too busy demanding someone else take care of their needs. They wanted control of the government and the economy to bring about their utopian world, but they've forgotten that by doing so, they've destroyed the system that allows that utopia to exist. They've very quickly found that without being able to get ahead by their efforts, they suddenly have nothing to offer."

James Rhoedraegon looked quizzically at his father, trying to grasp what he was saying. It was too abstract, too difficult for him. He finally sighed and looked away at the twins on Clarion Skeelar's lap. To James, they were far more interesting than all this talk of destruction and the economy, whatever that was.

"As you sow, so shall you reap, my son. Give nothing, get nothing. Give much, receive abundance. It's a fundamental principle that most people seem to have forgotten...again. I produce value and receive wealth. It's as simple as that."

"I suppose you'll take your family back to the mountains now," Clarion Skeelar said, trying to change the subject.

Hans nodded.

"We'll wait it out. When it's time to sort all this out, they'll find that we've not been idle while they destroyed a world's progress. In five years we'll be back to normal, our plants at full production and enough of what the world needs stockpiled to bring them back to a civilized level. The world will go on, but with those who have the intelligence and the will to lead in charge. There'll be no more of this nonsense about everyone being the same. It's a nice idea, but you and I know it is simply not true."

"Simply not true," Clarion repeated. "How did things get so twisted anyway?"

"Don't get him started," Beatrice Rhoedraegon said with a wispy smile.

But Clarion Skeelar was deep in his own thoughts. He didn't stand when his guests left for their shuttle, insisting apologetically that the two young charges in his lap would never allow it. When they had gone, he sent the twins on their way with their mother and settled back to stare at the cold empty fireplace.

He sighed a very heavy sigh.

"Yes, but is our way any better than theirs?" He mumbled to no one in particular.

Printed in the United States
74989LV00003B/232-264

9 781933 505077